Expensive Taste

BY TIPHANI

Essence Magazine Bestselling Author of
Millionaire Mistress and Still A Mistress

Life Changing Books in conjunction with Power Play Media
Published by Life Changing Books
P.O. Box 423 Brandywine, MD 20613

Library of Congress Cataloging-in-Publication Data;

www.lifechangingbooks.net

13 Digit: 978-1934230831
10 Digit: 1934230839

Copyright © 2008

Dedication

What Joe Jackson, Ike Turner, and my, Leslie Allen all have in common is their unwavering discipline to make sure everything they touch is perfect. And although they were all abusive☺ all who they were responsible for turned out to be stars. Leslie, there were times I wanted to run away from you and befriend a mouse under my kitchen table, and then there was that time you smashed the (imaginary) cake in my face when I turned in some bullshit to you.So, to my dedicated developmental editor, Leslie Allen, from Anna Mae (the writer), I say thank you for scaring me into finishing my book on time. Who needs those meds when I have you-lmao!! No seriously, you are incredible at what you do and I dedicate this book to you.

Thank you.

Acknowledgments

"There is nothing to writing. All you do is sit down at a type writer and open a vein." –Red Smith

Can you believe it? I'm actually on my third novel and counting.☺ Who would've ever thought that an undisciplined, emotionally unstable princess like myself would accomplish such a task? I am so extremely proud of myself!!! For some reason, this book was extremely difficult for me to write. It was equivalent to being in labor for five excruciating months, trying to vaginally give birth to a thirteen pound baby when only seven centimeters dilated and with no epidural.

Yes, it was really that painful!! And there were several reasons for this:

1. I am transitioning from relaxed to natural hair, which I'm sure had a lot to do with the struggles of my book writing process (only you true transitioners out there will understand the seriousness of this)!!!

2. I absolutely refused to take the A.D.D medicine that my doctor prescribed to me. I think that it's all a government set up like the Tuskegee Airman Experiment and they are all out to screw with my genius. (Don't worry…I won't let them take me alive!!)

3. I am a habitual doodler (anyone whose known me since I've been alive can agree to this) and for some reason, the doodling during this book got out of hand. I tried to stop myself until I had an AHA! moment that: DOODLING IS PART OF MY GENIUS…LEAVE ME ALONE!

And last, but not least, I just wanted to make sure that this book was my greatest one yet (which is very stressful in and of itself)

But nonetheless…it's here! Right now our economy is clearly not at its best, so to you, whose holding my baby in your hand, I sincerely thank you from the bottom of my heart for your support! It means a lot to know that you choose me over putting gas in your car (or paying a bill) and I pray that I don't disappoint you.

"Sometimes you have to go on when you don't feel like it, and sometimes you're doing good work when it feels like all you're managing is to shovel shit from a sitting position."
–Stephen King

Before I start to acknowledge anyone for anything, I just want to let EVERYONE know that it is 4:38 a.m. on Sunday morning. I'm tired.

1. Your acknowledgement might be 3 things:
Short…

2. Just a name drop

3. Or forgotten altogether

I try to take one hundred percent responsibility for all that I do in life, but for this, I can absolutely not be held accountable for my actions. I've started doodling again and I'm on the way to sleepy town. I promise to whoever I piss off, which is always quite a few people, I am truly sorry. Please don't call me to voice your concerns.

God, I stopped trusting you for a while. I thought I'd get more accomplished and done a lot faster if I did things my way. Then I end up further behind from where I started. You'd think I would've learned the process by now. I thank you for still loving me. I'm convinced that's what keeps me alive. I trust you!

Brenda "Mom" Ellison, you are the definition of brilliance, beauty, and wisdom. I hope that I'm just like you when I grow up! **Larry Ellison**, thank you for everything! To my sister **Carrie "Yah Yah" Montgomery**, I have tossed and turned for days trying to find the words to express how much I love you. I've seemed to piss you off in the last acknowledgements (actually it's been all of them) so this was extremely important for me to get right (I'm kind of being sarcastic). You're my fly baby sister and I love the woman that you're becoming. It seems like only yesterday that I was blackmailing you into being my slave for a week. Man I hated when you got old enough to catch on. I'm sure you'll hate this one too, but come on…you're related to me. Really, isn't that enough☺!!!!

To my first and only child, **Jaedah Kiss Hill**, I told you to stop talking, made you turn off the TV, go outside to play, take a nap, read a book, anything so that I would be able to finish my book. You had a slight attitude, but understood how much this meant to me. Without you, I wouldn't be the woman I am today. Mommy loves ya!

Pam "my other mom" Montgomery, it's scary to think how alike we are sometimes. I love you. My brothers **Thomas "T-Tom" Evans**, you really get on my nerves (most of the time), but that's because we're a spitting image of each other…mean, stubborn, and crazy. And **Cyrus "Spunge" Procter**, you turned out to be normal after all!!! I love you both. My aunts **Gail and Pam**, thanks a million! **Renee Cole**, thanks and I love you.

To my brother and sister, **Tex and Chey**, we are around each other way too much. You know what I'm going to say before I say it and do before I do it…and you stop me before I get out of hand. I love you guys. And I think I have a solution for the haters. I'll find someone to cut off all of their (you know what's) and hang them around their necks so that they can suck on them like pacifiers. Problem solved!

Azarel, thank you for putting up with me and understanding my "special" needs-lol!! Talking to my good friend, **Keisha George**, is not only like eating humble pie, but having it slammed down your throat and told not to chew! What would I do without you? Thanks for helping me out again and giving me your honest opinion about everything. To **Tonya Ridley**, thanks for it all…you're the coolest kid I know! To my publicist, **Nakea Murray**, who would not want you on their side when you have literary blood running through your veins? Thanks for it all! To my other editor, **Virginia Greene**, thanks for everything. Your role in this whole project is priceless.

My Power Play/ Life Changing Books family: **Azarel** (*Bruised 1&2, Daddy's House*), **Tonya Ridley** (*The Take Over, Talk of the Town*), **Capone** (*Marked*), **Danette Majette** (*I Shoulda Seen it Comin', Deep*), **J. Tremble** (*Secrets of a Housewife, More Secrets More Lies, Naughty Little Angel*), **Tyrone Wallace** (*Nothin' Personal, Double Life*) **Mike Warren** (*A Private Affair*), **Ericka Williams** (*All That Glitters*), **Chantal Jolie** (*In Those Jeans*), **Darren Coleman** (*Taste of Honey*), **Kendall Banks** (*Rich Girls*), **Sheree Avent** (*The Blackmail Diva*), **C. Stecko** (*Brooklyn Brothel*), **Marissa Monteilh** (*Something He Can Feel*), **Nissa A. Showell** (*Reign of a Hustler*) and to all the Teenage Bluez authors, this is incredible. I'm so happy and proud of you all.

To my cousins: **Shameika "Goldie" Moore, Bridget Johnson, Gina Merrit, Shawn, Gayla,** and **Juan Yarborough, Wally** and **Brandon Andrews, Sherri Evans, Stan Evans, Baby Sammy, Jamila Hartsfield, Stacey, Miko, Teddy** and **Terissa, Junebug, VJ, Butch, Marcat, Walter "Cuco" Gonzalez, Mahogany, Yahira,** and the rest of ya…thanks for the love and when are we going to have a reunion?

To my BFF's **Christie Monique Linton, Marla Dinkle, Yolanda "Pooh" Richardson, Karza "Friend" Walton, Jacque "Wildout" Harris, Shaunita "Skinny" Randolph,** and my newest edition, **Inf.** Thank you all for putting up with my crap and loving me through it all. You all are true best friends.

To my favorite city in the world **ROCHESTER, NEW YORK**, I've traveled all over the world and haven't found a city that had more heart than we do. I swear it must be something in the water because they don't bring them up like us anymore. To the great people at **104 WDKX**, I genuinely thank you for everything. I still stream online to listen to the Water Cooler when I get a little homesick. **The Rochester City School District (Young Mother's Program)** you guys are the best. I thank all the staff for your continued support and just want to let the students know that I was once a young mother and despite what everyone (including yourself) is telling you, you will make it. You have no choice, it's not just you anymore so stop complaining and take one hundred percent responsibility for where you are, write down some goals for where you want to be, and get moving! Time is money and both can't be wasted. I'll see you ladies at the top!

A special thanks to **Minnie Lee** and **Jackie Willliams**...you ladies are the greatest! **V**(Mad Flavors), **JaGood and Jerome** (It's Official Bookstore) thanks for the love!!

I graduated in 1999 from **Rush Henrietta Senior High School**, and wanted to give a big shout out to them. I'm a prime example that you can graduate with a 1.7 GPA and still write books!!! **Tia Linton**, **Nicole Dixon**, **Yoshida Baldwin**, **Melvin Cross**, **Will Mongeon**, etc., etc. etc...thanks!

RALEIGH, NORTH CAROLINA...I'm never moving away!! I'll just plant my palm tree in front of the mansion I'm having built! Thanks to **Shena J** for the love and I'm still waiting on that book you're writing to get written! To **Tisha** and **E** (Oakwood Mini Mart) thank y'all from the bottom of my heart for your open arms. I really, really, really appreciate everything. To my girl **Nikki** and **Latoya Lee**, I love y'all.

I'd like to give a special shout out to **Winter "Dog" Ramos**, **Angela Washburn**, and **Katrina Hill** all of who I called at the last minute to read my book and make sure everything was on point. Thank you all for being available and helping me out when I was down to my knees in despair.

Mo Vega, **Sunrise**, **Alf**, **Integrity**, **Shaun**, **Gloria**, **Kia**, **Carly**, **Carmie Nelson** (I love you), **Country**, **Dipsey**, **DJ Skills**, **Eric Terry**, **Jeff**, **Smurf** and the rest of the Dynasty 5 crew, **Jackie** (Rule the World), **Jah'Mal Brown** and **Naomi Odune**, **Stoney** (for buying so many books), **Lucky** and **Mina**, **Makeia Williams**, **Nekisha Gill**, **Quency Hawkins**, and **Sonya** "Hot Knocks." Thanks!

Thank you to all the bookstores: It's Official (Rochester, NY), **Tyson** and **Hakim** (Black and Nobel-Philadelphia, PA) you guys are a blast to hang out with!! **Xanielle** (Horizon-Philadelphia, PA), **Nakea and the crew** at As The Page Turns Bookclub (Philadelphia, PA), DC Bookman, Dynasty Books (Charlotte, NC), Books A Million, Waldens, Borders, Barnes and Nobles, and all the other independent black book stores. Thank you.

Thanks to **DC Livers** (www.blackpressradio.com), **Brandi Royal** and **Aiesha Little** (Triangle Catalyst Magazine), **Brian Regan** (B. Regan Photography), **Chakara** (MBrace Magazine). And thanks to my fellow authors, **Shannon Holmes**, **K'wan**, **Kiki Swinson**, **Freeze**, **SC Dikens**, **Control**, and **JM Benjamin**, **Nicolette**, and everyone else.

And to all my readers who made all of my books that have been published, Essence Magazine Best Sellers, I appreciate you. Thanks. I'd love to hear from you all! Please write to: P.O. BOX 40133, Raleigh, NC 27629 and I'll **try my best** to get back to you!

You can catch me via the web at the following:
www.TiphaniMontgomery.com
www.Myspace.com/TiphanitheAuthor
www.Twitter.com/Tiphani
www.LifeChangingBooks.net

"Writing is the only thing that, when I do it, I don't feel like I should be doing something else."-Gloria Steinem

And with that, I'm signing off,
Tiphani Nicole Montgomery
"Queen of Doodle Land!"

Chapter One

Big.
Plump.
Round.

It was finally here. What I always wanted...the ass of my dreams. I was on cloud nine and convinced that even Kim Kardashian's fat booty couldn't top this one. I smiled as the full length mirror shot back a reflection of the results from the silicone implants that had been inserted into my butt cheeks. I'd had them for two weeks, and couldn't wait to make them clap. And now, on top of all my other top notch features, I was a certified ten. Couldn't wait to show off my new assets in a pair of Rich and Skinny jeans.

Suddenly, my eyes darted away from my reflection for a quick second. I looked at the clock on the wall and released a huge sigh. I'd been in my plastic surgeon's cold-ass examining room for almost fifteen minutes now, and was becoming extremely frustrated. Didn't he know time was money? My money!

I was ready to show this new ass off to the world. And even though I knew the post operation follow-up was standard procedure, I was convinced that everything had gone smoothly. Besides, my surgeon, Houston's own Dr. Asura Khan, was world-renowned and had worked on every A-List celebrity in the business, so this visit was probably a complete waste of my time. I looked great...scrumptious, ready to turn some man out and take all his loot.

Turning my attention back to the mirror, I took off the pale blue paper gown to admire the rest of my body; the same regiment that I performed on a daily basis. With major arrogance, I flashed another cheesy grin. Call me conceited, but I knew I was the shit. My skin resembled the color of black coffee filled with three creamers, and my neck was graceful like an African queen. Not to mention the beautiful set of long legs that I used to sashay when I walked. Even my ear lobes were perfect, which by the way only rocked three carat flawless diamonds. To add to my perfection, my hair stayed in the most expensive front lace wigs and Malaysian weaves.

Yeah that's right, long jet black imported black hair…I was definitely fucking model potential.

Turning back around to see my most recent tattoo that rested on my lower back which read: 'Flyest of them all' I smiled again because it was the truth. I was the flyest of them all.

"So, I take it you like what you see," Dr. Khan said, while admiring what his expertise had done to my new figure.

I hadn't even heard him come in and didn't appreciate his ass forgetting the usual knock on the door that all doctors adhered to. I guess to him, I was no longer the average patient. Truth be told, he'd explored my pussy with his dick on several occasions. I guess you could say, it was an even exchange. He laced my pockets with Benjamin Franklins while I allowed him a piece of paradise, my coochie. I watched him carefully as he placed his clipboard down on the counter and accompanied me to the front of the mirror. His hands touched the base of my hips seductively.

He was handsome.

And of Indian descent.

His skin illuminated a dark olive tone, and his eyebrows were thick, dark, and mysterious. He wore his midnight colored hair, short and close to his face. There was no facial hair, which made him appear to be younger. At forty-five he could've easily passed for his late twenties.

A foreigner.

Yeah, I'd stepped outside my race and fucked with a muthafucka who could probably send a damn smoke signal. But it didn't matter to me what shade he was, or what second language he could speak. I was only interested in one color anyway. GREEN.

His hygiene was European. Not that musty-ass smell that most Indian people walked around with. His clothes…probably what I liked most. Dolce and Gabbana is what he'd become accustomed to. A savvy business man who'd taken over his father's business a few years ago. They had money. Old money. I guess that's why I went after his type, and not the typical street dude.

"Uugh!" I growled as he gently moved his cold hands onto my butt. "Why didn't you warm your shit up before touching me!"

"I'm sorry Mirror," he replied, as he continued to examine his work. "Wow everything looks great. You'll have a small amount of swelling for about five or six more weeks, and you still won't be able to sit down comfortably for another few days, but you'll be back to normal in no time." He grabbed his clipboard off the counter to mark a few things off. "Now climb up on the examining table and lay face down so I can check your incisions."

I smacked my lips. "Is that really necessary? Everything looks fine to me."

"Of course it's necessary. I still need to make sure there's no sign of infection, and that your scars are healing properly. Don't forget…you need to use the Mederma at least twice a day."

"I'm not…damn." He was starting to remind me of an annoying-ass school teacher.

The paper gown I wore made a lot of noise as it crunched and crinkled with every step I took toward the examining table. He might have to give me extra money today for holding me up like this, I thought as I was careful not to bump my new ass into anything.

"Before we get started with everything, I just want to know why you haven't been returning any of my calls?" Dr. Kahn asked, putting on a white pair of latex gloves. He looked as me as if I'd hurt him or something. "You didn't have to come into the office today. We could've done this follow up at your house." He displayed a crooked little grin.

Shit…now he wants to fuck. I climbed up on the table and laid face down. "Look, you know how this shit goes, Doc. Sometimes I want to fuck with you and sometimes I don't." I ended with a shrug of my shoulders.

"I can't believe you're treating me like this," he stated.

"I can't believe you're always whining? I've been busy."

He rushed to the top of the table, leaning near my face. He

looked at me with concern. "Busy doing what? You just had surgery. You're supposed to be resting."

I hoped his ass wasn't trying to be possessive because I didn't do leeches. Maybe I should've thought twice about getting this damn six thousand dollar surgery for free, I thought to myself.

"Can we just get this over with?" I asked with an attitude.

Dr. Khan moved back to where he belonged...near my ass. He lifted up my right butt cheek to see how well the scar was healing, and then did the same to the left.

"Everything looks great down here," he said, right before spreading my butt cheeks apart.

Instantly, I knew where this was going.

He was a freak.

Obviously, hypnotized by the sweet smell of my nectar, Dr. Kahn said nothing else. Seconds later, I heard his chair roll back slightly. When I turned around, his face was just inches away from my pussy. He blew in it, letting the warm air from his mouth tickle my clit.

"What in the hell are you doing?" I asked with my face pressed into the white paper. I turned slightly just to get a look at what he was doing behind my back.

He showed the same crooked grin he often displayed when his dick hardened. "I need to take a closer look."

He got a little closer.

Blew in it again.

We'd had sex countless times before, but he knew I hardly ever allowed him to go down on me, especially with my fucked up condition down there. However, his nasty-ass always tried anyway. You would think that he knew better. With all the shit going around now days you would think that his main concern would be to not bring anything home to his wife, but it wasn't.

I guess he was a selfish man.

Hell...they all were.

But I had to admit...even though sex with him always bored me, the light air to my pussy felt good. I twitched, then squirmed, ready to stop him before I let my emotions loose.

He forced his way inside before I had a chance to protest.

4

"Oh shit!" I screamed, completely caught off guard. He moved his tongue in ways I didn't think it could move. At this point, he was in too deep and I didn't give a fuck if his tongue fell off.

Damn, I'm so selfish. I laughed inside thinking about my medical situation. Apparently none of these thoughts ran through his mind because he was eating the shit out of my pussy. He licked, twitched, twirled his tongue, and one time even spit. A few seconds later, he began to do longer strokes then inserted one of his fingers.

"Ahhh!" I moaned by mistake. Just the sound of my juices squishing around had me holding onto the table. I gritted my teeth to keep from screaming again. I didn't want it to feel as good as it did. Didn't want him to think that he could eat the pussy whenever he wanted to. His slippery tongue was thick and warm. Everything about it felt good, but it wasn't supposed to.

What we did was always strictly business.

An exchange of services.

I wouldn't call it whoring, but it was damn sure close. This *understanding* between he and I had been going on for about six months now, and my feelings toward him still hadn't changed. I hated having sex with him before, but my hatred for it seemed to grow even more so now. He, however, enjoyed every moment of it, and the only thing that had me coming back repeatedly was all the financial benefits. It was a win win situation.

He continued to lick me, while I continued to pretend like his tongue game wasn't driving me crazy. All of a sudden, Kahn took it too far by rolling the tip of his tongue over my ass crack. An area that was completely off limits.

To anyone.

"Wait…hold…the…fuck…up. Stop!" I yelled.

Surprisingly, he took a few steps back from indulging in my juices to unbuckle his pants, letting them fall to the ground. His tight white Polo briefs followed shortly after, exposing what he lacked the most.

While still on my stomach, I turned around and was at point blank range with his dick. It was small…real small. Even with it being rock hard, it looked like it belonged to a ten year old little boy. He grabbed his dick, positioning it for a smooth entrance then began to take a step closer.

Is this muthafucka on drugs? Didn't he hear what I said? "Get the hell away from me!"

"Mirror, please…be quiet," he pleaded, while looking around, his focus mostly on the door.

"I don't give a damn who hears me. You need to put that little ass dick back in your pants!"

"So, you mean to tell me that I can't put it in just a little or even lick it?"

I squinted to make sure my vision was correct. A few pieces of my long black curly pubic hairs clung to his mouth.

He looked dumb. Sounded dumb too. Did he really think he was going to stick his shit inside my forbidden zone?

He was talking about my asshole, but he could cancel that. There would be no salad tossing up in here. "Lick it? " I repeated. "I'm still swollen you muthafucka! Why would you want to fuck me in my ass?"

Again, I didn't give a fuck who heard me. I couldn't believe it. My shit was literally still black and blue and all he could think about was sticking his little dick inside of it. My instinct told me that he was definitely one of those doctors who, if given the chance, would rape and fondle women while under anesthesia. No one would be raping me. Ever!

"Ssshhh. Mirror, please calm down," he suggested again. He had his finger vertically placed on his tiny lips.

"Hell no. Besides, you have a lot of nerve thinking that you deserve to get any extra perks. Look at these!" I pulled the annoying paper gown to the side and exposed my breasts. They use to be small, A cup, but now I was a healthy thirty-eight C. However, I still wasn't satisfied and had asked Kahn to make me a Double D, but he refused. Told me it would stretch out my skin too much and wouldn't look natural. I knew his ass was lying though. I'm sure he was probably just tired of doing surgery for free.

Before the butt augmentation, it was the breasts. Before the breasts, it was the lipo-suction... and before that, it was the lip injections. Which reminded me, I needed to fill them out a little more. At twenty-six, I had to admit, a lot of work had been done to my body, but Kahn had no right putting his two cents in. I didn't care whether he paid for the shit or not. His opinions were not wanted.

"So, when are you going to make these bigger?" I asked moving my breasts up and down.

He stuck out his tongue like a lizard, then looked toward the door again. Thought he heard something. When he turned back around I had a frown on my face. I wanted an answer. He knew it.

"Mirror, I told you before, that a C cup looks perfect on your slender frame. You're tall, but slim, anything larger would disfigure you. You know...you were very beautiful before you got all that stuff done. Don't go overboard," he suggested like he was trying to tell me something for my own good.

"I'm sorry, but a warning from a man that still has pussy hairs dried to his lips, won't be taken too seriously. Mind your fucking business! It's my body!" Then as if on cue, someone knocked on the door.

"Wait one second please," Kahn said hurriedly as he pulled his briefs back up, and then his pants.

I should've pointed toward the side of his mouth, letting him know hairs were still visible, but thought, *fuck him*! Whoever was at the door knocked again very impatiently. "I'm with a patient. Just one moment," he announced again.

"I know you're with a patient, so open the door, *Dr. Kahn*," a female voice replied, obviously still banging from the other side.

His eyes widened immediately. He then wiped his mouth nervously before looking at me. "Please fix your gown. I have to open it."

I started to say no, just to fuck with him because I knew who it was, but decided against it. After watching me place my boobs back under the paper gown, he turned around and quickly opened the door.

She stood there in her purple scrubs with one hand on her hip, the other on her clipboard and her eyes glued to me.

It was Nurse Khan.

His wife.

7

This dude had to be crazy. He'd just licked my pussy un-controllably while his wife was in another room. But shit, then again I didn't care. That was his problem.

"Everything is fine Nurse Khan, she was just experiencing a little pain on her rear, but I have all of it under control now," Dr. Kahn blurted out. You could see little beads of sweat start to pop up on his forehead.

"Is that so. Well, I think I'll just stay for the rest of her visit. You're supposed to have a nurse in here anyway when you're ex-amining a woman," she announced before pushing him to the side and closing the door behind her.

As if he doesn't already know that, I said to myself.

I smiled at the over-weight woman.

She didn't return the gesture.

Her size was typical for an Indian woman-short. It just meant I would definitely be able to fuck her up. I chuckled inside seeing her stand angrily with her arms folded. Out of the blue, Dr. Khan reached around his wife and opened up the door again.

"I said that I have everything covered. Please, I need you to go prep the other room for my next patient. I'm running behind and one of the other nurses called out sick."

She looked at him with spite in her eyes. I wasn't sure if she knew what was going on, or just didn't know how to confront the situation. "I'm well aware which one of our employees is not here," Nurse Kahn replied in her thick Indian accent. She stared at me again, before turning around and slamming the door behind her.

As I scooted my way off of the table, I could still feel the juiciness between my legs as I put back on my black tights and cranberry knit Theory dress. And even though it was a sixty degree day in the middle of January, I still put on my long black belted sweater. I couldn't wear jeans yet and recently, I'd been going panty-less because I didn't know what size my new derrière could fit. It felt so good not to have to wear the special panties that con-trolled my swelling anymore. Now, this ass could finally breathe.

I took my weave that I'd tied up in a ponytail at the begin-ning of the visit out and let all twenty inches of it fall down my back. Slipped on my knee high black Gucci leather boots, grabbed my oversized Hermes bag and headed for the door.

"So that's it? You're just going to put on your things and leave?" he asked.

"Why don't you take some of your expertise, build you a bigger dick and *then* come holla at me."

He looked down in the direction of his dick, almost in disbelief that I could've said something like that.

I'd attacked his manhood.

He was embarrassed.

"You know what," I continued, "you really got me fucked up! I don't need this stress in my life. Maybe some cash would make this all better."

I held out my right hand. The other one was on my hip. I had an attitude and depending on how much money he gave me would determine how long it lasted. Dr. Khan shook his head from side to side in disgust and pulled out his wallet, before sliding out two crisp hundred dollar bills and handed them to me.

"This is all I have on me," he stated. Kahn couldn't even look me in my face because his ass knew that wasn't enough.

"Two hundred dollars? Is this some kind of fucking joke? Is this what I'm worth to you now? What in the hell am I supposed to do with that?" I asked, after ripping the two bills into little pieces. I threw the pieces in the air, then watched them fall like tiny raindrops all over the floor. "I know what I'll do. I'll just have a conversation with your wife before I leave the office and maybe then you'll find a way to come up with some more money."

Fear spread all across his face. "No, please don't. She's already suspicious about where our money from certain accounts is going and I'm running out of excuses to give her. Not to mention all the free work I've given you. She only allows me so many pro bono cases a year, and I'm way over my quota."

I smiled thinking how he always sent his wife to go visit her parents, or on a spa retreat somewhere in the Georgia Mountains whenever I got my procedures done. "I need more money," I stated sharply.

"I don't have anymore," he whined.

I placed my hand on the door handle like I was about to

9

open it. "Then go get some from your wife. I'll wait."

Kahn shook his head back and forth. "Mirror please... no. I can't do that. She'll ask what I need it for."

"That's not my fucking problem," I replied making him aware of all the sympathy I didn't have for him.

"Listen, all I'm asking is that you give me some time and the money will come in again as fast as it did in the beginning. I promise."

"Fuck that. Your time is up. It's over!" was the last thing I said before opening the door.

Surprisingly, I was greeted by his wife again, making me wonder if she'd ever left from outside the door. Her eyes were cold, so I turned my back. "Bye Dr. Khan and thank you for *everything*," I said as seductively as I could.

Mrs. Khan continued to stare me down from behind, never letting up. I smiled again and added a wink for fun. She turned away from me and stormed into the room with her husband, slamming the door behind her. From the looks of it, she was getting ready to chew his ass out. I laughed, knowing that my work had been done.

I rushed outside thinking about my plans for the day. Had a smile on my face until I saw it. Stopped me dead in my tracks. My car, my baby, my Benz... was *keyed up*. Somebody got me. Quickly, my mind raced. I thought back to Mrs. Kahn. I knew scratching a car up with a key was a black girl move, but she could've snuck out the office and touched my prized possession. The question that had me puzzled was did she have time.

The crazy part about the situation was that it could've been a host of people. I'd fucked over many, and most had vowed revenge against me. The mental list inside my head seemed to scroll as each name came to me. Jared, Keith, Lance, and of course... I immediately thought about Donnell, my lawyer trick. Had his whole life in shambles. I remember taking half his paycheck every week, plus dipped into his savings that he shared with his wife.

I leaned against my car and rubbed the new indention as I thought about his wife. She was probably the culprit. The bitch was crazy. She'd told me to my face the day Donnell put her out, that she'd get me back. Told me she'd follow me to my grave for destroying her family if she had to. That threat was crazy and unnessasry because I left that nigga once he lost his position in the firm as partner. I didn't do regular niggas. I needed dudes with clout, or with some type of prominence.

Suddenly, I felt someone watching me from above. My eyes did a three-sixty, then I saw the blinds move. There was movement from Dr. Khan's office. I knew it was his wife, so I flicked my finger and hopped in my ride. Little did that bitch know I would be living in *her house* by next week!

Chapter *Two*

Late.

As usual.

But really didn't care.

"Hey ladies," I said, rushing past the group of fifteen or so anxious women ready to shop. I could barely walk with the four large garment bags that were laid across my forearm. Bags that were full of brand new merchandise for my boutique. It was five o'clock in the evening and the sun was starting to settle down as I bumped into the wave of bodies, fumbling to get my keys together. I had a million of them attached to my key chain and it was always impossible to find the right one.

"Whatever! You always do this shit Mirror. A little consideration for our time *and* our money would be appreciated!" one customer had the audacity to yell out.

Her name was Kippy and she had her hands on her hips and her posture read attitude. Her oversized Bvlgari shades were pushed down on her nose and her hair was in a tight bun like a scholarly librarian. She had the appearance of an angry black woman, and acted like it too. Although her attire was always on point, her face resembled the bottom of my shoe.

Worn.

Scuffed.

Black.

I ignored her. Didn't think she deserved an explanation. It had been three days since my doctor's appointment with Kahn and I felt better than ever, especially every time I caught a glimpse of my ass in the mirror. Hadn't been this happy in weeks, but now this broad was trying to fuck with my happiness.

After searching for what seemed like forever, I finally found the right key and placed it in the door. I knew it was foul to open my boutique so late, when most stores downtown closed by six, but she was the only muthafucka complaining. Besides, my store didn't have operating hours. I simply opened the shit when I got there and closed when I left. Came in after hours when I needed to and closed up early when money called. I was the boss and that was how I wanted things to run. There were fourteen other women directly behind me ready to shop, but it was Kippy, who was about to fuck it up for everyone. That's probably why I still hadn't let anyone in yet.

She kept fucking talking. I checked her physique just to see what I was up against, just in case I decided to jab her in the mouth. She had decent height, but I was taller, 5'7 to be exact. My legs were long and firm, and ready to kick her in the torso as soon as I got the chance.

Kippy continued..."First you close the store down for days at a time and now you open this bitch up at five o'clock in the afternoon? What's up with that? I mean seriously, what kind of business are you running here? If you can't show some professionalism then I'm not coming back. There are a lot of other people who would appreciate my business," she ranted.

She motioned her hand to show off her Diane von Furstenberg print shirt. The sleeves mimicked a kimono and the shirt hung loose and sported a low split V-neck that showed her D cup breasts, the breasts that I wanted. She was, at this point, the center of attention. A show off.

"I swear some black people shouldn't own shit. I wonder how you got a store down here on McKinney Street anyway. Maybe you should open up your store in the ghetto-ass Sharpstown Mall instead of downtown," Kippy continued.

I'd finally had enough. "Bitch, you know what…you got me all fucked up. You don't have to buy shit from me!" I guess you could say I didn't have the 'customer's always right' attitude.

Even though Kippy was one of my best customers, I wasn't gonna let her ass keep talking shit, and definitely not in front of an audience. I knew she was a rich bitch and used to having things done her way. Kippy made it known every time she shopped that she was a trust fund bitch whose father left her everything. She

14

was used to being catered to, but I put her in her place, somewhere she wasn't used to being.

"Are you serious?" she asked with her hands planted firmly on her hips. "I've spent a lot of money in your store. Is that how you're going to talk to me?" Kippy stood there and waited for an answer. When she realized that she wasn't going to get one, she yelled to the crowd of women, "Come on ladies! We'll take our business somewhere else!" She turned around and took a few steps forward before looking back. I guess she expected her girls to have her back, but no one moved. "Sash, Caton, what's up? I know you all aren't going to patronize this business after she talked to me like that?"

"I'm sorry girl, but I've been waiting on this new Rachel Roy Apache dress for too long," her friend Sasha said, not long before the other friend, Caton shook her head in agreement.

"Yeah, we'll holla at you later on girl."

I grinned wickedly, then turned to Sasha. "And that dress just came in too." I patted one of the garment bags before turning back to Kippy. "Looks like you're outnumbered," I continued, trying to conclude her tirade.

"This ain't over," Kippy warned before storming off. "This shit is not over!"

Unmoved by her dry threat, I laughed out loud and watched her dumb-ass storm off to her little 3 series BMW. "You need to take some of your dead daddy's money and upgrade to a better car!" I yelled to her backside.

Not waiting for any type of response, I turned back around and finally opened the door to my boutique. I welcomed everyone in with a frustrated smile, trying to forget about the drama that had just taken place. I flipped the lights on in my twelve hundred square foot space, which exposed how well organized and clean everything was. Walls that were kissed by warm yellow paint brightened the open space and everyone went their separate ways like a swarm of ants, trying to be the first to grab whatever caught their eyes.

"When can I see that dress?" Sasha asked.

Damn can I at least put my fucking purse down....maybe

even turn on the register, I thought. "Umm, just give me a minute. I'll pull everything out."

"Great. I just want to make sure nobody else gets it. What size is it? I ordered a six right?"

I swung my weave in frustration, then gave Sasha a look that said she was about to pinch a nerve. She turned her head then walked away. I proceeded to walk away as well, but was stopped in my tracks when I glanced down and noticed several scuff marks on my floor.

The cream colored marble tile that cost me nine thousand dollars in pussy labor to have installed, were all messed up. Floors that I had polished on a monthly basis. The maintenance was expensive, but I had to keep the sheen on it flawless.

A few pieces of Italian leather furniture, which provided rest from the exhausting exercise of spending money, sat in the middle of the store on a red Persian rug that also cost one of my men a pretty penny. To top things off, fresh red roses were placed sporadically throughout the store in crystal vases. Everything in the store including the merchandise was exclusive. That's how I rolled. Top notch, one of a kind. That was my style. There was always just one of everything and I carried nothing but the best. More importantly, my profits were nothing short of great. I brought in almost one hundred percent of the retail price because it was all stolen.

Yes, I have an addiction.

I'm a shoplifter.

Professional Booster is what I called it.

Had been doing it since the age of ten.

Started with twinkies and blow pops. Now, it was more like Prada and Valentino.

It's something about what I do that fills a void, fills an emptiness that I have inside. There's something about brand spanking new shit that appeals to me. The store was full of new clothes and accessories, nothing out-dated. The two weeks I took off for my ass to heal, I used that time to replenish my boutique with the hottest shit. Went on a boosting spree to several high end department stores in the area, and stole as much shit as I could carry out. The ladies had plenty to choose from and I had spared myself a week or two before I had to go back out boosting again.

As I went behind the counter to grab a cloth for the scuff marks, I placed the garment bags down just as my cell phone began to ring. Pulling the new Sprint touchscreen Instinct phone from my purse, I became hesitant for a moment after looking at the caller ID, but decided to take the call anyway. I hoped Kahn hadn't decided to call from an unknown number. He'd been blowing up my phone since the day I left his office.

"Hellooooooooo?" I asked, the anonymous person on the other line. My voice revealed that the call was irritating to me because private calls were something I didn't answer frequently. But there were times when I made exceptions.

"Is this Mirror?" the female voice asked.

I had no idea who the woman was. My first thought, maybe it was Kahn's wife. But then I thought, the woman didn't seem to have an accent. "Yes, it is. Who is this?"

"It's me…Rich," another voice on the line chimed in.

Answering the phone had been an instant mistake.

Rich was a nigga from New York, who I'd fucked with a while back, but he was locked up for distribution of crack cocaine now, and of no more use to me. Someone who didn't deserve that fucking name anymore because he was far from that. He should've gotten the point when I stopped accepting his collect calls over three months ago. This time he'd obviously gotten someone to call me instead.

"What the fuck do you want Rich, and why do you keep calling me? I don't do visits and I damn sure don't send commissary."

"Yo', Ma you need to stop all 'dat cursing wit' my moms on the phone and all," he replied.

"So what? I didn't tell your ass to call me with her on phone. As a matter of fact we can hang up now. I don't have shit to say to you anymore," I shot back.

"Look, you been duckin' my calls for the longest. I just need you to send my moms all my money that you holdin' for me!" Rich yelled.

"Money? What money?" I asked sarcastically. I knew he

was referring to the ten thousand dollars that he'd given me just in case his lawyers needed extra money. Little did he know that shit had been spent up as soon as it touched my hands.

"Don't play games wit' me B. Where my money at?"

"Games? Huh! I'm for real, B," I mocked. "That shit is gone. Go ahead and take it as a loss."

"A loss? What the hell you talkin' 'bout. I shoulda never trusted you!"

"Trusted me? I should've never trusted you. Do you know what the hell your dirty dick gave me asshole? I think about it everyday. It's not like there's a cure for that shit. I can't even believe I'm still talking to you after what you did," I responded

"I done told you before B...I didn't give you that shit. What 'bout them otha niggas you fucked?"

"Fuck you nasty dick! Does your mama know how dirty you are?"

"Young lady you sure do have a nasty mouth," the old woman finally interrupted.

"Shut up lady! I'm not talking to you," I replied.

"A yo', don't fuckin' disrespect my moms like 'dat. You know what, I'ma fuck you up when I get out of here!"

"You mean *if* you get out. Fuck you. I hope you drop the soap nigga!" I shouted. "And don't call my damn phone anymore!"

And with that, I hung up. Couldn't take anymore of him crying like a bitch. Besides, I didn't really know if he was the one who plagued me for life anyway. Shit, all that talk about my condition actually reminded me of what time it was...time to take my pill. As if on cue to all the drama that was going on, my head started pounding. My muscles had already been aching all night, and I'd worked up a slight fever. I walked over to the register, and sat my purse down before placing my cell phone inside. Then, I fumbled around inside the huge tote until I reached my bottle of prescription pills. *I can't believe that I'm gonna have to take this shit for the rest of my life*, I thought as I twisted the bottle open and took out the white pill, swallowing it without any water. "This should do the trick," I said to myself hoping that it would work as fast as possible. The medicine wouldn't stop all the aches and pains, but it would stop me from getting sick.

"Hey, excuse me Miss, do you work here?"

She was big...damn near Amazon-like with mocha colored skin. She rocked a badly done wrap, which indicated her lack of style or unconcern for the welfare of her hair. Her clothes were average at best, which meant she damn sure wasn't one of my normal customers.

Her ass must've waddled in here while I wasn't looking, I concluded as I walked over to address her question. She's someone that I would've never let in.

"Yes. I'm the owner," I responded.

"Great. Do you have..."

I cut her off instantly. "No, I'm sorry, but our restrooms are not for public use."

"Oh, no I don't have to use your restroom," she said, obviously missing my sarcasm. "I was wondering if you all carried any Apple Bottoms or Baby Phat jeans."

My face looked like I smelled something foul. "Apple Bottoms? Baby Phat?" I repeated, making sure I'd heard her correctly. I was offended in her choice of clothing. *I hate when fat women try to wear that ghetto shit. Her big-ass needs directions to the nearest Lane Bryant anyway.* I placed my right hand on her shoulder and directed her back to the door. "Sweetheart, I doubt that you can fit or afford anything in here." I gave her a once over look one more time from head to toe, which confirmed my statement. "I don't carry that ghetto-ass apparel."

"Excuse me?"

"Yeah...maybe you didn't hear me. Do you see what I have on?" I asked, using my fashion sense as an example. I struck a brief modeling pose and pointed to the 'Genius Jeans' that I'd stolen from the Gucci store a while back. They fit my new ass perfectly. The distressed ripped jeans with African beads was well worth the thirty-one hundred dollar price tag. "This is what Savvy Girl Boutique is all about. Class, custom, couture. There is nothing here under three hundred dollars and I'm sure that it's too much for you."

"You have a lot of nerve talking to me like..."

"What kind of shoes are those?" I cut her off, then pointed at her feet.

"Steve Maddens, why?"

"Exactly. You *can't* afford my stuff."

I shooed her away like a fly.

She called me a bitch.

I smiled and said, "I've been called worse by better."

She left…with an attitude of course, but it wouldn't be the first time. If you weren't spending big money up in my spot, you had to get ghost.

The women that remained in the store hardly noticed what was going on, and besides they were all pretty much my normal customers and should've been used to my rants and antics. I was known to put people out. I was also like the soup Nazi on the classic T.V. show, *Seinfeld*. There was only one way…mine. If there was one thing I hated; it was for a lower class chick to step foot on my property. I only catered to the rich and that was only when they stayed in line or else they would find themselves ending up like Kippy. Once in a while I had to use one of them as an example.

That's probably why I didn't have any employees. Couldn't trust them. Just like people shouldn't trust me. Anything that wasn't bolted down I stole and the rules of karma kept me from trusting anyone else. I knew I had it coming back one hundred fold one of these days, but until then, I had plans to ride this shit all the way out.

"Hey Mirror, when do you think you'll get another Chloe tunic dress in?" the girl Caton asked, holding someone else's dark grey dress. "I don't know how you do it, but these designer clothes are so much higher in other stores."

That's because I have a special way of getting my shit, I said to myself. "Oh, I have a special distributor." I gave a smirk. "You know my merchandise has a 'get it now or never policy'. You know I don't want my savvy girls wearing the same stuff that everyone else wears."

The truth was I could only steal one of each item from the stores I usually boosted from anyway. Security was too high, and my philosophy had always been to get in and out as quickly as possible. I didn't have time to hang around one area too long.

"Hey ladies, remember to pick up the merchandise and place it neatly where you found it." I picked up a couple of pieces of clothing that were lying around on top of fixtures and hung them back up where they belonged.

My arch nemesis.

Clutter.

Reminded me of how dirty my mother's house was. She was a hoarder when I was growing up…still is. Just like some of the guest you see on Oprah. Until then, I never knew that the shit had a name other than junky. A fucking pack rat. She created chaos in her life that demon transferred over to mine. Growing up we never had friends, family, or neighbors visit us because she didn't want anyone to see the mountains of shit that left us isolated and imprisoned in our own home.

That was my past.

My future would not be a duplicate.

Someone once said that I had Obsessive Compulsive Disorder. I didn't care what name they had for it as long as it wasn't a 'dirty bitch'. A name that I was frequently called all throughout my childhood. Thinking back, my school-mates never had anything good to say about me. They always made me feel inferior. Called me names like dirty…trailor trash…worthless.

"Oh, but if they could only see me now," I boasted to myself.

Suddenly, my cell phone went off again. This was getting aggravating. I walked back over to the register, and picked it up realizing that I still hadn't taken all the new clothes out of the bags. *Shit, I need these bitches to see all the new stuff I stole.*

"Hello," I answered quickly. I didn't even look at the caller ID. I hoped like hell it wasn't Rich.

"Yo', what up Mirror?"

It was distasteful the way he asked for me. Whoever it was wasn't a real man and obviously didn't know how to treat women.

"Who is this?"

I was stern.

To the point.

"King Pen."

"King Pen? Are you fucking serious? Who the fuck is this?"

"Shawty, chill out. Yo', I just met you yesterday while I was takin' a break from the studio, remember? I was drivin' the Navigator Truck."

"Oh yeah…you," I mentioned unenthused.

I was turned off by his introduction just as much as I was turned off by our initial contact from the day before. We met at the bank. He rolled up in the drive- thru pumping his awful rap music. My Benz was parallel to his truck when I noticed him winking at me. *Who in the hell still winks?* I thought as I rolled my eyes.

I remembered him turning down his music and trying to get my attention by calling me 'Shawty'. He shot me a motion with his hand basically telling me to write my number down.

I could tell he was a wanna be rapper.

Damn sure talked like one.

I turned my radio up, high as it could go, and watched as everyone turned their attention to me, including the tellers. With my foot on the break, I was seconds from moving the gear shift from park to drive until I spotted him placing five big bank bags individually into the tray.

My deposit had been weak, while his looked strong. Without a second thought, I turned down the radio, rolled down the window and gave him my number. I immediately overlooked his wanna-be flaws because he obviously had a couple of dollars. I was bored anyway. Needed a new man in my life. Some new money. Guess he got lucky, he was at the right place at the right time.

My mind snapped out of it when his raspy voice rose higher. "Yo lil' Mama, you was so fly yesterday, I can't get you out of my mind. Feel me? I just wanted to know when King could see you again?"

Why is this lame- ass dude talking to me in third person? I wondered while he fell silent. "Yeah, whatever. Look, I have to go…"

"I ain't tryin' to hear that! Where you at now? I'll come

22

scoop you."

"Scoop me? Nigga, I don't get scooped."

He laughed. "King got a feisty one...he likes that."

I thought, this nigga is insane. "Call me in about an hour," I suggested just to get him off the phone, then hung up before he could respond. I'd had enough of his antics and was relieved that he had no idea where the boutique was. I was convinced that he would just show up and probably make a scene. He seemed like that type, an overdramatic bitch-ass nigga.

"Ok ladies, let's rap this up. If you're finished shopping bring your items to the register. If not, hurry up. The boutique will be closing in twenty minutes."

Of course I got slapped with crazy looks, but surely didn't care. I took my time and opened up the garment bags one by one. "Here are all the new items. I don't have time to hang them on the racks. Oh, and if I have any new customers in here, no I don't do holds, or those dumb-ass lay-aways."

"But you just opened up thirty minutes ago," someone said sounding extra pissed.

"Yes, I did. And now I'm *just* closing. So like I said, you got twenty minutes." I pulled my watch close to my face. "Oh, now you got nineteen."

I listened to all the "Ahs and uhs, and no she didnt's." I wasn't concerned about anyone's business or their attitudes. It was all about me, and at the moment I was ready to leave for the day. Furthermore, I wasn't worried about them not coming back. These women loved the fact that they could get all this designer shit for a fraction of the price. It was like crack to them, and I was the fucking dealer.

● ● ● ● ● ● ● ● ● ● ● ● ● ● ● ● ●

Twenty-five minutes later, I'd checked out the last lady and closed out close to six thousand dollars in less than an hour. "Not a bad day at the office," I said to myself just before straightening up what little bit of items were left. I knew this meant I would have to go out and boost again real soon, but that went along with the territory. After making sure everything was in place, I turned out all the lights, and walked outside closing the door behind me. While scrambling inside my bag for my keys, I recognized a familiar sight. A sight I hated with a passion.

Today was a bit warmer, about seventy two degrees and she was covered in what looked like layers of clothes. Her dirt covered filthy hands, dug through the garbage can that was overflowing with trash. She was so determined to find something to eat, sell, or keep that she never even noticed my presence. My feet were glued to the spot I was standing in, and they wouldn't allow me to move.

I thought back to the old days.

I remembered being laughed at.

I remembered how my mother used to drag me along with her to do our shopping in the garbage cans. We lived a life of disgust. My mother had plenty of chances to leave my father, but declined every one; always making excuses of why she had to stay. None of them were ever good enough for me. After awhile, I figured that my mother believed that she didn't deserve any better.

I agreed.

An alcoholic is what she became. She funded her habit through her welfare checks that came every month which were supposed to keep food on the table. This had become her life. She hadn't changed, and was still content.

My mother finally turned around. "I was just coming to see you." I didn't expect her to talk. She had snapped me right out of my thoughts as she inched over cautiously. She noticed that my face didn't welcome her advance.

"See me for what!" I shouted.

Her facial features hadn't changed. But the alcohol had been doing a devastating job on her skin. Both ash and wrinkles had set in, along with the permanent crust that laced her lips. When I looked at her matted grey hair, it took me overboard. I shouted, "Didn't I tell you never to come here!"

"I just wanna talk to you about something important. Really important," she reiterated.

"No, get the hell outta here!" I shooed her with my hand.

She didn't move. But she knew I was serious. "Of all the fucking trash cans in Houston, why you gotta fuck with the one by

24

my boutique?"

"Well, can you at least spare me some change?" she asked me pitifully. She sounded like a real homeless woman. Acted like one too. "I caught the bus all the way down here just so I could talk to you."

"I don't give money to people like you! Look at yourself!" I pointed to the reflection in my store window. "Stop begging people for shit. Why don't you try something different? Go get a damn job."

And with that, I walked away. I hopped into my 2009 Diamond White CLS 550 and left smoke in her face as I screeched away. I was her, before I was even fifteen years old.

Alone.

Deserted.

I really was homeless at the time.

The only difference was that I didn't ask for any handouts. I bought what I needed and stole what I couldn't afford. But I never asked anyone for shit and promised myself that I would never be in that position again.

Chapter *Three*

"What the fuck? It feels like Alaska up in here," I said to myself as a slight chill ran through my body.

I grabbed my black and gold Roberto Cavalli hoodie jacket out of the hallway closet and put it on. Obviously, one of my Mexican housekeepers had left my air conditioning on blast because it was freezing. Shit, I could've sworn I even saw my breath.

"Who the hell turns the AC on in the winter? Just because this is Texas doesn't mean it's hot all the damn time." When I made a b-line over to the thermostat, it read fifty-six degrees. I was beyond pissed. "Is any of them non talking muthafuckas gonna pay this bill when it comes?" I said out loud like somebody was listening.

It was no way I was gonna let those three bitches think they could touch my shit and get away with it.

They would be fired.

Immediately.

Shutting off the AC, I turned around and scanned the living room and instantly noticed that one of the pillows on my couch was turned the wrong way. I don't know why I keep dealing with these damn cleaning companies anyway. I'm already on my fourth one, I thought as I marched over to the couch and placed the pillow in the correct position. I didn't bother fluffing it because they'd at least gotten that part right. A hundred and fifty dollars a week is what I spent to have these illegal immigrants keep my apartment exceptionally clean and this is what I had to come home to damn near every time. I was a stickler for perfection and despised anything less. That's what I deserved...that's what I demanded.

Besides, I no longer lived in the hood where filth was expected. I'd been living in the posh Post Rice Lofts for over two years now and enjoyed every inch of luxury the building offered.

My two bedroom, twenty-three hundred square foot home, which was on the 17th floor gave me the best downtown view of Houston and always made me feel like I was on top of the world. Hardwood floors and vaulted ceiling where also perks, but the best part was the exposed brick on the wall. It gave my apartment an immense sense of openness, and a chic sense of style which definitely represented the Mirror I had become. All my furniture was a mixture of West Elm and Z Gallerie, and several of my beautiful Jacob Lawrence paintings were displayed throughout. Yeah…where I was from, one could only dream of having a place like this, so I knew I had to do whatever it took to keep it.

When my cell phone rung a few minutes later, I quickly went into my purse and moved a few things around before grabbing it. For some strange reason, I felt as if the conversation was going to be about me getting some money, so I was quick on my toes. No, I wasn't a physic, but more so a muthafucking blood hound when it came to paper.

"Hello."

"What up for tonight…we still on?"

This time I recognized his voice. It repulsed me. "What do you want KP?"

"It's King Pen actually, or you can just call me King, baby."

"Look, I'm not fucking calling you either one of those stupid-ass names. I've made my decision, it's either KP or nothing at all."

"Damnnnnnnnnn. I guess I'll take what you give me."

"What do you want?" I repeated sharply.

"Did you forget?"

"Forget what?" I was completely annoyed.

"You told King to call back in a hour. You rollin' or what?"

I let out a huge sigh. "It must be hard for you to get pussy."

The line went silent for a brief second. "Hell no! Why you say that?"

"Because you have absolutely no game that's why," I replied.

He laughed like I was joking. "Who needs game when you got my kinda money?"

My expression changed instantly. "So, you mentioned something earlier about taking me out. Where do you want to go?" I decided to change my tone quickly, especially if I wanted to get some of that money he was talking about. I couldn't wait to see how deep his pockets really were.

He laughed again. Maybe he knew my MO. "King wanna take you somewhere special baby. Where you live at so I can be on my way?"

"Umm...I'm actually out and about already so I'll just meet you somewhere." His request wasn't an option. There was a fee to get inside my house, and KP hadn't paid his bill yet.

"Oh, okay that's cool. Well, meet me ova at The Vault Recording Studio. It's near Hunter's Creek Village. That'll just give me the chance to lay down a few mo tracks."

"Uh...whatever," I blurted out, very unimpressed with his rapping skills. "I'll be there in about thirty minutes then." After KP gave me the address to the studio, I hung up.

Quickly.

I really wasn't up for his annoyance, but since I'd cut most of my men off, and Khan was on my shit list, I needed someone to come in and fill the top position right away. I treated these men like insurance policies. Lapses were not tolerated.

Ten minutes later, I'd already jumped in the shower to freshen up and was headed into my favorite place in the house...my bedroom. Looking at the comfortable king sized brocade-canopied bed along with the five goose down Ophelia pillows, I wanted to take a quick nap, but decided against it. Especially when I realized what time it was. Seven thirty is what the clock read, and I hoped to be out of the house and on my way to the studio by eight at the latest. That was my ideal time for dates. Anything before seven thirty cried desperate and anything after nine screamed whore.

I was a lady...most of the time.

I took a step into my walk in closet, which by the average persons standards, could've fit another king sized bed inside of it. But not me. I wasn't average and my entire wardrobe took up the walk in closet and the second bedroom. I had clothes for years…literally.

Everything was color coded and separated into specific categories. My lingerie, dresses, jeans, shirts, and suits all had their special places in the store-like space. I had mirrors covering every wall from inch to inch, so that I was always guaranteed the best possible view and angle. One would think that the boutique brought in enough to pay for all of this, but it was my skill to steal anything that wasn't nailed down and good old fashion nigga hustlin' that provided me with all these luxuries.

I ended up putting on a black, tight sweater dress that was romantic, bold, and flirty…everything I knew that this date wouldn't be. I dressed my eyelids with soft black eye shadow, giving them the illusion of mystery and then glided on some Chanel lip gloss over my pouty lips. I was so glad I got them injected. They were so full now compared to their former life. I combed my weave into a very messy ponytail, stepped into my leopard print Manolo pumps, grabbed my Anna Sui clutch, and made my way to the front door.

However, before I got a chance to open it, there was a knock on my door. Just one. One that made me wonder if it had been done by mistake. Under any other circumstances, I probably wouldn't have given it too much more thought, but since I was already headed out anyway, I placed my hand on the knob to open the door.

I always thought she was beautiful. Jet black, bone straight hair ran over her breasts, while a red dot that I hadn't noticed before sat in the middle of her forehead. The small diamond ring that was pierced in her nose glistened from the light in the hallway and her dark mysterious eyes stared at me with conviction.

"I came here to warn you. Leave my husband alone."

She never moved.

Kept her body in an intimidating position. Just her words, laced with an Indian accent and a warm vodka scent warning me to leave Dr. Kahn in her bed at night.

"How in the fuck did you find out where I lived?" I asked.

Mrs. Kahn smirked. "It wasn't hard. You're my husband's patient remember? I went through your records."

"What happened to patient confidentiality? You're not supposed to do that!"

"And you're not supposed to be fucking my husband either," she replied. "Besides, any woman who's trying to keep her family together will go through great lengths to make that happen. She'll become an investigator when necessary. And she'll follow whoever to get the answers she wants."

"So, you've been following me!" I shouted, still not sure after the strange riddle she'd just hit me with. I could tell that she'd been drinking. The proof was in her slurred words and glossy eyes.

"Maybe." Her voice was monotone. Almost scary.

"Well, you better hope I don't ever catch your ass following me."

"You know what, I'll be damned if I let some nigger bitch come in and ruin…"

Before she knew it, I'd slapped her in the face so hard that the shit echoed through the hall. She stumbled a few feet back and quickly cupped her cheek to hold in the stinging pain that I'm sure she felt by now.

She never fought back.

Had the nerve to come to my house, talking all that shit and never once even attempted to defend herself. The whole outline of my hand was now imprinted on her face while she straightened herself up and continued to stare at me with even more hate than before.

"I will only warn you once and then I will kill you," she said, still never raising her voice.

I snapped, then rushed her. I took both of my hands and wrapped them around her neck. Watched as her eyes got wide and she gasped for whatever air she could catch. I whispered in her ear. "Don't you ever come to my house with your fake fucking threats again bitch! I'll kill *you*," I said mocking her. "You better take your drunk-ass home before you get hurt."

I let go of her neck and watched as she bent down and inhaled as much air as her lungs would allow. She coughed a few times and inhaled some more before she straightened back up to her original position.

"I will only warn you once. And then I'll kill you," she had the nerve to repeat.

With all my might, I pushed her into the wall. But she kept making threats.

She just wouldn't shut the fuck up.

"Back down bitch," I warned shoving her body toward the elevator, then grabbed her by the arm.

I let her go as soon as she stumbled closer to the elevator. When she pushed the button, the door opened immediately. After stepping inside, she turned around, faced me, then mouthed for the third time, "I will kill you."

Once again her eyes said something weird.

They were scary in a strange sort of way.

"I'm serious," she said. Then the door closed.

Chapter *Four*

Fifteen minutes later, I was sitting outside the studio waiting for KP. That was the luxury of living downtown; I was never too far from anything. Going into a slight daze, I still couldn't believe everything that had just gone down with me and Kahn's wife, and was already trying to figure out how I was going to handle the whole thing. Just in case her dumb-ass got bold and decided to come back, I needed to be prepared.

"Damn girl, you look good!" KP yelled, catching me off guard. I had my window rolled down which gave him the chance to sneak up on me.

I couldn't believe I'd conned myself into going out with this loser, but my rent was almost due and I had no intentions on coming out of my pockets to pay for anything. I needed a replacement for Kahn who was my top money maker, but still couldn't figure out why I'd stooped so low to get it. KP dressed ghetto-fabulous and was too old to be participating in the 'Soldier Boy' movement. Normally, I went after the clean cut Armani suit type men, but lately they were nowhere to be found. The good ones seemed to be extinct.

KP was a lot shorter than I thought, and reminded me of a smaller version of Busta Rhymes with dreads. His mouth was full of gold; neck and wrist draped in what were probably silver and cubics instead of platinum and diamonds. He wore an outfit that someone would only wear if they were in the rapper Paul Wall's entourage. The dingy black t-shirt and baggy jeans were a complete turn off.

"How old are you again?" I asked looking him up and down.

"Thirty-two."

"Yeah…I thought that's what you said." *You're too damn*

old to be dressing like that.

"Come on, get out and ride with me in my car," he suggested as he began walking away.

I looked at him like he had three heads. "Excuse me? Are you not going to open up my door?"

Damn, a loser who didn't open up doors. I was really beginning to re-evaluate how I picked my victims.

KP stopped and turned around before showing those awful gold teeth. "Oh, my bad Shawty." He returned back to my car then opened my door and waited awkwardly as I stepped out. At thirty-two years old, it was a shame that he had never done this before.

I could tell.

"Damn!" he shouted before swinging his hand over his heart. "Yo' Shawty, you got the biggest ass I seen." He stepped back to admire it. "Yeah, I'ma have to snatch you up before another nigga does! When King make it big, I wanna classy chick like you on my arm." He placed his hand on the small of my back and before I knew it, I'd grabbed a hold of his finger and bent it back.

"Don't you ever put your hands on me again without permission...understand?"

"Yeah," he said shaking his head. "Ouch...dat shit hurt, Shawty!" When I let go he stared at his finger to inspect the damage. "You crazy girl."

"I can be."

Now this time, he looked at me like he was having second thoughts. "Let's go."

We walked a couple of feet to his black Lincoln Navigator and surprisingly he followed the pattern and opened the door for me again. Maybe he could be trained? I hopped inside the truck slightly optimistic.

The fresh smell of 'new' entered my nose as I looked around for any evidence that the truck was used.

I found none.

"So how long have you had this?" I asked, watching him pull from the curb. I could tell he was a cautious driver by the way he studied the rearview mirror before mingling in the busy traffic.

"I just got it this year…it's my baby," he replied admirably as he rubbed the dashboard.

"Oh really. What year is it?"

"Umm…a 2008. I guess."

My face frowned instantly "You don't know what damn year your car is? Besides, didn't they have any 2009 trucks on the lot? You need to upgrade."

"Yeah, but '09 trucks be like a ten thousand dollar difference and…"

"Ten stacks…that's all? That seems like nothing for someone in your status, but hey, maybe you're not balling like I assumed."

"Ballin? Yo' do you see dis shit?" he asked tugging on his jewelry. "I got two five-row diamond chains hangin' from my neck wit the bracelets to match and I sleep in a half a million dollar crib. Dey don't call me King Pen fo' nothin' Shawty."

He was defensive.

Uncomfortable.

I'd obviously pushed a button and took him off his game. My intentions were successful.

"As a matter of fact you wanna hear how a nigga like me did his thang in the studio today?"

It really wasn't a question. I could tell that the option for me to decline wouldn't be taken seriously since he had already inserted the CD into the system.

> *They don't call me King Pen fo nothing*
> *Other niggas be frontin'*
> *I roll around in Bentleys*
> *And bitches be buggin'*

I blanked out.

I saw nothing. I heard nothing. I reared back in my seat and wondered why I had stooped so low. A kindergartner just learning their ABC's had more skills than KP did. I caught a glimpse of him from my peripheral view and saw him singing along, confident that he had the hottest shit since Jay-Z's *Reasonable Doubt.* I hoped he wasn't lying to himself like that though. A few seconds later, his phone went off, sounding off with it the same wack- ass beat that the song had.

He answered, "What's good?" The caller on the other end obviously had a lot to say because KP was silent for a while, then he got hype. "I'm tellin' you Yo', I really think that this track right here is a winner! Man, I stayed in that damn studio all night, high as hell. I'm telling you Yo', I was in a zone and this song here is the one."

Again, silence

Even though I was sick of all the studio talk, I was hoping that whoever had him hostage on the other line would continue the conversation until we got to where we were going. But I wasn't so lucky. Suddenly, his telephone call came to an abrupt end. My bubble had been burst.

"Yo'…I'm sick of niggas hatin' on Yo' Boy. Day just mad cause day ain't never seen nothin' like me befo. Wait till dis shit drop Yo'…I'm tellin'' you!"

"Whatever," I said after rolling my eyes. "Where are we going to eat?" I noticed we'd passed several restaurants, and I'd gotten hungrier by the second.

"I was thankin' that we could hit up somewhere nice like the Cheesecake Factory over at the Galleria and then…"

"The Cheesecake Factory? What the fuck do I look like to you…some corny bitch? That's your business if you want to ride around in this cheap-ass old truck, but I only eat, ride, live, and travel with the finest things. Cheesecake Factory is low budget. I'm not. Take me to an upscale restaurant or take me back to my fucking Benz. You know a real car," I demanded, before crossing my arms and pouting like a toddler.

I was serious.

He could tell.

"Calm down. I ain't mean it like dat Shawty. Whatever you want…it's yours. King got you."

Now he was speaking the language I understood. Me.

"Well, in that case we're going to Perry's Steakhouse because they have great Salmon. We can go to their new location in Memorial City." *Plus that's not too far from where we're at. The sooner I can get this date over with the better.*

36

"I love it when you get feisty wit me boo."

As we drove up Katy Freeway, KP got another phone call.

"Do you have any tissue in here?" I asked, while opening up the glove compartment. It was the perfect time to perform my usual I-spy routine. Whatever car I got into, I always made sure to check the glove compartment for the registration. Really, I wanted to find out if my potential really owned the vehicle, where they lived, and any other personal information I could find.

He didn't hear or respond to my question. Instead, he just kept complaining to someone about the drum beat on one of his tracks not being right. Looking inside, the glove compartment was bare, except for a pink piece of paper that was folded in half. Under normal circumstances that would've been okay except this piece of paper had the words Thrifty Car Rental located at the top left corner. *This lying muthafucka*! I said to myself, while my snooping continued. Everything inside the truck looked standard. Nothing seemed customized. No booming system…no base. Now, it dawned on me that I hadn't even seen any rims on the damn truck. What rapper didn't have rims?

It was the first sign that he might be broke. *Damn, I hope I didn't fuck up this time*. However, I kept my fingers crossed, and hoped like hell his Aston Martin or at least a Range Rover was being serviced.

As soon as we pulled up to Perry's, KP got off the phone and pulled directly in front of the restaurant. At least he had sense enough to know that front door service was something that I expected. A few seconds later, two men dressed in slacks and crisp white shirts appeared. They were valet, which must've been something new. An added plus to the already award winning restaurant.

Both doors opened simultaneously. "Welcome to Perry's," the valet on my side greeted. He was short, but handsome for a white guy.

"Thank you," I replied.

"Your car will be in great hands," the other valet said to KP. He seemed to be rushing and as I turned around, I realized why. A convoy of cars had lined up behind us in the thirty seconds that we'd been there.

"It better be," KP demanded after getting out of the truck. "I just got this car buffed after the valet at the Westin Hotel scratched my baby up."

I was beyond annoyed that this nigga was still acting like this truck belonged to him. "Ain't nobody thinking about this cheap piece of shit!" I said loudly. I wasn't sure if he was talking to me or the valet anyway, but wanted to make it clear to him that I didn't give a fuck. The valet guy chuckled under his breath when KP looked at me, shocked that I would say something like that I guess.

"Look," he said in an attempt to recoup whatever dignity he had left as a man. "You better watch how the fuck you talk to me Shawty fo, real! I ain't one of dem punk-ass niggas you been dealing wit'." He was serious and it was written all over his face.

I didn't give a fuck had been written all over mine all along.

"And you better watch how you fucking talk to me!" I demanded. We instantly gained the attention of a few people. After the episode that I'd just had with Nurse Khan I was ready to fuck something up anyway.

"Yo'...fo real tho Shawty..."

"Let's go so we can get this shit over with," I said again while walking past him. I didn't even bother to wait for a response.

He followed like a good little boy.

As soon as we walked through the front door and I glanced at Perry's beautiful upscale décor, and warm color scheme, I was even more embarrassed that the wanna be rapper was my date for the evening. His pants, which were several inches lower than his belt loops looked extremely ghetto, an appearance I didn't associate with. Not to mention, it was a huge difference from the oxford pants, button up shirts, and loafers everyone else seemed to have on.

"Good evening and welcome to Perry's. Do you two have a reservation?" the female hostess asked. She seemed kind of hesitant. Studied his long dreads for about ten seconds. I bet she was wondering if the 'thug' could afford the meal. However, one look at me though, and I'm sure that her question would've been answered.

"No, we don't," I responded quickly before he had a chance
to.

"Okay, well I think we had a cancellation, so if you can
wait right here, I'll go and check on that for you." I followed her
with my eyes as she walked away and caught a glimpse of the interior design again. It was contemporary. The dining room looked
like it carried an intimate mood and that damn sure wasn't the im-
pression I wanted KP to get.

The hostess came back quickly. "Thank you for waiting.
Our last reservation did cancel so if you two want to follow me."

"Umm, is there any way that we can just sit in the bar
area?" I asked. I didn't want any of these upper class people to see
me with this dude.

She looked confused. "Oh, of course. I didn't realize you
wanted to sit in that area. Right this way." She seemed relieved that
his ghetto presence wouldn't ruin the decorum.

So was I.

When we took a seat at the bar, the hostess handed the both
of us a menu before leaving.

No sooner than I could place my purse down, the bartender
appeared with a huge smile. "Hello and welcome to Perry's. Can I
start the two of you with something to drink?"

"Hell yeah. Yo', I'll take a Henney and Coke," KP blurted
out. Evidence again that he wasn't used to taking out a *real* woman
like myself. He ordered first. That was a big no no.

"And for yourself ma'am?" the bartender asked.

"Sparkling Pellegrino, please."

"Certainly!" he said before walking off.

I detested alcohol. My family had been addicted forever
and I refused to be anything like them.

"This is a nice spot you picked, Shawty. You come here
often?" KP asked looking around. He seemed way out of his ele-
ment.

I was so relieved when my phone vibrated, which meant
my conversation with Mr. Wanna Be would have to be postponed. I
pulled the phone out of my clutch and saw that it was private

caller.

On any other occasion I wouldn't have answered the phone, but whoever was on the other end couldn't have been worse than the knucklehead I was with.

"Yes, may I help you?"

"Mirror it's me, Dr. Khan. Listen...I..."

"No, you listen," I warned through my teeth. "You better keep your fucking situation in check! Do you understand me?" Called it a situation because I didn't want KP to know what was going on. Wished I could've taken this phone call later, but this was important and it couldn't wait. It was something that had to be addressed right away.

"Situation? What are you talking about?" he asked. He didn't know what was going on. I could hear it all in his voice.

"What the fuck were you calling for then?"

"I was calling to tell you that I deposited that money into your account. What situation are you talking about?"

My eyes lit up instantly. "Oh really. How much?"

"Ten thousand. What situation, Mirror?"

"Your wi..." I looked at KP who was damn near looking down my throat. I turned my head slightly before continuing. "Your nurse came by today."

"My wife? Came by where?"

"Let's just say that bitch made a house call. Must've thought I was sick or something," I said trying to disguise what really happened. I hoped Dr. Khan was swift enough to catch on.

"My wife? Came by your house? Oh my God! What...what happened? What did she want? Does she know? What did she say?"

"Oh, she knows. Suggested that I change doctors or else I'd have a price to pay."

"She threatened you? That's not like her...you sure it was..."

"Muthafucka, I know what the fuck that bitch looks like!" I said impatiently. "Look, I can't talk right now...I'll hit you up later!"

"Wait...but..."

I hung up the phone.

"So, I'm saying tho. Who was that…yo man?" KP asked.

"No. And if it was, it's none of your business."

"Why you ain't got no man as fine as you is?"

"Because I don't want one."

"You gay?"

I wish, thinking that anything would be better than this, even a chick. "No, I'm not gay. Are you? You know, there's a lot of that *down low shit* going on these days…"

"Hell, fuck nah I ain't gay Shawty. You tryin' to play me!" He'd made a scene. People were looking. I had him frustrated…again.

"No more than you just tried playing me."

He went into his back pocked and pulled out a wrinkled pack of Newports, and slid a cigarette out. Visibly upset about the accusation of his homosexuality, he shoved the cancer stick in his mouth and quickly followed up with a lighter. Before the flame ever touched it, the bartender ran over with our drinks and said, "I'm sorry sir, this is a non-smoking establishment."

"What type of shit is dat?"

"I'm sorry sir, that's our policy." I put my head in my hands while KP debated with the bartender for a few more seconds, before he finally placed the cigarette back in the pack. He'd obviously been defeated. "Are you all ready to order," the bartender asked with pen and pad in hand.

"Absolutely. I'll begin with the Cherry Pepper Calamari for my appetizer. Then I'll move on to the Bosc Pear and Pecan Salad, along with the Salmon De Paris and sautéed spinach for my entree. Actually, you can bring the salad out with the salmon."

"Great choices Ma'am. And for you sir?" the bartender asked looking at KP.

"Yeah, y'all got some fried chicken wings?"

I was so fucking embarrassed.

"No sir, we don't carry those," the bartender responded with a smirk on his face.

I bet the curly head white guy was positive now that all black people ate chicken. I was just waiting for KP's hood-ass to ask for a big juicy slice of watermelon next.

"Damn…King like dem thangs fried hard, too. Uh, just give me a steak."

I rolled my eyes at his lack of etiquette.

"Oh, we have so many choices of steak, Sir. Which one would you prefer? May I recommend the Peppercorn New York Strip?" the bartender suggested with a smile.

"Man, King don't know nothin' 'bout that. Just give me a steak," KP chuckled, laughing at his own damn stupidity.

I couldn't take it anymore. "What kind of steak do you want and how do you want it prepared dumb-ass. Medium rare…well done. Have you ever been anywhere other than Wendys?" I asked. It didn't matter that the bartender looked like he was about to watch an episode of Jerry Springer. KP was insulted…again. I could tell.

"I just want my shit cooked, a'ight!" he yelled.

The bartender quickly collected the menus that were in front of us. "Thank you. I'll make sure I put your orders in right away," he said before walking away.

We were silent.

Just had nothing to talk about.

We lived two totally different lives. Mine was elite, his hood. I glanced at him for a second and caught him bopping his neck to a beat that was only in his head. Then the worst came. He had started to rap.

In my heart I knew that this entire date was a mistake, but the only thing that kept me sane was the image of those five bank bags of money that I remembered him handing the bank teller the other day. If he had it, I was determined to make his ass withdraw every fucking dime.

"Can you please stop?" I begged him. He was way too old to be rapping at a restaurant.

"Yo' you need to stop naggin' me and shit. Besides, you gonna be all on me when dis song blow up. I'll probably spend the whole day at the studio again tomorrow." He took a huge swig of his Hennessey, leaving nothing but the ice cubes in the glass.

Don't flatter yourself, I thought as the bartender came over and placed my appetizer in front of me before asking KP if he wanted another drink. I loved their fast professional service, but wished they would've waited before offering his ass another drink so soon. When he accepted, all I could do was get even more frustrated. Like we needed his ghetto-ass to be drunk up in this classy restaurant.

I wasn't sure if it was the stress of being out with Mr. Wanna-Be or what, but the headache I had earlier today had come back even stronger. I shuffled around in the chair trying to ease the discomfort in my lower back as well. While he guzzled down his second drink, I went into my purse and placed another one of my special pills in my hand and swallowed it, this time with a little help from the water. I knew I wasn't supposed to take more than one a day, but it seemed necessary. My symptoms seemed to be getting stronger. I knew what that meant.

KP let me eat my calamari in silence as he continued to move his head and let out a corny sounding beat box at the same time. I covered my plate so his ass wouldn't get spit all over my fucking food.

"Look, can you just sit here like a normal person? I'm trying to eat."

"Then eat," he said in between several crazy sounds.

"Who does that shit anymore anyway? This ain't 1983." I took another bite of my calamari before shoving my plate away. He was starting to ruin my meal.

"Say what you want. These beats gotta play out in my head. Dis shit is how I make my loot." KP went into his pocket and pulled out a raggedy business card from his wallet. "Actually here's my manager's card. Pass dis to someone who might wanna book me for a show." When I didn't hold my hand out, he tossed the card and the wallet on the bar.

Yeah, I was definitely ready to go.

Several minutes and several beat boxing tunes later, a waitress came by and placed our entrees and my salad on the table then placed her hand on the calamari plate. "Are you done with this Miss?"

I looked at the plate that was probably covered in tiny spit balls by now. "Yes, yes I am."

She swooped the plate up. "Well, you all enjoy your dinner," she said, flashing a huge smile before walking away.

"I certainly will. This looks absolutely delicious!" I raved, just as excited to dig in.

"Is this it? Dis is all the food I get for all dis money?" KP asked loudly. "Where the hot sauce at!"

"Would you shut up? This is not a fucking soul food restaurant!" Again, I'd had enough, and was sick of his damn whining. I picked up the steaming hot piece of salmon and began eating it, hoping that he was able to learn by example in a matter of seconds.

I wasn't so lucky.

"You know what…you look good and all, but yo' booshie-ass up on a real fucking high horse or some shit. Yeah…I know Yo' kind. You probably ain't use to eating dis type of shit either. Probably tryin' to run from where you really came from, trying to be somebody you ain't."

I placed another piece of salmon in my mouth while watching my entertainment vent all his frustrations out on me. In the midst of him still talking, I began to clap. And then I stood up. Gave him a standing ovation. Everyone at the bar stared at us again. I'm sure hoping we would leave soon.

"That was so cute. Do you feel better now?" I asked as if I was talking to a child. "I hate to bust your bubble, but I grew up in an estate that sat on fifteen acres. My father owned jets, yachts, and everything else you could think of. My mother was well taken care of until the day that she died, so to answer your assumption, no. No, I'm not used to things like this. I'm accustomed to the finer things in life. I only agreed to come here because this was all I thought your ass could afford!" I didn't care if he believed all my lies.

He'd begun eating his steak during my speech. "What the fuck ever," was all he said as he cut himself another piece and shoved it inside his mouth.

I too, continued on with my meal while trying to pretend that he wasn't there. However, the smacking sound that came from his mouth was a constant reminder that he was low class. I lowered

my head and tried my best to ignore him until I heard several muf-
fled type noises. When I looked back up, KP's eyes were widened
with fear. He seemed to be gasping for air.

Unable to communicate to me verbally, he placed his hands
around his neck to translate the universal code for, 'I'm choking
bitch, help me!' I sat there and placed the last piece of fish in my
mouth while I watched.

"Hey, I think that guy is choking," a woman said to her
date. The man, who was only a few bar stools away from us,
rushed over and proceeded to give KP the Heimlich maneuver instantly.

"Oh, just let him die," I instructed the helpful bystander. I
took a sip of my water as the guy looked up at me in disbelief.
"I'm serious. Just let him go up to be with the Lord. He's no good
down here…believe me."

I laughed after saying that one.

Cracked myself up.

It only took three good pumps before his filet went flying
across the room. After coughing for the next few seconds, KP put
his hands on his chest and took several big breaths before getting
up and hugging the man that had saved his life. Everyone, including the manager, came over to check on him. It was a special moment if you were into that type of shit.

When he walked back over to the bar, KP seemed relieved
and pissed all at the same time.

"Are you okay?" I asked rubbing his arm.

"Get the fuck off me!" he yelled. "What kind of person are
you? Why the fuck would you just sit there while I was chokin'?"

I tried to make it sound good even though he was right.
"I'm sorry. I thought you were just joking with me."

"Bitch why would I joke about somethin' like dat!" he
yelled.

That was it for my so called niceness. "Bitch? You know
what, maybe they should've let your ass die." I knew that was a
low blow, but I didn't care. At that point, all I wanted to do was
get out of there, so I didn't waste time flagging the bartender down
for the check. I still continued to mumble insult after insult under

my breath until the bartender reappeared with the bill.

"You sure you're okay Sir?" he asked KP. "You scared us for a little bit."

When KP shook his head, the bartender placed the black little folder in front of him then walked away.

"I don't know why he placed the shit in front of me. You got fuckin' money, right? So, you take care of it then. Especially since you think it's cool to sit and watch somebody die," KP stated angrily as he shoved the check next to me, then stormed off. I guess he was attempting to leave me stranded at the restaurant.

And his dumb-ass probably would've gotten far had he not left his cell phone and wallet right on the bar. I knew it would only be a matter of time before he realized it, so I quickly motioned for the bartender to come toward me, then opened up KP's wallet. Looking back every few seconds, I pulled out a gold American Express card, then placed it in the black folder before sending the bartender away.

Hmmm...a gold American Express, I thought. Another sign that he could possibly be broke. I was expecting a Black card or at least a platinum one.

Suddenly, I saw KP rushing back inside, and patting his pockets at the same time. When he walked up to the bar, I waved his ugly leather wallet back and forth, teasing him like a little child.

"Look, I'm not in the mood for fuckin' games. Give me back my shit!" he demanded. Everyone in the restaurant seemed to be looking our way. We'd definitely been their entertainment for the evening.

I tossed him both the wallet and the phone. "There you go, but just to let you know your wallet might be missing a gold Amex card." When he looked at me with a cold pair of eyes, all I could do was laugh. He was in no way a threat to me.

"Who told you to touch my shit? I didn't tell you to do that!"

"This food will get paid for with *your* money. Do you think that you can just walk out on me? Muthafucka, I don't get walked out on, and I certainly don't pay for meals."

46

I could tell by the way his eyes moved up and down my body that he wanted to kill me. Possibly strangulation.

The way his life had almost ended.

"Bitch…" was all he managed to get out before the bartender returned.

"I'm sorry Sir, but your card has been declined."

He just stood there looking stupid.

"Dat can't be right. Yo' try that shit again!" he suggested obviously forgetting the fact that he refused to pay the bill in the first place. It was something about having a card declined that brought out the bitch in me.

"Sir, we ran the card several times and each time it declined. Do you have another payment method?"

A declined credit card. Fuck the signs…now I knew this nigga was broke.

"Give me a second," he asked while digging into his pockets. I guess he still felt like he had a point to prove. That he could afford what I had lied and said I was used to. An expensive lifestyle.

"You fake balling-ass nigga! How do you have me out here with no money? I can't believe this!"

"Shut the hell up, Shawty. All you do is run yo' damn mouth, King tired of hearin' it for one night!" KP yelled back at me.

The bartender had a look on his face that begged the both of us to hurry up and get out of the restaurant. When I parted my lips to fire something smart right back at him, KP shouted again, "Shut up!"

He placed his hand in his pocket and shuffled around a bit. The anticipation was killing me. What the fuck was he looking for…lint? Suddenly, he pulled out a large wad of money that was tightly wrapped in a rubber band, a reminder of what I was here for in the first place. A confirmation of what my plans were for him. I used my expertise to scan the thickness of the bills. When he peeled off a couple of hundreds and handed them to the bartender, my guess was about eight thousand.

"I'll be right back with your change," the bartender said before walking away.

"Nah, you straight," KP responded before placing the rest of the money back into his pocket.

"Thanks, Sir. You all have a great evening," the bartender stated. He seemed pleased with his tip.

KP quickly made sure he had his wallet and cell phone this time before turning around and walking out the door as fast as he could. I got up and walked swiftly behind him as he bolted straight for the valet. He then handed the young man the ticket and waited impatiently as he retrieved the keys to his Navigator.

"Actually, you can just give me the keys, and I'll go and get the car myself," I heard him say to the valet.

"Are you sure, Sir?" the guy asked, recognizing that this wasn't proper procedure.

"Positive."

As directed, the valet handed KP his keys and then pointed to him where the truck was. We both looked in that direction at the same time, and saw three trucks sitting only three cars away from where we already were. Obviously, trying to leave me for the second time, KP's short legs took off walking faster than a crack head until he reached his truck. I had to run in order to catch up with him, but by the time I reached the passenger side door, he already had the engine running and the doors were locked.

"Let me in," I said, banging my fist on the window. "Muthafucka, let me in the damn car!"

Surprisingly, all he did was turn up his music.

Chapter Five

"Please let me in the car!" I'd changed my voice from demanding to more of a pleading tone. The crazy thing is, it obviously worked because he cracked the window open just enough to hear my cries, but not wide enough for me to stick my hand through. "I'm sorry for acting like a bitch all night, King," I said, after he turned down the music. Thinking about the wad of money in his pocket, it was time for me to finally turn on the charm for this nigga. I knew he would be pleased that I'd just called him by that stupid-ass name.

"I just had a very nasty breakup and I've been bitter ever since." I pried my eyes away from his and looked down at the ground.

Tried looking sad.

Wasn't sure if any it was working.

"I knew it was too soon to start dating again, but you seemed so nice and handsome. It's hard to find a good man nowadays and as selfish as it sounds, I didn't want you to get away." I lowered my head again, and tried to make myself shed a few tears, but couldn't. I guess my tear ducts had dried out over the years, especially from all the crying I used to do as a child.

This time he rolled the window down a little bit more. "Get in," was his only reply just before I heard the doors unlock.

Trying to hurry up before he changed his mind again, I quickly opened the door and climbed inside, then shut it with ease. I looked him in the eye, then placed my hand over his. "I'm so sorry," I whispered, like an actress in a drama filled movie.

"Listen, I know we ain't been gettin' along too good, and I'll put some of dat on me. Wit all 'dis music stuff happenin', I been a lil' stressed and shit. But you a firecracker yo' damn self. I really fuckin' like you Shawty, so cut all yo' bullshit out!"

49

I would be so glad when the name *Shawty* turned into Mirror. "It won't happen again King. I promise."

He leaned his head back on the head rest and took a deep loud sigh. "Man…what a fuckin' night. I still can't believe I almost choked to death. Dat shit was wild man."

"Yeah, I know. I've never seen anything like that before. I know you think I was trying to be mean, but actually I was just scared." I wasn't sure if he would believe me or not, but it was worth a shot.

The look he gave me said that I was full of shit. "My fuckin' life flashed in front of me, Yo'. All I could think about was the shit I ain't got to do yet. Like my yacht. I ain't even had the chance to wild out on it yet."

"A yacht?"

"Yeah, it's just another toy, but it's somethin' I always wanted."

If this dude was rocking yacht status, his ass was definitely a long term keeper, but I still had mixed feelings. It had never taken me this long to figure out if a guy was paid or not. I guess I just had to keep investigating.

While he rubbed his head back and forth, I dug in my clutch and took out my lip gloss, and slowly glided it on my lips. If he was stressed, I knew just what to do to make all that shit go away.

He watched just like I wanted him to.

Licked his lips.

I rubbed mine together and then poked them out a little more.

"Damn, dem lips is so juicy. King wanna taste 'em."

"They taste good too," I replied slowly running my tongue across the top.

Without warning, he leaned over, pressing all his body weight on top of me. He tried kissing me wherever his lips landed. I could smell the yack on his breath as his breathing got heavier.

"Get off of me!" I yelled with one hard shove.

"My bad you just look so good."

"I know, but you could use a few breath mints," I said, trying to sound a little nicer.

I didn't like to be kissed in the mouth.

It disgusted me.

Maybe it was a phobia. Either way I wasn't going to try to overcome it with his dirty-ass mouth. We could play around a bit, but not that way. "Look," I said with a much softer tone. "You've had a rough day. Let's go back to your crib and chill." I needed to see where and how he lived.

"Bet," KP replied with a huge smile. He was damn near breaking his neck trying to pull out of the restaurant's parking lot.

I was thankful that I wasn't going to have to catch a cab from the restaurant back to my car.

Public transportation.

It was disgusting.

No one spoke a word the entire ride to his house for some reason. It was as if we were trapped in a marriage to each other and had nothing else left to say. There was no more interest in getting to know each other better.

He wanted sex.

And me, I wanted money.

Lately, all I'd been thinking about was pulling up to the front of my boutique in a 2009 Bentley Continental GT. I'd already been to the dealership on West Loop South, and picked out the two door beauty. Silver with piano black interior was my choice. Once I found someone to write me a check for the $180,000 price tag, I'd be straight.

A stop at the gas station and thirty five minutes later we ended up in Copper Lakes, which was a beautiful subdivision and one that I was well familiar with. The neighborhood was quiet and well kept, and majority of the houses started at four hundred thousand, so I knew I could get down with KP.

So far so good, I told myself as we cruised through the neighborhood and turned onto a street called Red Leaf Hollow. Seconds later, we pulled into a huge Mediterranean style house with a three car garage. It had a stucco exterior, which always gave homes a certain flair.

"Nice house," I said, admiring the landscaping. Things

seemed to be picking up a little bit. I started to think that maybe I was tripping about the car rental receipt and the gold card. Maybe I just needed to give him a chance.

"Thanks. Dis rappin' shit is really pickin' up fo yo' boy. Yo', just wait...I'ma be on MTV Cribs and have billboards of my face everywhere when my first single makes #1."

"You know it," I said stroking his ego.

I was more concerned about the house. It sat in the highly desired water view section of the subdivision and was accompanied by two other houses. His seemed to be the biggest though. Looked like it was at least five thousand square feet.

KP didn't waste time getting out of the car, and just like clockwork he came over to open my door. I'd trained him well in that short period of time. "Yo' you sho blessed you wit' a phat ass," he said, twirling me around to get a better view once I stepped out.

"Yeah, it runs in the family," I bragged with confidence. Little did he know that my mother's ass was as flat as a damn pancake. I hated the fact that she'd given me her shape.

Walking up to the house, I could barely control my excitement as KP took out his keys and unlocked the door. Although I was hoping we would go through the garage, so I could see what other cars he was working with. But if the inside was as nice as the outside, I could see myself moving my bags up in here in a matter of weeks. As beautiful as this house was, I could get ear plugs to drown out that stupid rap shit.

As soon as he opened the door an alarm rang out throughout the house, startling me in the process. I stood in one spot as KP turned to the wall and punched in a seven digit code onto the key pad. The alarm beeped a few times then stopped, letting us know that it had been disarmed. I watched as he turned on the light in the foyer, then took a few small steps before taking off his sneakers.

Oh now he wants to have some manners, I thought. He'd acted like a straight hoodlum in the restaurant and now he was treating his floors with more respect.

"Can you do me a favor and take yo' shoes off?" he asked.

"Ah, no."

He gave me a strange look. "Baby, dis floor is marble. You

can't wear shoes on dis."

"Nigga, I have marble floors and actually mine are a better quality," I shot back after a little inspection. "This floor is cold. I'm keeping my shoes on!" I knew me turning back into a bitch so soon probably wasn't the best move, but it was hard for me to put on a front. I guess a bitch was who I really was.

"Yo' fuck it!" he yelled, throwing his hands up. "I'm tired of fuckin' arguin' wit' you." He sucked his gold teeth and walked into the kitchen that was a few feet ahead of us.

I followed.

Walking up to the granite top kitchen island, the stainless steel Viking kitchen appliances and cream colored marble back-splash spoke volumes, and told me he had nice taste. Not to mention, the nicely decorated great room, which sat right off the kitchen displayed a beautiful view of the lake.

I love my apartment, but I deserve to be living in something like this, I thought as I watched KP pull three styrofoam cups out of his custom made cherry wood cabinets.

The infamous styrofoam cup.

Houston, Texas.

It could only mean one thing.

Born and raised in Houston, that 'lean' was the *only* thing that these niggas put in styrofoam cups. He took out a bottle of sprite, poured it into all the cups, and mixed them in with some Robitussin. He then took a bottle of prescription Vicodin out of the drawer and crushed three pills up before throwing it into his three separate concoctions. After it was all said and done, he topped them off with an apple jolly rancher. They didn't call this the city of syrup for nothing.

"You want some?" he offered, right before chugging down one of the eight ounce drinks.

"No, I'm straight."

I walked over to his entertainment center in the great room and turned it on. It didn't come as much of a surprise when DJ Screw's music blasted through the surround sound. It played in a super slow motion in what they called 'chopped and screwed'. However, because DJ Screw had died of a 'lean' overdose, I thought that everyone would've gotten the message and left that shit alone, but I guess some dumb-ass people just loved to play with death.

While he got high on that shit, I snooped around the crib, trying to figure out who the man was in all the pictures. They bore no resemblance. This man was much cuter. Handsome actually. Besides, even if they were family, it was still kind of creepy that he had this many pictures of one dude.

"Hold up. Are you fucking gay?" I asked over the music.

"What the fuck? He snapped, then strutted his lil' short ass over to see what I was talking about. "What did you say?"

"Nigga you heard me. Are you gay?"

"Oh, no. That's my manager. He's the reason why my music even allowed me to get a crib like dis, so I posted up a lot of his flicks. I owe him my life." He reached out and grabbed my waist. "Don't worry baby, I'm all man."

I flinched when he pulled me in closer because his dreads dangled in my face. I almost gagged at the smell of cough syrup and alcohol, which at this point seemed to be seeping out of his pores.

He kissed me.

I gagged again and then mushed him.

"What the fuck is yo' problem!" KP yelled.

"Don't put your mouth on mine and we won't have any more problems."

Kissing was for lovers, and we were far from that.

Besides, there was no attraction. Nothing that we had in common, except he wanted something from me and I damn sure wanted something from him. He *wanted* pussy. I *needed* cash. Looking at how frustrated he was, I knew I had to make a move in order to get some of his money before the night was over. I needed him comfortable and incapacitated. And there was only one thing that could make that happen.

Pussy.

It was the one sure thing that would do the trick.

Pussy made kingdoms fall.

I knew if he lived in this neighborhood, he had to have

money. I had no doubts about it…the money bags, the type of cash he carried in his pockets, this house in Copper Lakes, it all spelled out m-o-n-e-y. Money that I was determined to get.

"Can I see your bedroom?" I asked in a sexy voice.

As if he already knew what was about to happen, KP showed a wide gold tooth grin. He was already on his second syrup cup when he led me up the black wrought iron staircase and into the massive master bedroom. He pushed a switch, which turned on several lights.

"I wanna be able to see that body," KP said, looking at me like a hungry lion.

I had to play the role. "No problem, Mr. King Pen."

Not wasting much time, we both walked over to the king sized platform bed, which was the one thing in that house that I didn't like and sat down. KP attempted to kiss my neck a few times, but I quickly turned my head. I didn't understand why he was so determined to put his lips on me. Didn't he get the memo that I wasn't into foreplay? Not from him anyway.

In an attempt to speed things along, I undressed myself, then folded the clothes neatly on the cinnamon colored leather chaise lounge that sat alongside the bed. He ended up downing the second cup of syrup and was happy to follow my lead.

It didn't bother me that I was completely naked in front of a stranger. Besides, Kahn had hooked me up with a beautiful body that I didn't mind showing off to anyone who wanted a peek. As long as they had money for the admissions fee, I was down. However, what did bother me were the two additional pictures of his so called *manager* sitting on the nightstand which only sat a few feet from the bed.

"You sure you aren't gay?" I asked with a high level of concern. I was already sick, and didn't need any other problems by sleeping with a homo.

"Hell…nooooo. Would…a…gay dude dick…loooook like diiiss," KP replied. It was obvious that the cough syrup was finally starting to take effect because his words were beginning to slur. He was in a zone, and it showed. "Coooome…over herrrreee wit' yo' fat assssss…and sit on dis." His dick was hard, tall, and covered

with the latex condom that he'd slipped on without me even noticing.

Even though I was still concerned, he did have a point. I
guess a gay dude wouldn't be able to get his dick up for a female.
Oh, but shit. He could be bi-sexual, I thought looking at him again.
*But then again…fuck it. He does have on a condom. I just gotta
make sure that shit don't break. Besides, he would be just as mad
at me if it did.*

Not thinking about it any further, I finally followed his orders and straddled him, rubbing my big lipped pussy along his
shaft.

I was turned off and dry.

I started playing with his shit a little more and thought
about Donnell, the only dude who'd ever made me cum like clockwork. I thought about his long, curvaceous dick, and felt my juices
start to flow. I looked down at KP only to see his eyes rolling back
up into his head. I guess he thought his shit was already inside of
me.

Putting his dick in, I moved my body up and down and listened as my ass clapped against his thighs. Music that didn't exist
until after the surgery. I closed my eyes, trying to escape from this
disaster, riding him harder and faster and doing whatever else I
could to make him cum as quick as possible.

I even tried moaning. "Ohh King. This dick is so good
baby."

I got nothing.

Not even a sound.

I was certainly expecting him to fuck me back or use some
type of movement.

I opened my eyes just in time to catch the drool trickling
out of his mouth. His eyes were closed and his arms lay motionless
to the side. *This muthafucka*! I thought while coming to an abrupt
stop. I couldn't believe he had passed out. As I went to get off his
dick, which at this point was limp, he suddenly woke up and
grabbed my ass as hard as he could.

"Fuck me harder. Don't stop!" he demanded. I cocked my
hand back and punched him in the chest as hard as I could. He

gasped for air for the second time tonight.

I went into shock. Although my butt had healed, it was still tender and the pain sent shocks up my spine. A regular ass could handle that kind of pressure. This one was still new and fragile. As his blinking got slower, drool continued to slip out the side of his mouth. He was officially under the influence and before anything got a chance to jump off, he'd passed out…again. I sat there for a few moments, counting how many times his chest rose and fell.

He inhaled.

Exhaled.

Then nothing happened…for a while. *I hope this dude doesn't die on me,* I thought as I recounted the days of Pimp C. He didn't seem to be breathing, but then suddenly, he started snoring.

Now, it was time for me to do my thing. I quietly got up, slipped my underwear and dress back on, then tiptoed to the other side of the bed to grab his jeans. In a way, I was glad that KP had decided to keep the lights on because it was easier for me to see. But then again if he woke up and saw what I was doing, he would be pissed. I had to make it quick.

I made it over to his side of the bed without making a peep and then picked up his jeans. *These fake-ass True Religion jeans.* I could tell that they weren't authentic by the stitching that was falling apart.

He moaned. Turned over and faced where I was *supposed* to be. I froze. Didn't make a move, until I heard his snoring resume. Seconds later, I dug the big knot of money out of the back pocket, and thought that I'd hit the jackpot until I began peeling away at the cash. The knot that I assumed was consumed with hundreds and maybe even twenties turned out to be a stack of mostly one dollar bills. There were at least two hundred of them with only three hundred dollar bills on top.

I was pissed.

He was a deceiver.

I dug back in his pockets to see what else I could find, and pulled out the keys to the Navigator along with his ugly leather wallet. There was nothing inside except the declined American Express card, which I didn't even bother to pull out, a fucking library card, his license and a tattered social security card. I couldn't believe this. What kind of fucking rapper walked around with a library card?

"Where the fuck is all his money? All that shit from the bank?" I asked myself while I held his social security card up. When I read the name Wolfgang Monroe Deans, I was even more pissed than before. "What the fuck? Wolfgang!" I said in a low tone. "That shit don't even sound like somebody getting paper."

KP moaned again, this time louder. Maybe he'd heard me say his dumb-ass name. If he did, I didn't care. Obviously, this muthafucka had fooled me, and I knew there was only one way to find out. I looked around to see what else I could take in order to compensate for my time, and my eyes locked in on his jewelry. He'd taken it off and placed it on his nightstand.

"I guess this will just have to do it," I said, scooping up the diamonds.

I grabbed my clutch and placed the ridiculous stack of ones inside along with the jewelry, then picked up the keys to his truck and headed downstairs toward the front door. As knocked out as he was, I could've walked around the house and tried to find more money, but for some reason my gut feeling told me there was none. Why he'd decided to fuck with me, and waste my time dealing with his broke-ass, I wasn't sure. But maybe after he finds out that all his shit is gone, he'll think twice before trying it again. I frowned one last time as I opened the front door.

Oddly, the picture of his *manager* seemed to be looking directly at me.

Scary.

Real Scary.

"Fuck you too," I mouthed as I shut the door.

Chapter Six

The next afternoon, I hopped up from my own bed, and drove down to my old stomping grounds. Located on Houston's southwest side, not far from the crime infested Fondren neighborhood, is where I was from, the Shady Grove Community. Home of loss, destruction, and death. This is ultimately who had raised me.

The streets.

Already a fucked up place to live, the hurricane Katrina evacuees made it worse by migrating in. The sky was perfectly blue and the fiends were working hard to get their next fix. I hadn't been in the old neighborhood in a while and I was hoping to keep it that way. When I got out of the trailer park, I was out for life, except when I needed something, like now.

Feeling another bad headache coming on, I also began to notice that the lymph glands in my neck were swollen, which was a sure sign that I was trying to get sick. However, I was used to all of this by now. It was the same thing over and over, and was unfortunately going to be a part of me for the rest of my life. I just had to deal with it. Taking out the prescription bottle from my purse, I unscrewed the top then popped one of the tiny white pills into my mouth and swallowed.

My daily regiment.

What a life.

After placing the bottle back in my purse, I got out of my car and walked toward the pawn shop, which sat by itself like a corner store. I'd been thinking about it all morning, and couldn't wait to get inside so I could see just how much Mr. King Pen's jewels were really worth. But not only was I excited about that, I was also hyped about finding out who that nigga really was. You see, the owner of the pawn shop, Bubba was what you could call the hood's very own private investigator. Anything you needed to find out about someone, all you had to do was go to Bubba and he could make it happen. He was an old head, in his mid seventies, and had owned the pawn shop ever since I could remember. He had connections that no one would believe. Fortune 500 CEOs and Politians checked for him...on the low. He ran numbers and could get anything you wanted, for a small fee of course. He'd been doing a background check on all my niggas for years, so it came as no surprise when I called him a few hours ago and gave him all KP's information. I needed the 411 on that muthafucka, and Bubba was the man who could provide it for me.

Walking up to the front door, I hit the buzzer and waited for Bubba to answer. It was like Fort Knox getting up in his spot. Normally, his voice came over the little speaker that sat right outside the door within a matter of seconds, so when he didn't answer I hit the buzzer again.

"Who the hell is it?" Bubba finally said through the speaker.

His comment was strange. Why would he ask that when there were several cameras posted up outside the door as well. *Damn, I hope he's not getting robbed or some shit, I thought. Maybe I need to do this another time.*

"Who is it?" he asked again, interrupting my thoughts.

"Umm...Bubba it's me...Mirror." *Shit, if he's getting robbed I shoulda gave him a fake name. Damn...I could be a witness.*

Without saying another word, he buzzed me in.

I was scared as hell to walk inside, and actually told myself to turn around at least three times, but then I thought about Bubba. What if he really was in trouble? The man had looked out for me my entire life, so I couldn't just stand there and allow him to get hurt. When I was a little girl, Bubba would always buy my stolen stuff whether it was valuable or not because he knew my mother wasn't shit, and that I used the money to eat. He was a good man. I had to do something.

Slowly, I took several small steps inside before calling out his name. "Bubba!"

"Yeah. Are you gonna take all day? I have some business to

get back to," he called out.

When I finally made my way over to the jewelry counter where he normally operated, he looked suspicious, as if he had been doing wrong. And then I saw her, still on her knees, wet mouth and all. A fiend that had the nerve to look a little pissed that I had ruined the party. Never moved to straighten herself up.

She wasn't ashamed.

They never were.

When I looked down, he'd obviously tucked his dick back inside his pants, but didn't bother to zip the pants back up. I could only imagine what Bubba's dick looked like by now. The first thing that came to mind was a raisin. He was already losing weight, appearing to be slighlty over one hundred fifty pounds. I remembered when he was a chubby guy, always laughing, making me feel good inside.

"Bubba, I'm going to get you. You were acting so crazy, I thought you were in here getting robbed or something. But now I see you're in here getting your little raisin sucked," I said rolling my eyes.

"Well, as you can see, I still got it," he replied cracking himself up. "Besides, ain't nobody gon' rob me. I been in this neighborhood fo' over forty years. Everybody knows not to fuck with Bubba. Plus, I got a big-ass shot gun waiting for 'em if they do." He continued to ramble on until he caught a glimpse of my backside. "Damn girl. Where you get all that ass from all of a sudden? You gain some weight recently?"

"No. And I see you didn't either. You starting to look frail."

He brushed my comment off as if he didn't care. My head shook even more after closely looking into Bubba's mouth. He was supposed to wear dentures, but hardly ever had them in.

Then I smiled, thinking about the comment he made about me. I realized that my surgery had definitely paid off. But I was wondering why nobody ever noticed my boobs. I guess black men just weren't into them. "Yeah, I guess I've been eating good."

He ignored me as if he knew I was lying and asked, "What you got fo me? I gotta get back to work." He looked over at the broken down chick that had been slobbing him down to make sure that she was still there, then went back to focusing his attention on me.

"How much can I get for this?" I asked holding up KP's jewelry.

Bubba grabbed both five row necklaces and bracelets with his narrow, worn hands and studied them carefully, then grabbed his diamond tester. It registered positively almost instantly. I had to admit I was shocked. Bubba studied the jewelry a few more seconds, and seemed pretty unsatisfied with the results. Or so I thought.

"So, the jewelry is real right? How much can I get for it?" I asked getting antsy. I could feel the money in my hands.

"No, something ain't right." He took out another tester and placed it on the stones. It registered positive with that machine as well. "I knew it. This here ain't diamonds, this Moissanite."

"Moissanite? What the hell is that?" I stuttered, "but it came up positive."

"That's cause that Moissanite shit is so close to the real thang, it's hard to tell 'em apart. It ain't real diamonds though. I been doin this shit fo' years…I know a diamond when I see one."

I was pissed.

Looked pissed, too.

Anger fumed through my nose.

"Did you get this fake shit from that boy you asked me to check out this morning?" Bubba asked.

"Yes," I said sounding disappointed.

"Well, that boy is broke, so I wouldn't waste too much time with him anymore."

All I could do was shake my head. "I knew it."

"The boy stays with his older brother."

"Older brother? What's his name?"

"I'm sorry, baby girl. I had to buzz my best customer in right before I was 'bout to find out that part. I can still get the information if you want."

I was a little offended. I always thought I was his best customer. "No, that's okay."

"Yeah, they say the brother some wealthy hot shot. His

place is out there in Copper Lakes. Well, one of his houses. From what I hear, he got more than one. They say he paid, but he's dangerous. A thug turned businessman."

I couldn't believe it. That nigga had played me with his brother's shit. "But what about the money bags I saw him with the day we met?" I was so confused.

"I checked that out fo' you too. He was making a deposit into his brother's account. As a matter of fact, that boy only got a couple of hundred dollars in his bank account."

"So, does he do anything in the music industry?" I asked. *If KP's brother is so paid why he got him walking around in fake shit.*

"Well, his brother does own a record label, but your friend is not even on the roster. Maybe he just follows behind him, like an assistant."

"I can't believe this shit. Is he from New York? He's always trying to talk like he is. "

"Nope. Born and raised right in Houston," Bubba responded. "Shit, it looks like you need to go find the older brother to me. He's the one you need to go…" Bubba stopped then looked at me with a slight smirk. "No, that shit ain't gonna work either. I forgot my sources told me he beats women just like he fucks up dudes in the street.

Every time he told me something else it was another blow. *I bet it was his brother who was in all those pictures around the house.* "Damn, who are these sources? I guess I should get his brother's name." I had no idea why I'd just asked that question. Maybe I was hoping to make sense out of everything.

"Now, you know better than to ask me that. You know I don't give up that type of information. What's wrong with you?"

Bubba never did. Everyone's secret was always safe with him.

I pushed Bubba's two hundred dollar background check fee across the counter, then headed toward the door.

"Wait Mirror," he said once I reached the front. "I'll still take that piece of shit. I'm sure one of these young hoodlum boys around here will buy it from me," he said holding five hundred dollars in his hands. He was still the same, buying stuff from me that wasn't worth shit. If I believed in love, he would be the first person on my list.

"Thanks so much Bubba."

"Mirror, you're still my favorite," he reminded me with a wink. It was something he'd been telling me since I was a little girl. He was never able to have children and always let me know that if I were his, he would've given me the world.

"I know Bubba. I know."

● ● ● ● ● ● ● ● ● ● ● ● ● ● ● ●

I made it to the boutique shortly after two, which was unusually early for me. Rushing out of the car, I headed for the store with my mind full of things I had to do. I was running low on merchandise and wanted to check my inventory before my customers showed up. But I was too late.

Seven women had already congregated in front of my door, and a few of them had cupped their hands to the window to get a better view as to what was inside. Kind of annoyed that I wasn't going to be able to check the stock, I barged passed them without speaking, unlocked the door, and held it open while all the ladies walked through.

"Late again, huh," someone said to me from behind.

When I turned around, I noticed that it was Kippy. The girl who I'd put out my store the day before. "What the hell do you want? I'm not in the mood for any of your bullshit today."

"And I'm not in the mood for any of yours. I'm just here to shop like everybody else," she said, walking past me and into the store. I guess it hadn't dawned on her that I didn't necessarily want her ass inside.

I followed right behind her. "But why are you shopping *here*?" I asked, pointing my index finger toward the floor. "I thought you didn't like the way I operate my store."

Kippy picked up a black Alice & Olivia ballerina dress and held it up her to body. "I don't like the way you do business, but you have cute stuff, so I guess I have no other choice, but to shop here." She looked at me and tried to force a fake-ass smile.

A part of me wanted to tell Kippy that she did have other choices…hell, tons of them, but I decided not to. I really didn't have the energy to argue with her at the moment. Instead, I walked over to one of my many display tables and began folding a few pairs of skinny jeans.

"Hey Mirror, do you have any other clothes in the back? It's looking kind of empty out here," Kippy said.

She hadn't even been in the store five minutes, and she was already dancing on my last nerve. "No, Kippy I don't, but I have a shipment coming in next week."

"Shit…that's gonna be too late. The All Star Game is this weekend and that's what I was shopping for."

"Aren't you a little too old to be going to shit like that? Isn't stuff like that for kids?" I asked. "I don't do those little girl trips, I go to places like Dubai." *Little did she know I had checked the fares for flights headed to New Orleans already. All I needed was an opening at one of the hotels, and everything would be confirmed.* I loved to act classy. That was my shit.

I'd fixed my lips to tell more lies as my phone vibrated on my hip. I picked it up to see who was calling before the bitch, Kippy asked me what Dubai looked like.

I had no answer.

I had never really been.

"Hel…"

"You fuckin' bitch! Where's my shit?"

He sounded mad.

Real mad.

Probably wanted to whip my ass.

I flashed a wicked smile. It was King Pen or should I say…Wolfgang.

"Smart. Calling me from a different number, that was very smart," I admitted while continuing to take inventory. "Where's *your* shit…or do you mean your brother's shit?"

The line went silent for a quick second. "What are you talkin' 'bout?"

"Your brother…you know the one who you live with?" When he didn't respond I continued. "Don't you think it's about time that you stop fucking lying? Your gig is up nigga. I know that your brother owns that house in Copper Lakes, and that he's the one who's actually got all the fucking money. Not your dumb-ass. Actually you're his follower, slash-assistant right? Don't you need to go get your brother coffee or some shit?"

"I ain't no fuckin' assistant. Yo', I'm not playin'…"

I cut his ass right off. "And stop talkin' like your ass is from New York or some shit!"

"Where my jewels at? And my truck?" he asked, obviously ignoring my requests.

"Please…those fake-ass diamonds are in the trash, and I sent your *rental* car to a chop shop. Just go ahead and charge all that to the game."

"What? I'ma fuck you up!" he yelled breathing insanely heavy over the phone. "My brother knows how to deal wit' bitches like you. You just wait...you fucked wit' the right family! You ain't nothing but a high class whore!"

"I'd rather be a whore than broke, so fuck you."

I hung up on him when I saw three of my customers, NBA wives to be exact walking past the window. I knew they were coming inside my store, so I quickly finished straightening up the table, then went to greet them at the door. Everything had to be perfect for them. Absolutely perfect.

I made a mental note to change my cell phone number, something I usually had done every few months anyway. It was a way of me getting rid of all the men, who were disposed of.

"Hey ladies," I said, greeting each of my long time customers with cheek kisses.

"Hey Mirror. It's been a while since we've been here," one of the wives, Carmen replied.

Carmen was the nicest one out of the three women, and the only one who stopped to make conversation. The other two women were straight bitches majority of the time, and walked straight to one of the racks.

"Mirror, is this all you have?" one of the other women, Alexa asked me as she pointed to the scarce selection. The All Star Game is this weekend and that's what we came here for. Don't tell me you're falling off with all the hot stuff."

I hated her slick-ass comments.

I also hated her. She was light, damn near white, but acted like the elite.

I was envious of her position. Not to mention, she was a bitch.

Who told her she could act that way while sporting freckles on her face?

I still hadn't figured out who Alexa's husband was because she hardly ever bragged like the rest of the women, and surprisingly didn't even wear a ring. But whoever he was must've been paid because the bitch wore nothing but the best, and had a different car every time she came to my store. However, I'd taken note of her 3.1 Philip Lim trench coat which was quite expensive, but already worn twice in my store. I didn't understand how a woman of her stature would do such a thing. She should never wear the same thing twice. I certainly didn't.

When I grew up, I only had three outfits to my name. On the days that they were too filthy to wear, I had to put on my mother's clothes and that didn't look too good on an eight year-old girl. My mother also made me wear shoes that were always three sizes too big because she said that my feet grew too fast. That's why to this day, I never rock the same thing twice. It's forbidden.

"All Star Game, huh? Well, my inventory is low because I had plans on going to the MAGIC show in Vegas. That's why there's not much to choose from right now. I was going there to pick out the season's newest clothes." Little did they know, I hadn't been to boost yet, so that's the real reason why the inventory was low. "Where's the game going to be this year?" I asked trying to act like I didn't know. I knew Kippy was probably wondering why I now had such a deep interest in the event.

"It's in New Orleans this time," Carmen replied.

I thought to myself for a moment and said, "Yeah, I should have some new inventory coming in over the next day or two, so you all can look great in New Orleans. Hell, I might go too now." I knew once I said that I had no other choice, but to go boost now.

"My, my, my how convenient," Kippy said unable to keep her comments to herself. "That's funny, just a couple of minutes ago, the All Star game was for kids. You're an ass kisser! I mean you told me your shipment wasn't coming until next week, but for a NBA wife, it'll be here in a day or so."

The store fell extremely silent and all eyes were on me. Everyone wanted to know what I was going to do next, so I had to make my words memorable. I couldn't believe that she had the audacity to call me out, in front of the wives at that. They lived the life that I was determined to live. The life of prestige, and power. The wives had been customers of the store since it opened and every time they told me a story of their luxurious lives, I followed up with one of my own. I just made sure that it was always bigger and better. They always say that birds of a feather flocked together. If I flocked anywhere, it would be with them. I was going to fix Kippy's ass.

I snatched the Missoni draped tunic that she'd been holding onto for a while, walked over to my register, and grabbed a pair of scissors.

"Hey, I was going to buy that," she instructed as she ran over to the register.

"Too bad, bitch. Maybe next time you'll learn how to stop talking so much shit." I held the tunic that was priced at nine hundred and forty dollars up in the air for everyone to see and began cutting it into large uneven pieces. I heard several gasps throughout the room and a few 'no she didn't,' but didn't care. I grabbed the hanger that the tunic was on, and threw it in Kippy's direction. "Now, get the fuck out *my* store, and don't come back!"

"You know, I don't think that's necessary. You can be a little over the top sometimes," Alexa butted in.

"I don't think I was talking to you," I replied giving her the evil eye.

"That's it!" Kippy screamed before running outside. Everyone watched as she made a scene outside the store calling me everything other than a child of God.

"Fuck her. I don't need money that bad," I said, as I turned my back and faced the small group of women who were still watching her tirade. However, suddenly each one of their eyes became much bigger.

I quickly turned back around to see what had happened and watched in slow motion as Kippy took a brick that she'd obviously picked up from the construction site next door and slammed it into my passenger side window.

"What the…"

Before I even decided to finish my sentence, I took off running out of the store. I tried my best to grab a huge piece of her long-ass weave, and snatch her head backward, but just couldn't get a good grip. She slipped away from my grasp, and took off running in the other direction.

"Bitch, you better fucking run!" I yelled.

I couldn't believe what had just happened. I paced the sidewalk for a few seconds, then stopped. Quickly turning my head left to right, I searched the street for Kippy's BMW, but didn't see it anywhere. Something wasn't right. She normally parked that piece of shit right in front of the boutique, but today it was no where to be found. I was starting to think that her ass had it all planned.

"She better not ever show her fucking face around here again," I said to myself. "Fuck that…or anywhere else in Houston for that matter."

I walked over to my own car, and stood there for at least two minutes before I began to examine the damage. It was pretty bad, in addition to being added to the damage from days before. I knew it was going to cost me a liver in order to get it all fixed.

My face felt flushed but I had to gain my composure. "Damn," I said, walking back inside.

"Are you going to call the police?" one of my customers asked.

I shook my head, no. The police were the last people I wanted snooping around my establishment, considering all the stolen shit that was inside, and I didn't want my car insurance involved in the situation either. My expenses would just have to be paid out of pocket, but that bitch, Kippy was going to pay me back one way or another. I would make sure of it.

Everyone that was left in the store I'm sure had a line up of questions and comments to make after what had just happened, but all of that was put on hold as we watched an older woman walk into the store. She staggered a bit, and you could smell her sour skin from afar.

"Can anyone spare some change?" she asked, with her dirty hand out. I froze in place and forgot to blink as I watched Carmen reach in her Miu Miu clutch and handed her a wrinkled dollar bill.

"I have some food in the back, come and follow me so that I can pack you up something nice," I said as the woman went to reach for the measly dollar. "Ladies, I'll be right back out." I had to intercept the deal with a forced smile. I walked the filthy woman to the back of the store into the storage room. She followed me and when we reached our destination, I shut the door calmly, then lost it.

"Cookie, what the fuck are you doing here?"

My mom.

The bum.

"Well, I really want to talk to you about something..."

I cut her off with a simple hand movement.

"Seems like you're busy," she slurred. "So maybe you could spare your mama a few dollars. Since you doin' all good for yourself, Tyonka. Maybe you can help me out some?"

"What did I tell you about calling me that? My name is no longer Tyonka. It's Mirror. Mirror Carter."

I absolutely hated my birth name.

Born Tyonka LaVaughn Reid, I decided to change that ghetto shit as soon as I turned eighteen. To me, Mirror was classy, rich and sophisticated. Everything that described me as a person. I changed my last name because I refused to walk around with any-thing that belonged to my father. Carter was what I chose...some hopeful connection to Jay-Z.

"Well excuse me Ms. Mirror Carter. It's still hard for me to get used to that booshie name." Her teeth wore the color of cocoa brown, and were no longer white.

"You're disgusting. I told your ass never to come around here again!"

"Watch your mouth. I'm still your mama," she warned with

70

a reprimanding tone.

"My mother? As far as I'm concerned, you're a dead woman."

"You should watch what you wish for," she warned again.

"If wishes did come true, I'd be a lucky bitch! Now get the fuck out! I demanded right before shoving her out through the back door. She fell to the ground.

Not even waiting to see if she was okay, I slammed the door so hard it almost broke in half. I swayed back to my customers as if everything was alright. For some reason, their smiles had turned to frowns.

"Did you give the woman money?" Alexa asked.

"Of course. A crisp fifty," I told her with a straight face.

Chapter Seven

Shady Grove Trailer Park.
This is where I grew up.
This is where she still lived.
My mother.
I drove over immediately after closing my store. Even
though I frequented Bubba's pawn shop quite often, which was
only a five minute walk away, I hadn't been over to the actual
trailer park in a while. A place that I had vowed to never come
back to, but I had a bone to pick. My mother, Cookie Reid, had
crossed the line by coming to my boutique again, and I showed up
to make sure it never happened again.

This piece of shit that they still called a community looked
exactly like a landfill. Abandoned cars, animal feces, and litter
made a home where grass once grew. I took my purple silk Hermes
handkerchief out of my pocket and pressed it against my nose. No
matter how many years I inhaled it, the smell of rotten flesh that
floated in the air was nothing that I was able to get used to. They
needed to tear this fucking place down, and also needed to make
sure my mother went right along with it.

Nothing at Shady had changed, much like the people that
lived here. Everybody, from the kids to the old people, was stuck
in the misery of their own company. They were worthless and
would never amount to anything. *They should be more like me*, I
thought as I watched a group of women that looked to be in their
early twenties interact with one another. They were dressed like
whores and I could tell that they fucked for sport, always for a ride
or some new sneakers. Never for real money, like myself.

I walked up to my mother's beat down trailer, taking a few
steps up the unstable stairs and opened the door. After all these
years she still had never bothered to lock it. She was a creature of

habit, which was a very dangerous thing.

The small, cramped space that she called a home was musty. Black mold crept up the walls as well as the corners of the ceiling next to the water damage. Just like the olden days, shit was never right. I tried my best not to touch anything, but the mountains of trash that she had collected over the last thirty years made no way for easy entry.

She still hoarded.

Everything.

I heard some sniffling as I made my way in the hell hole a little further. The more I walked, it got louder and louder until I stumbled upon her. She looked pitiful as she lay buried under the rubble that symbolized her life. She was sprawled out on an old flowery pattern couch that she stole off a moving truck when I was five years old.

It used to be white.

Her head rested face down on the arm of the tortured couch and she never looked up to acknowledge my presence.

"Cookie!" I said angrily, waiting for her response. She continued to sniffle and still didn't look up. I grabbed her matted, gray hair with my hand and lifted her head up roughly. "COOKIE!"

I never called her mom. Not since I was twelve. That was one of the many things that she didn't deserve. She finally took a quick glance at me before rolling her eyes and yanking her head from my grasp.

"Don't touch me!" she demanded, with the sour smell of gin creeping off of her tongue. Her whole face was covered in tears, and the bags that sat under her eyes were now swollen more than ever.

"I don't know what the hell you're crying for. If you had listened to me and not brought your sorry-ass to my store like I tell you all the time, I wouldn't even have to be in here right now!"

She kept sobbing.

This time uncontrollably.

"Seriously, stop playing that dumb-ass role. This isn't the first time you've been kicked out of there, or from in front of my house. Aren't you used to it by now? Don't you get it? I don't want you around!"

"Oh Doc," she whaled, totally ignoring what I was saying. She clenched her heart and called his name again. "Doc, why did you leave me?"

I squenched my eyes as my face tightened up and eyebrows darted down. My arm pits began to sweat profusely and my knee caps were losing control of themselves.

"You fucking bitch!" I slithered through my teeth angrily.

Bruce Reid.

Also known as Doc.

My father.

He wasn't a real physician like his mother had hoped for him to become, rather a cheating-ass, woman beater who also abused alcohol and cocaine. Doc was his nick name though he tricked many people into thinking it was an occupation of his.

I remembered the day he died. I remembered watching his body jerk violently back and forth before collapsing on the same yellow and brown stained couch that she laid on.

I remember when he clutched his heart.

Then I clenched my teeth.

He died on my twelfth birthday, a day my mother would mourn forever. The same day that I would celebrate, except more than the average celebration.

He abused us. Yet she still loved him. If that's what you call love, then fuck it…I didn't want it. I couldn't recall loving anyone my entire life anyway, so I wasn't missing out on anything.

As if she had been reading my mind, she looked up at me with red stained eyes and said, "You'll never understand true love!"

"True love? True love? True love wouldn't have left your ass black and blue every other day from him stomping you out! True love would've kept his ass home sometimes instead of out creeping with every woman in the fucking neighborhood. Your true love needs to be money. Men and love don't go in the same sentence. Money, that's what you use them for. That's all they're good for. Anything else from them is a waste of time. Money-always-over love. Remember that shit, okay?"

She turned her back to me. Didn't want to hear what I was saying, just like when I was a child. I hated her. More now than ever before. I thought about pushing her damn head into the wall, but instead decided to dig myself out of the graveyard she called a house.

"I hope this piece of shit trailer catches on fire while you're trapped inside! Anything to get you back with your *husband*," I continued as I walked out the shabby door. "You never know. Maybe I can make it happen!" I screamed from outside.

This visit proved to be more stressful than it was worth, and I needed some immediate gratification to help me forget it all.

As if on cue, my phone rang.

"Hello?"

Dr. Khan spoke gently and asked, "Can I see you?" I hadn't spoken with him about the deposit and the stunt his crazy-ass wife pulled since KP and I were at the restaurant. I figured I could use some more money for my pain and suffering.

He was always reliable.

"Maybe I can make arrangement for tomorrow."

"But I need to see you now."

"I don't give a fuck what you need. Whatever it is, that shit can wait," I told him. "As a matter of fact, now I'm gonna make your ass wait two days." Although I didn't have anything else to do for the rest of the day, I couldn't let him call the shots. I was in control.

I was always in control.

Chapter Eight

Two days passed.

Just like I'd warned Kahn's ass.

But I'd held out long enough anyway. Needed more money in my bank account badly.

The sun was setting when I pulled up at the gated community of Orman Place. An exquisite community where Dr. Kahn built his dream home. He had five others scattered in Miami, Los Angeles, New York, Atlanta, and one, of course, in India. This house was the biggest though. It was a little over ten thousand square feet, had five bedrooms, a tennis court, and a huge Olympic sized swimming pool.

This is the home that he shared with his wife.

This was the home that at times he shared with me.

I parked my car in his driveway like I paid bills there, got out and walked up to the front door. Ringing the door bell, I stood there seductively and played with my hair before Khan opened the door with a huge smile.

"You look beautiful," he said grabbing my hand.

"Where's your wife at?" I shot back while walking into the house. "I got something for her crazy-ass," I added along with a devious grin. He never asked what it was. Instead, he attempted to defend her.

"Please leave her alone, Mirror. She has nothing to do with this."

"What are you talking about? She has everything to do with this. When she crossed the line and came to my crib, she invited herself into this." Little did she know that I'd crossed the line into her territory plenty of times in the past. "Why the fuck am I even here if you want to defend her?" When I turned around like I was leaving, he didn't waste anytime jumping in front of me.

"Listen," he said planting both his hands on a decorative table near the front door. He dropped his head not knowing what to do next. "She still hasn't mentioned any of that to me." By the tone of his voice, he seemed confused, and he wasn't alone. I too wanted to know why she hadn't said anything to him about her fucking with me. About her unannounced visit to my house. About the ass whipping she got before she left.

"Where is she now?" I asked.

"The office."

"This late? It's almost nine o'clock. What in the hell could she possibly be doing there this time of night? You sure she's not fucking around on you?"

I smiled.

He didn't.

It's funny how men thought they could do whatever they wanted, but women couldn't.

"She's at the office doing billing. I timed it perfectly. It's enough to last her at least until eleven. Had it set up that way so I could see you." He took his hands off the table and walked over to grab mine. "Do you want to take a dip?"

"Take a dip where?" I questioned with an immediate attitude. "In your pool? Do you know how cold it is outside? You've got to be out of your fucking mind."

"No, Mirror, I meant in the hot tub."

"Look, I need some more money," I blurted out. At this point, I really wasn't interested in anything else he had to offer.

Kahn frowned. "What do you mean you need some more money? I just put ten grand in your account."

"Yeah, I know and that was for an apology acceptance. I accepted your apology, didn't I? Now, I need some more money for the anguish your wife caused me. She stepped out of line and now you're being fined. You should learn to keep your bitch in her place and maybe you won't have to come out your pocket so often."

He shook his head back and forth like he wanted to call me a greedy bitch before walking into his study. It had only been a couple of minutes before he came back carrying a small stack of money in his hand.

I smiled immediately. *That's a good boy. Come to mommy.*

"This is only a thousand."

My smile faded. "You're not serious...are you?" I asked, taking the money out of his hand. "How the hell am I supposed to get my Bentley Coupe like this? Speaking of cars, I need money to fix my Benz. Your wife vandalized my shit!"

"Mirror, are *you* serious? I'm sure she didn't do that. You must be mistaken."

"She did!" *And even if it wasn't her, you can help me with the Bentley anyway*, I thought. "Now, come up off some more paper because a thousand dollars can't help me get shit."

"But I just gave you ten thousand."

I placed my hands on my hips. "So."

"Well, I'm sorry that's all I have for now. I'm kinda on a budget."

I was so mad, I bit the insides of my lip. Could've sworn I tasted blood. "A budget!"

"Yes, my wife's birthday is coming up in two weeks, and I plan to do something nice for her. I think I'm going to buy her that new Jaguar."

"What? So, this bitch gets anything she wants, huh?"

"She doesn't want it, she just deserves it."

The nerve of this muthafucka talking to me about her like I gave a shit what she deserved. Didn't he care that she came to my house and threatened to kill me? Oh, it was on now. "You know what, don't even worry about it," I said, thinking about what I was about to do to get him back. I had something up my sleeve and I was sure it would teach him a lesson not to fuck with me.

"So, where do you want to fuck me at?" I asked. He loved that type of kinky talk.

Kahn's eyes lit up like a hundred watt bulb. "Right here...can we do it here. Can I bend you over and fuck you on my wife's favorite table?"

This sick bastard. He'd just talked about what his wife deserved, but wanted to fuck me on something she obviously cherished at the same time. "Sure, why not."

While I placed the lousy thousand dollars in my purse, he was busy in front of me taking off his clothes. The Armani t-shirt, cargo shorts and the dingy boxer shorts he wore were on the floor in a matter of seconds.

"Can you take off your clothes now," he asked, wishing he had the balls to demand shit from me like I do him.

I wore the pants.

He was my bitch.

I took off my black Jimmy Choo pumps followed by my Maison Martin Margiela Jeans and left them along with my purse on the floor. After that, I lifted my shirt over my head and stood before him in just my red laced underwear. La Perla, of course.

"Oh shit! I just remembered that I was supposed to pick my girl up from the airport at nine thirty. She's going to fucking kill me," I said, with a worried look on my face. Before anything jumped off between us, I bent over and grabbed my purse then pulled out my cell phone. "Maybe I can find her another ride."

I dialed seven digits and placed the phone to my ear waiting for a response. Nothing. I dialed the number again. And then again. The truth was no one was coming from out of town. I didn't even have any friends. The number I'd been calling was to an office. His office. The one his dumb-ass wife had been working diligently toward making a success. She just wouldn't answer the phone. I didn't have plans to give up. I called again.

"Maybe you can leave her a voicemail and tell her to catch a cab," Khan suggested, as the phone rang. He was trying to come up with anything that would allow me to stay a little while longer.

"Khan's Plastic Surgery Center. How can I help you?"

It was his wife. She finally answered.

She finally took the bait.

"Oh well," I said, placing the phone down on the special table, closer to Khan of course. "I'm sure she'll call me back soon."

My only hope now was that she would stay on the phone long enough to hear how fucked up her marriage really was. Although I was sure that this was something she was already aware of, she needed to hear the proof. I saw the minutes counting on my cell phone by the second before the back light went out. She was obviously still listening.

Taking my underwear off, I was completely naked within seconds.

"Your body is amazing," he whispered, while stroking his dick with his hands. "I did a great job." It grew with every stroke, and even though I didn't get the money that I was expecting, this revenge would be sweet. It was like pissing off two birds with one stone. I knew his size wouldn't satisfy me, it never it did, but like Tupac said, *'Revenge was like the sweetest joy next to getting pussy.'*

"Oh…Doctor Khan," I said in a girlish pitch, almost mimicking Marilyn Monroe. "You feel so good." My words sent him into a frenzy. He started dry humping me, making his tiny dick grow a little longer. He was becoming more excited. Poor thing, he didn't know that I had a motive. That his beloved wife was hanging on to our every word. I had a show to put on. I had a relationship to break off.

I bent over the antique table in the foyer, resting my head right next to the phone and said, loud enough for everyone to hear, "Put it in. Put your dick in and fuck me hard."

"I don't have any condoms," he said, looking disappointed.

"That's all right, just put it in and pull it out before you cum. You don't have any STDs right?"

"Of course not," he replied with his dick already inside.

"Fuck me harder and say my name," I ordered.

His dick slipped out. It always slipped out. My pussy was too big and his dick was too small for it to ever work the right way. He couldn't satisfy me. He never did.

"Mirror," he called out, trying to quickly get it back in.

During his struggles I discreetly pressed the volume button to make sure that my plan was working. It was. She was still on the phone.

"Say my name again…louder this time."

"Mirror…ahhh…Mirror…"

He pounded.

My ass bounced.

81

"I bet your wife doesn't fuck you like this," I added as I threw the pussy at him. "Does she fuck you like this?"

"No...she ...doesn't...fuck...me ...like...thi..."

Muthafucka couldn't even finish a sentence. Beads of sweat started pouring down his forehead and he licked his lips while digging deeper.

"Call me her name," I demanded. He didn't answer. Even though I knew he heard me. Probably just didn't understand what I was asking him to do. "Call me by her name. Pretend I'm her. Cum in my face and call me that bitches name!"

His pumps got wilder. Harder. More violent.

"Say her name! I'll let you cum on my face."

I contracted my pussy muscles, putting his dick in a serious choke hold, and then let go. Felt his knees almost give way under him. Needed him to say it before he bust a nut. Needed her to know how he really felt.

"Dia!" he finally screamed. He took his dick out and started jerking it. If his ass thought that I was really about to let him cum on my face, he needed to get his head examined. Everything that I'd just said was for entertainment purposes only. I hit a button again on the phone to make sure that she was still there and she was. I could hear her irregular breathing letting me know that her face was pressed against the phone and she was hanging on to every word.

"Call her a bitch!"

"Dia...you bitch....aahhhhh....fuck yeah," was all he had left to say after he released himself. I'd stepped out of the way just in time, letting his babies squirt all over his wife's beautiful Indian furniture.

When I pressed the phone again, I noticed that the call had already been disconnected. I guess *Dia* had heard all that she needed to hear. I was sure that by now she was on the way.

I laughed to myself thinking, we never made it to the hot tub.

"So, how long does it take to get here from your office?" I asked as he casually walked to the kitchen butt naked. I'm sure that there was someone in the neighborhood who was watching all of this unfold. He didn't have any curtains. Rich people never did.

"About thirty minutes. Why do you ask?" He opened up his cabinet, showing his collection of liquor and took out a bottle of Louis the Thirteenth. He unscrewed the top, poured a generous shot and drank every last drop.

"Oh, I don't know. Just trying to respect the wife…you know? I can only imagine what she must be going through right now. The last thing I want is for her to catch us here." I was impressed. I lied so well.

"I told you before, she has enough billing to last her a while. There is really no rush."

"Yeah, but I have to be on my way anyway. My girlfriend is stranded at the airport, remember?" I walked back into the room where we'd just violated their vows, and put my clothes back on. Then I thought about it, I had one last thing to do for my finale.

Taking the bottle of pills from my purse, I opened it up like I was about to take one, then walked back into the kitchen.

"What's wrong? Not feeling well?" he asked, noticing that I had a pill in my hand. "What's the med for?"

"Nothing too serious. Just a headache. Can you pour me a glass of water please?"

"Sure."

When he turned around, I placed the bottle of pills on the counter next to the wall. I wanted him to see what I had. Wanted him to know what he'd walked himself into.

"Here you are," he said handing me the glass

I held another devious grin. "Thanks." After acting like I'd swallowed the pill, I sipped a little bit of water, then handed the glass back to him. "Listen, I really have to go."

He escorted me to the front, still in his birthday suit, and opened the door. When I walked out, I never looked back and went straight to my car. Disarming the alarm, I hopped inside, started the ignition, then quickly backed out of the driveway. Once I made it onto the street, I was about to place my gear in drive when all of a sudden headlights came from nowhere.

I knew exactly who it was.

My timing was slightly off.

This bitch had made it home much sooner than I antici-pated.

She parked her car directly behind mine. I knew she was about to jump out and cause a scene, which was fine with me because my job here was done anyway. However, she did the total opposite. Obviously putting her foot on the gas, Dia drove her car forward and ran directly into the back of mine.

My Benz was done.

Had been through enough.

Now missing a tail light.

I'd be kicking that bitch's ass if it was my Bentley.

Luckily, she wasn't going at a high rate of speed, or the damages would've been a lot worse.

I turned around and looked at her through her windshield. She looked deranged the way she gripped the steering wheel. Her lips were tight.

"Dia, please stop!" Kahn yelled as he rushed out of his house with only a pair of pants on. *When the fuck did he put those on*, I thought as I watched him run up to her car.

She finally got out. "How could you!" she screamed to the top of her lungs. "I heard you yelling my name while you were with her. How could you?"

"No…no, Dia. She just came to get some medicine that's all. Tell her Mirror," he said in hopes that I'd add to his defense. Little did he know…this was it between us. He'd short changed me one too many times and I'd made the decision to move on.

I rolled down my window. "The bitch is right. She heard everything because I called her while you were fucking me on her favorite table. While the phone was next to my face and you were screaming her name, she was listening. Oh, and before I forget, I left the two of you a little gift on your counter. Enjoy!"

Kahn looked at me in disbelief.

As I listened to Dia's cries grow louder, I put the gear in drive and hit the gas, making my car screech down the street. After noticing that I wasn't being followed, I slowed down a little bit, so that I could make my way out the subdivision in one piece. I was unsure whether or not she would kill her husband, and it didn't matter to me if she did. This was a chapter in my life that I would consider closed.

Chapter *Nine*

New Orleans, Louisiana.

Home of the Mardi Gras.

Legacy of hurricane Katrina.

Surprisingly, the government had cleaned up the place a bit. Well, maybe only the places that brought in the city's revenue, like the French Quarter and the Super Dome. Everywhere else was still a disaster and no one seemed to give a fuck. Thousands of people had come to party in a city that had lost it all. To me, that was fucked up and didn't make much sense, but I guess that was just how the world worked.

Bourbon Street still held a scent of shit, vomit, and piss that seemed to have been rolled up in an air freshener and dispensed upon the entire street. The flood water never washed away the filth. It just seemed to add to it. Trumpets sang in the air as jazz bands floated by, and locals as well as tourists danced around to celebrate their lives.

Their existence.

Their survival.

My initial plans were to spend the whole weekend in New Orleans, but after the back of my car got banged up three days ago, I'd switched my plans from driving to flying first class. My weekend getaway had turned into a one day stay, but it was cool. As long as somebody told me where I could find Bird Man or Lil' Wayne's paid-ass, it would be well worth the trip.

I was just excited to be here; in the midst of real men and real money. So excited, that for a second, I'd forgotten about my crazy world in Houston. I'd even forgotten about my boutique, the only thing that brought me joy anyway. I'd closed it down until I returned home. There was no warning to my customers, no note on the door; I just figured that they would find out when they got there. Even though, I'd gone out and boosted a few items before I left, my inventory was at it's lowest, so I didn't see a point of being open anyway. Besides, I'd hit up most of the good stores in my area anyway, and didn't want to make myself hotter than I already was. It was a good thing that I was out of town. Now, I could do my job and take a vacation all at once, which lead me to Saks Fifth Avenue on Canal Street.

A booster's dream.

A booster's worst nightmare.

Just like all the other luxury retail stores, security in Saks was always, tight, but it was a chance any professional was willing to take. And I was a pro; like Michael Jordan is to a ball, Denzel to a movie, Super Head to a dick. If I was careful and played my cards right, I could hit up a few places around town and make it back home with plenty of shit to resale.

Before walking through the doors, I pulled out two old Saks bags from my handbag that were in perfect condition. The reason I was so successful at this was because I acted as though I belonged. When I walked in, I was shocked to see how many people were actually inside. The store was flooded with celebrities, ball players, and regular people who had enough money to hang with the elite. I made a mental note to make sure I got my flirt on after I was done taking care of business. I walked past a mirror and was pleased at what I saw. The temperature in New Orleans was about seventy six degrees and I'd put on an black Martin Grant jersey dress that cost a little over a thousand dollars along with a fly-ass pair of peep-toe Christian Louboutin's. I blended in well with the socialites. I moved at a non-suspicious pace trying to blend in with the crowd and made my way over to the women's section.

"Hello Ma'am, welcome to Saks. Is there anything I can help you with today?" the sales person asked me. The salesmen was gay and stylish, seemed to be happy to have a job here, in heaven.

"No, I'm fine, but I'm sure I'll need some help in a few. Just keep checking up on me," I instructed. If he thought I was up to something before, the advance for more help certainly would throw him off.

"Were you in here earlier?" he asked, referring to the empty bags I had in my hands. He seemed a little suspicious, but I quickly brushed it off.

I was mad at myself for letting my empty bags show. "Yes, I was and forgot to get a couple of things, so I came back to grab them before heading to my room."

"Well, let me take those for you so that you don't have to lug them around…"

I jerked away from his helping hands. Probably made a scene, something I didn't want. He seemed to take offense, and I didn't blame him. The move was extremely ghetto.

"Is there something wrong?"

"I'm sorry, I'm just in a rush and I won't be in here for long. Besides, I need to compare what I'm getting to what's in the bag."

"Oh…I see," was all he said. I smiled nervously and walked away, at this point, knowing I needed to get out of the store as quickly as possible. "Oh, and by the way…," he continued, "your shoes are amazing."

I turned around, gave him a wink, and moved along as if I had all the time in the world.

His eyes were still on me.

I could feel them.

I walked past all my favorite designers, Fendi, Carolina Herrera, Badgley Mischka…the list goes on, and checked the price tags on all of them. I looked around to see who was within eye distance. Before anybody could count to ten, I'd slipped three Emilo Pucci dresses into one of my bags. Dresses that retailed for twenty-one hundred dollars a piece, but I would sell in my boutique for at least eighteen hundred. I knew the multicolored print pieces would fly off my racks as soon as I got them home. *That was too easy*, I thought to myself as I realized no one was paying me any attention.

I took a few steps forward to see what my next score would be and noticed that the store, which was once flooded with people had thinned out considerably. Either everyone had left or they were at the checkout counters preparing to leave. However, it was going down, I would soon be in the store alone, and that was a no-no. I looked down at my diamond bezeled Philip Stein watch, and checked the time. It was only 4:00 p.m. The store didn't close until 6:00 p.m. With my profession, I needed the store to be crowded to keep all unwanted attention away from me. Then out of nowhere two security guards seemed to just pop up around me and the faggot that had initially greeted me was only a few feet away as well.

Panic consumed by body.

"Can you point me in the direction of your fragrance counter?" I asked him, trying to weasel my way out of the booby trap.

He stared at me for a few seconds. "Sure, right this way."

Although the gay blade directed me in the right direction, his entire attitude had changed from before. Something was definitely wrong.

He led me to the section that carried a million different aromas from fruity to woody. There was so many different smells in the air that I was starting to get nauseated.

"Do you have Annick Goutal's perfume?" I asked the older woman behind the counter.

"Goutal's huh? That's a great fragrance."

I looked back at the gay guy who was still staring at me. *Damn, I need to get out of here.* "Umm…thanks," I replied to the woman's compliment .

She walked away for a second and came back with the beautiful butterfly bottle. I picked up a small glass of coffee beans that sat on the counter and took a deep breath. It cleared out the other fragrances that I smelled. A light mist came out of the bottle as she sprayed the fresh citrus smelling liquid on me. I brought my wrist up to my nose and fell in love with the scent of grapefruit, lemons, and cypress on my skin.

"I'll take it," I instructed as I noticed a man dressed in a business suit standing in a close range. He looked important, dressed well, and didn't smile. I'd been in the game long enough to spot a plain clothes security officer when I saw one. But then again, his suit looked kind of expensive for a toy cop. A black Dior three piece suit with a pair of Acetate Dior logo cufflinks to be exact. *Damn, I hope I didn't fuck up this time. Maybe they just have extra security because all these people are in town.* However, the crazy thing is the more I looked at the man, the more familiar he looked. Like I'd seen his face somewhere before. *Man, this stealing shit probably got me tripping*, I thought shaking my head.

I pulled my credit card and my lip gloss from my purse and handed the card to the woman. I was certain that buying a two hundred and fifty bottle of perfume would be enough to get anybody off of my tracks, but he wasn't letting up. I watched her as she swiped the card through the machine and then used the mirror sitting next to me to touch up my gloss. I was doing everything I could to stay cool, but he and a couple of the employees seemed to be keeping tabs on my every move. I was nervous and had to find a way out of the store.

"Here you go Miss. Would you like your receipt in the bag?" the woman asked.

"No, I think I'll hold on to it," I replied, after grabbing the receipt and the small Saks bag out of her hand. I turned around and walked as quickly as I could toward the door. The next thing I heard just as my left foot hit the outside of the store was, "Ma'am, do you mind stepping back inside the store for a moment? We need to talk to you?"

Chapter Ten

I thought about running. Everything in my being said to haul-ass like a cheetah until I got to my rental car, but it was too far. Besides, I refused to ever look like a fool. I took one step back into the store and watched as the door closed behind me. Even though most of the customers had left out of the store, security had commanded that all eyes remain glued on us.

This was it.

I was trapped.

In the sixteen years that I'd been a professional booster, I'd finally gotten caught.

Damn.

"Ma'am, do you have anything in your bags?" one of the two officers asked sternly. He was chubby. Not fat, but just a little chunkier than his partner. My underarms became drenched. It was something that always happened when I was extremely nervous.

"Yes, of course I do. This two hundred and fifty dollar bottle of Annick Goutal perfume I bought just a few minutes ago," I told them, holding up the evidence for everyone to see.

"And what about the items in your other bag?" he asked referring to the dresses I'd obviously stuffed in the old Saks bag. I had to come up with something quick.

"Sir, I bought these things earlier today and forgot a belt to match one of them. That's why I came back. Is there a reason for all this questioning?" I asked, taking offense.

"Did one of our employees give you those bags when you purchased your items...today?"

I wasn't sure if that was a trick question or not. "Yes...yes they did," I responded. My arm pits felt like Niagara Falls, but I still had to keep my cool. "What's this all about?"

"Well Ma'am, that's funny because our store hasn't used those bags since last season."

I felt like a fucking loser.

Like I'd lost my boosting credibility.

I'd completely forgotten that Saks along with a few other stores changed their bags up seasonally.

"A few employees saw you confiscating unpaid merchandise. Do you mind if we take a look inside your bag?"

This was it. My first time in New Orleans and I was going to jail.

"Excuse me. I couldn't help but to overhear the commotion that was going on. Is there a problem here?" It was the man that had been staring at me while I purchased my perfume. The guy in the expensive looking suit who I thought was security.

"No, not at all sir, there's no problem. Sorry to disturb your shopping experience. We'll take her in the office," the fat one responded while grabbing my arm and pulling me toward him. The cutie in the suit looked more and more attractive the closer he got. But there was no time for fornicating.

I needed to act crazy. "Get off me!" I shouted, yanking my arm back. "I patronize your store and you accuse me of shoplifting? I've never been more insulted before in my life. Wait until my husband gets a hold of this. He's the biggest lawyer on the east coast. He's going to sue the shit out of you guys. I'm going to own Saks!"

I hoped like hell my little scene would work.

However, security seemed unenthused with my outburst and demanded that I follow them again before they tried to cuff me.

"She's with me, so if you don't mind, I'd like for you two idiots to stop making a scene and let me get back to shopping," the gentleman in the suit announced.

They looked at him and then back at me. I followed suit by looking at them then back at the man. I was just as surprised as they were to hear this stranger speak in my defense. His hair was jet black, but carried a hint of grey. He was a slightly older guy, but didn't look a day over fifty. His teeth were white with no gaps, a perfect smile. Whoever he was, he was well maintained... had clout and obviously lots of money.

"But sir...," the chubby security guard chimed in, holding his index finger in the air as if he were asking a question in school.

"But sir?" the well-dressed business man interrupted. "I paid over twenty thousand dollars to have everyone leave the building so that I could shop exclusively and...," he stopped in mid sentence. "You know what, you just lost my business."

"That won't be necessary!" Someone yelled from behind. "Mr. Towers, I'm the store manager and I apologize severely for your inconvenience. Please, go back to shopping. Your business is appreciated. I'll take care of this matter personally," he assured us while giving security the eye.

"Is that all?" this Mr. Towers guy asked. "You give me your word that you'll address this personally and I'm supposed to be okay with that?" He gave the store manager a chance to answer before he continued. The manger just held his head down. "Your employees embarrass my guest in front of everyone and your apology is supposed to make everything better? Well, I'm not satisfied with that and it's simply unacceptable!"

"You're absolutely right, Mr. Towers," the manager turned, looked at me and asked, "Ma'am, what's your name?"

"Mirror...Mirror Carter," I answered, figuring that there was no point in lying about my name at this point. The coast was clear.

"Mrs. Carter, I'm incredibly sorry for what has happened with you." He then turned to the stranger. "And Mr. Towers, I will be more than happy to return the twenty thousand dollars you gave us to shut the store down. Enjoy yourselves on us." He walked away quickly, I assumed before his offer was rejected.

Now that's what the fuck I call power, I thought in amazement. I couldn't believe that one black man could shut this whole department store down on a weekend like this. Not to mention, get my clepto-ass off the hook.

I was turned on.

Extremely.

For the first time ever, I was attracted to someone on first contact. I'd never met a man that demanded something and got it on the spot. Either they were too passive or weak, but never the leader. He was cocky, powerful, demanding and I loved that about him.

"So, Mirror Carter?" he said with his hand extended toward mine.

There was no ring, which determined his eligibility.

I made sure to give him my left hand which determined mine. "Yes, my name is Mirror Carter, but I'm afraid I don't know yours?"

"Brice Towers." He kissed my hand and then held on to it while he continued to talk. "I'm sorry for everything. They probably just did that to you because of this." He pointed to our skin.

His was dark brown.

Mine caramel.

A perfect mixture.

"It's okay. Believe it or not, stuff like this happens to me all the time. I guess they just don't expect *us* to have anything."

"Listen, the store is empty. It's just me and a few friends. Would you like to go and pick out something nice for yourself?"

"No, I couldn't."

"Really, I insist. It'll be on me. Consider it an apology from me for your troubles. I'm sure your husband won't mind!" My eyebrows curled up in confusion, but it didn't take too long for me to remember that I'd used my fake husband as a threat against the store.

I flashed my ring finger slightly in the air. "Oh, no I'm not really married," I confessed. "I just wanted to scare those security guards." His eyes sketched the outline of my body and paused at my big, perfectly round ass.

"Good, because if I had a woman as beautiful as you, the rock would hold your finger down." My pussy dripped instantly like a faucet. Any more time spent with a man who could shut a whole fucking store down would make me show my true colors. "So what do you say?"

"If you insist." I tried to play the shy role as he led the way.

"Let me introduce you to my friends, Tommy and Patrick."

96

I shook the hands of the men that weren't as attractive as Brice, but seemed to be just as wealthy. After our introduction, they excused themselves and let Brice know that they were going to the men's section, letting us have our privacy.

"That dress that you're wearing looks very nice on you," Brice said, giving him another reason to sneak a peek at my booty. I pretended I didn't notice.

"Thank you."

"So, where should we head?"

"Let's go and look at some jewelry," I suggested. Although I needed some more clothes for the store, it had been a few weeks since I'd gotten some nice things for myself. I hadn't helped myself to any nice jewelry recently, and since he was buying, I couldn't think of a better time to get some. We walked side by side, past the shoe section and then the fragrance counter until we reached the fine jewelry section. There was no hiding the excitement in my face as I studied each piece that sat behind the glass with devotion.

"Good evening. Would you like to try on a piece?" an older Asian woman asked.

"Yes, I'd like to take a look at that one," I said, pointing at a David Yurman necklace. It was eighteen carat gold with huge whiskey colored stones that the saleswoman took out of the case and placed around my neck. I was up on expensive shit, so I knew how much it retailed for.

"That looks beautiful on you," Brice said as he ran the tips of his fingers along my collar bone. "Do you want it?"

"Do I want it…of course I do."

The $6,600.00 Chantelaine collection necklace was stunning, just like me.

"Go ahead and box it up," he instructed to the saleswoman.

"Am I being punked or something?" I looked around then gave off a silly giggle. I was expecting Ashton's white-ass to jump out at any moment.

Brice laughed displaying an addictive smile. "No…no. Not at all."

"Well, thank you so much."

I know that the happy glow on my face showed how appreciative I was, but I thought it was nice to offer my gratitude up verbally. I could barely control my excitement as the saleswoman handed me the small bag.

"You're welcome Mirror. But honestly, this is nothing. Just a little apology gift that I hope will make everything better."

"Apology...for what?" I asked, letting him know that all had been forgotten. "And besides, you had nothing to do with that."

"I know, but you still were the one embarrassed at the end of the day. An apology from the store manager doesn't really fix that, you know?" I nodded my head. "Well, I have a few more hours before the All Star Game later on tonight. Do you want to grab a few more things?"

"Um...no. I better get going."

I could've kicked my own ass for turning down a proposal to go on an exclusive shopping spree, but I still had all the stolen shit on me and needed to get out of the store while I had the chance. My new jewelry would have to be enough for now.

"Are you getting ready to do a Cinderella on me? Run off into the New Orleans night and leave me with a shoe?" he asked. We both laughed because that's what it seemed like. "You know you have a beautiful smile."

I blushed, then thought to myself, *just wait until I get these porcelain veneers*. "Thank you." We left the jewelry section and walked back to the front of the store.

"Listen, if you don't already have plans, I would love for you to join me at the game tonight." Before I could say anything he continued. "I won't take no for an answer. Let me know which hotel you're staying in and I'll have my limo pick you up."

I gave him my information and watched him take out something from his pocket. "What's this?"

"Your ticket."

"Oh my goodness, you're being too sweet to me. Thank you," I said before leaving out of the store. I wanted to ask more questions like where he worked or what business he owned. Or if we would have great seats. But I needed to jet with my stolen shit. Besides, I had the feeling that I'd hit jackpot!

Chapter Eleven

"Ms. Carter," the concierge said on the other end of the phone. "Your limo is downstairs waiting for you."

"Okay, thank you."

After almost landing myself in jail, I was still in shock by being rescued by a total stranger. He was definitely a man of his word and two hours after meeting him, he had his limo positioned outside, The W Hotel, in the French Quarter just as he'd promised. Going over my long ass list of men in my head, I couldn't even think of anyone who had Brice's sophistication, charm, and more importantly…his money. He was the perfect package, and I was looking forward to seeing him again at the basketball game.

Before heading downstairs, I took one more look into the mirror to make sure everything was in place. My yellow and black Dolce and Gabbana silk tie dye mini dress was skin tight and the knee length Dolce and Gabbana black leather boots went perfectly together. My loosely curled weave, which was parted down the middle, fell graciously over my shoulders and down my back. I was sure that all eyes would be on me.

I grabbed my Gucci Indy bag and my room key before heading out of the door and took the elevator down to the lobby. When I proceeded outside, my mouth fell open when I was greeted by a black Phantom Rolls Royce. Just when I thought maybe it was a mistake, the driver opened up the coach style rear door and said to me, "Good evening Ms. Carter."

I turned around just in case there wasn't someone else behind me with the same name. "Does this belong to Brice Towers?" I asked him, trying to make sure this was the right car.

"Yes Ma'am and tonight it belongs to you."

I wanted to pass out, but knew my smile still wouldn't dis-appear. I was expecting some long stretched boring-ass prom limo, but not this. I couldn't believe how much I'd been treated like a queen so far. "Thanks," I said to the driver before stepping inside.

I never would've imagined being inside a car of this magnitude. Rubbing my hand against the buttery, seashell colored seats, I couldn't help but notice what I'd been missing all my life. This was something that I could get used to and for a slight second I allowed myself to wonder what life would be like without the boosting and all the drama. Who knew what I even saw in guys like Rich and King Pen in the first place.

"Would you like some champagne before we head off?" the driver asked.

"No thank you. Water would be fine."

After handing me a bottle of Voss, we pulled off from in front of the hotel and headed toward the arena. The driver and I didn't make much small talk on our way there because it literally only took us about four minutes to arrive at the Superdome, and that included the traffic lights and the small amount of congestion.

I laughed to myself thinking, *that was the best four minute ride of my life.*

Once we pulled up, I was greeted by Brice's friend, Patrick who I'd met earlier. He was quick to open the door and help me out of the car. Everyone I'd met so far behaved like true gentlemen.

"Hello Mirror. Brice is looking forward to seeing you," he informed before slowly looking me up and down. "And trust me, he won't be disappointed."

I was flattered. "Thank you. I look forward to seeing him as well."

His eyes still followed me.

I could feel them.

I was a little late, but had managed make it to the game just before the first quarter started. The orchestrated intros that both teams had were all a thing of the past, but none of that mattered to me. As long as I was in the building, that's all I gave a shit about. Following Patrick into the arena, I was in complete awe at the thousands of people sitting in the stadium. My eyes were still on the prowl for any nigga I thought had some cash. Brice seemed to be a great catch, but I was used to being disappointed so I needed a Plan B just in case he switched up. Yeah, my mind was corrupt. I guess that's what I got for fucking with these sorry-ass niggas. Every dude in the stands watched in awe as my ass danced the whole way down the stairs in my tight fitting dress. All I could hear on the way down was, "damn girl" and "look at the ass." I knew this outfit would bring the heat, and tonight I wanted to start a muthafucking fire.

The more we walked, the more I realized where we were going.

Court side.

Damn.

He was sitting where everyone else dreamed to be. Where all the celebrities and A-list people sat. It was hard for me to believe that the only empty seat in the entire dome belonged to me. Brice stood up, kissed my cheek, and then my hand.

"I'm so happy you made it."

"Me too!" I said, probably showing way too much excitement. "Floor seats? This is crazy!" I hadn't had time to take this all in and it showed.

"This is nothing," he assured me. "Hey Tracy, come here for a second," he screamed. When fine-ass Tracy McGrady came over and stood by me, I thought somebody was gonna have to pick me up off the floor. "I would like for you to meet a friend of mine. This is Mirror Carter." From the introduction, you would've thought Brice was trying to hook me up or something, and if he was…that shit was cool with me. Money was money, no matter how you looked at it or whose pockets it came from.

Tracy smiled then shook my hand.

I couldn't believe that I was face to face with a rock star ball player who made nineteen million dollars a year. I was in heaven. Damn near intoxicated, and I didn't even drink.

"This is unbelievable. You know Tracy McGrady personally?"

"Yeah well, I pay him enough. They all at least pretend to like me."

What the hell does he mean? "What do you do?"

"I own the Houston Rockets." I blinked. *Did he just say that he owned the entire basketball team,* I asked myself. *Shit, if Tracy makes nineteen million I can only imagine what the fuck Brice makes.* My eyes lit up, unintentionally. This was the man I'd been looking for my entire life, and here he was pursuing me.

"For real," was all I could say.

"Yup, I've been living my dream for about five years now. I actually own a few other businesses, but the basketball franchise is closest to my heart."

"How old are you if you don't mind me asking?"

"No, not at all. I'm forty-two."

At that point I knew our age difference would never be a factor. He was sixteen years my senior, but that nigga could've been walking with a cane or wearing Depends, and I wouldn't care. He was paid.

The fans roared throughout the arena when someone made a basket. I wasn't paying any attention. I was too busy pinching myself. I wasn't interested in the game at all, but I was in love with the city of New Orleans. I'd gotten everything I came here for and more.

All throughout the game, the audience cheered, booed, heckled and cursed out all the calls that they agreed and disagreed with. I didn't know what was going on. Was never really a fan of the sport. I just sat and enjoyed the moment; something I didn't get a chance to do too often. I especially enjoyed every time a VIP came up and spoke to Brice. Everyone from Chris Tucker, Terrell Owens, and even that little Asian Kung-Fu guy named Jet Li, all knew who I was before they walked away. Brice had gone out of his way and introduced me to every single person, like I was already his girl. It felt good to be treated so special.

"You know that the basketball union didn't want to have the games here this year," Brice said to me, after he had finished up a conversation with what looked like to be another very important person.

"What do you mean?"

"After Katrina, the media had made this place out to be

where Satan himself camped out. After all of that refugee talk, people were afraid to vacation here. Then the murder count went up. People refused to come here."

"So, what did that have to do with the game?" I asked. I really wasn't interested, but when Brice talked, I was all ears. This nigga could talk about how many craters were on the moon, and I would listen.

"They advised the players and their families not to come. Said that it was too dangerous. But this was the only thing that was going to revive this city. The tourist money. They knew this and just didn't care." Brice shook his head like he was disgusted. "That's why I made sure I donated two million dollars to help build homes for the hurricane victims. So they could come back. So this city can get back to the way it used to be. You know I love giving money to help people better themselves. I just wish other people did the same."

He seemed angry about it.

It showed in his forehead.

He could definitely give me some to help better myself.

"But enough about all that. The game is here now and that's all that matters."

"That's right," I agreed as I extended my hand to rub his back.

He smiled.

Bystanders stared.

And they were more than welcomed to. They were staring at the future Mrs. Brice Towers, and didn't even know it.

● ● ● ● ● ● ● ● ● ● ● ● ● ● ● ● ●

When the game was over hours later, we gathered our things to go.

"I had a great time tonight. Thank you for everything," I said as his security surrounded him, seemingly ready to wisk him away. He motioned for them to back up.

They obliged.

"You're certainly welcome. Do you have plans for the rest of the evening?" Brice asked.

"No, probably just a night out on the town. I'll try and find a nice jazz club." Even though I was far from being into jazz, he didn't have to know that. Brice seemed like he wanted a classy, mature lady and I wanted to be the perfect candidate.

"Well, I would love for you to join me for the night. I know some people who are throwing a few after parties, and I don't want to go alone."

I looked around at the army of men he had surrounding him and said, "I'm sure your nights are never lonely."

"Believe me, they are."

"Okay. I'll take you up on that offer," was all I had to say before we were escorted to the Phantom.

Minutes later, we were driven to the Loews Hotel downtown where Diddy was throwing one of his famous parties inside the tenth floor ballroom. It was a different atmosphere for Diddy because he was known for his club events, but nevertheless the shit was still the place to be. Security walked us in as we were greeted by every famous film star and music mogul in the business. Brice kept his conversations short, and didn't seem to mind letting everyone know the reason.

Me.

"Oh, this is my song," I whispered to him as I began winding my hips to *Fiesta,* an old R. Kelly tune. I moved my body to the Spanish style beat of the music, like I wanted to be fucked.

Slow.

Nasty.

Brice summoned someone to fetch him a drink and asked if I wanted one as well.

"No thank you," I replied as I continued to move to the rhythm. I moved my body up and down his as if it were a pole. All the men that stood around stared as my body made a name for itself. Nothing could touch me. I was the finest thing up in the spot.

"I love the way you move," he told me. His lips brushed against my neck making my nipples hard. "Are you a dancer?"

"Not professional."

I took his hands and placed them on my hips while I moved my body in a slow, seductive motion. He felt so good, so I grinded even more.

He smiled and said, "I like that."

"I bet you do."

"Come with me, I have to show you something," he instructed before grabbing my hand. We moved through the thick crowd of people like something was on fire.

"Where are we going? You didn't even wait for your drink," I said just before we made our way past some giant glass doors and into another section of the ballroom, which overlooked all of New Orleans. The lights were low. The room…cozy. Even the music was different, more somber.

I would've preferred to stay inside the real party. Dry humping him while everyone watched. I wanted to show those bitches the prize that I'd just won, and show the niggas what level I was at. In this room, no one could see us. We were alone. It was almost as if Brice paid for it to be that way. I wouldn't have been surprised.

"I just wanted to come in here and clear my head a little bit. It was too loud to do that in there." From the expression on his face, I could tell that wasn't the only head he wanted to clear up.

I turned around to face him after looking out one of the huge windows. "Wow. The city is so pretty at night. This is beautiful," I lied. I would've much rather been back in the party showing him all the dance moves I knew how to perform, but there was no use in complaining to him. I knew what Brice wanted, and why he'd brought me here.

Looking around to see if anyone was coming, I went straight for the kill. I took my hand and rubbed it along his dick then stopped once I felt the head.

It was hard.

Just like I thought.

An affect that I seemed to have on men.

I got down on my knees and unzipped his pants. I could tell that Brice was a man who was used to getting his way, so I was definitely prepared to do whatever he wanted. It had been quite some time since I had to go down on a man, but for Brice I was willing to do it. Shit, if it meant I could get my Bentley or some money inside my purse, I was willing to do anything.

Chapter Twelve

"Wait!" Brice yelled. He stopped me just before I pulled his dick out. "Not here. I have a suite upstairs." He quickly zipped his pants back up and helped me back to my feet. "If you were just some random chick, then I wouldn't give a shit about your dignity, but I really like you."

Call it a strong case of puppy love, but I was falling for Brice by the second. Any other nigga would've taken that blow job, without a second thought. "That means a lot," I responded.

Hugging each other around our lower backs, we carried on like teenage kids while walking as fast as we could to the elevator. After pressing the up button, Brice groped my breasts in front of several bystanders who were waiting for the same ride. He obviously didn't give a shit about his own dignity.

They watched.

Shamelessly.

A minute or two later, the elevator doors opened wide; as wide as my legs would be in several more minutes. As wide as my mouth would open to take in all his manhood. We followed four other people inside, then stared at our reflection through the mirrors that covered all four walls.

"Can you please hit twelve for me," Brice asked out loud. When someone pushed the circular button for his requested floor, and the elevator doors finally closed, surprisingly Brice hemmed me against the back wall. He kissed me in the mouth, an area I never allowed anyone to go, while slipping his hand up my dress at the same time. He touched my secret place gently. A place where wishes were granted.

"I can't believe this shit," one of the people said, talking to no one in particular. The dude was young. Around twenty-two.

Probably wishing that he was getting fucked, too. No one else responded although I was sure that they all agreed.

Why wouldn't they? They were all men.

They just watched.

Moving my thong to the side, Brice took his index finger and circled the opening before pushing his finger inside my pussy. I did everything I could to keep myself from moaning as his finger plunged deeper and deeper into my walls. Moving my hips slowly, he could tell I wanted more, so he added another finger, this time allowing his thumb to brush against my clit. I bit down on my lips several times, just to hold my composure.

I'm sure the nosey male viewers were enjoying each second of our little porno, and were probably ready to whip their own dicks out when we finally reached our floor.

Someone cleared their throat. "Umm…12th floor."

When Brice heard that, he quickly removed his fingers, which were now soaking wet, out of my sweet vagina, then led me out of the elevator like nothing ever happened. Every pair of eyes were glued on us.

"Can I watch?" was the last thing we heard from behind before the doors shut in their faces.

As horny as I was, I'm glad we didn't have to walk far in order to get to the room. It was only two doors down from the elevator. I waited patiently as he pulled the room key out from out of his pocket, slid it in the slot, and turned the knob after the green light appeared.

I walked inside.

He followed like a perfectly trained puppy.

After the door closed behind him, he swept me off my feet like we were newlyweds who'd just eloped and carried me over to the king size bed. He laid me down gently on the crisp white sheets and proceeded to unzip my knee high leather boots. He threw them down on the floor and thoroughly inspected my feet.

"They're pretty," he said, before licking each toe individually.

He obviously had a foot fetish. This had become a scene that reminded me of Eddie Murphy's character in the movie

Boomerang. He devoted the same amount of time to each toe, never discriminating against any of them.

I loved the freaky side of him already.

After he showed my feet how special he thought they were, Brice undressed himself from head to toe as I watched in awe at what I saw. He lifted weights for sure. Not so much to the point where he looked like a body builder, but enough to make you say *damn*! His body was toned, tight, and cut. My body was the same except plastic surgery was what took care of the imperfections that I was born with.

His dick was long, hard as a rock and curved slightly to the right. Something that I knew was going to work in my favor. Putting his head under my dress, the warm breath from his mouth sent chills up my spine as it breezed past my thighs, and made its home on my pussy. He moved my thongs to the side, ready to enter the Bermuda Triangle.

"No, wait!" I yelled as I scooted my body up and pushed his shoulders down at the same time. I had to make a move before he licked it. As much as I liked getting my pussy sucked, this just wasn't the right time for that.

He brought his face back uptown. "Why, what's wrong. I want to taste you," he insisted while trying to make his way back down.

I pushed him off me again.

"Why do you keep doing that? Does it stink down there or something?"

I was offended. "No, it doesn't stink. You were just down there. Why don't you tell me how it smells?" I uttered seductively.

Brice paused for a moment like he was thinking about it. "Well what's wrong?"

"It's just that…I don't really like oral sex," I lied. "But I bet you do. Let me taste you." I had to think of something quick to get his mind off my coochie.

I also didn't have to ask him twice because before I knew it, Brice was laying on his back with his dick standing at full attention. Propping myself up on my knees, I wrapped my mouth around his shaft, then licked him like my favorite red, white, and blue popsicle.

Slow. And then fast.

Soft. And then hard.

I sucked his shit until he was swollen and his breathing mimicked a dog in heat ready to fuck. I already knew I could give that porno chick, Heather Hunter a run for her money.

"I don't wanna cum yet," Brice said, stopping me in mid stride. "Take off your clothes."

I'd almost forgotten. Following his instructions, I wiggled my way out the dress and threw it along with my thongs on the floor before laying next to him in my birthday suit. He kissed every part of my body, nice and slow.

"Aahhh…don't stop," I moaned.

"Tell me why you deserve more," he asked in a deep and low voice.

"Because I've been a good girl."

His hands were soft like he hadn't worked a hard day in his life, and when he pinched one of my nipples, the pleasure was incredibly intense. I guess I had Kahn to thank for that. I was grateful I still had sensation in that area. Brice bent down and took one of my breasts into his mouth, before moving to the other. Everything he did to me at this point felt good. Especially his dick that had brushed up against my leg several times.

I couldn't wait any longer.

I wanted him inside of me.

As I wiggled my way into a position for easy entrance, I suddenly remembered that I didn't have any protection. Hadn't asked him if he'd brought any either.

Shit.

"Wait," I said in between moans. I attempted to push him off, but he wouldn't budge. He was too determined. Horny. "Baby, do you have any condoms?"

He smiled. Kissed me on the neck and said, "Of course." He quickly climbed off the bed, grabbed his pants, then went into his pocket. Several condoms fell to the floor while he only tried to pull out one.

"You come prepared, huh?" I asked sarcastically.

"Better safe than sorry," he answered climbing back on the bed. He was right.

I took the pleasure of placing the condom over his dick, caressing his balls with one hand as I rolled it down his shaft with the other. My legs were spread like a bald eagle, almost shaking from the anticipation.

Then suddenly he entered my love nest.

Not slow, but more so rough.

He worked his magic stick inside of me as if he was my man that just came home from doing a ten year bid. A man who was aware that society questioned his sexuality after spending that much time away from his girl. A man who had a point to prove to everyone. Our body language would call us addicted.

Obsessed.

Crazy.

His dick squished around in my wetness until it made a puddle on the sheets. What was once cool and crisp had now been taken over by my warm and dampness.

My juices.

Caused by his lust.

We moved to the same rhythm, like we'd been sexing for years. We were that much in sync with each other. His mouth connected to mine once again and I enjoyed every second of it as his tongue swam around in my mouth like he missed me. Like someone told him that I was running away forever. Small pants escaped my mouth as my waist moved in circular motion.

He let out another sound. This one louder.

"Please don't stop," I pleaded with him as his hands investigated my body even further. His touches were soft and firm all at the same time.

He was experienced and rich which was something that usually didn't come in the same package.

"Let me ride it," I whispered as he quickly repositioned himself up under me.

I climbed on top of him.

My big ass followed.

His dick did a disappearing act as I rose and sat on top. I

twisted my waist from side to side as his thick, long pole rubbed along the right side of my pussy, hitting my g-spot every time.

"Oh shit…I…think…I'm…," I moaned as he said nothing. His eyes did all the talking as they drifted to the back of his head. "Fuck…I'm going to…" I placed both my hands over his shoulders and rode even harder.

Faster.

As if I had somewhere to go.

"Jesus!" I screamed.

A word I didn't use often.

Hardly ever.

I just couldn't find another word to describe how good it felt. How unbelievable the cum felt gushing out of me. Jesus' name was the only one I could think of at the time.

I felt bad.

But the damage had already been done.

Together we came and I laid on top of him while we both struggled to catch our breaths. Both of our bodies were hot, sticky, and wet.

"Damn!" was all he could muster up to say.

I felt the same way. I rolled off of him and onto my back. Stared at the ceiling in satisfaction. He did the same.

"Tell me more about you," he asked a few moments later. His dick was still covered in the dirty condom.

"Well what else do you want to know?" I asked as if we actually knew anything about each other. As if we weren't total strangers who had only met earlier today.

"Everything."

He asked as if he cared.

He asked as if this wasn't just a one night stand.

Brice rubbed my stomach in a trance of satisfaction. He had got what he wanted, and I felt like we made a connection in the process.

"Well, I was born and raised in Houston by my mother who is a celebrity stylist. My father died in a car accident when I was smaller so she remarried a big time movie director." I could lie very well.

"What's his name, I might know him?" Brice asked as seriously as he could.

"Yeah, well one day I'm sure you'll meet him. I don't like doing any name dropping. I'm sure you understand, right?"

"I love you already," he said hugging me. "Tell me more."

"They sent me to Harvard's law school when I graduated high school and I went on to finish there with honors. Law was never really my passion so now I own my own clothing boutique in Houston, which does really well."

"Any children?"

"No, I've realized that I don't really want any. I'm too spoiled for that."

"Well at least you're aware of that already. Look how many children are in the world today with parents who don't give a fuck about them. It's a shame."

Shit, it sounds like you're describing my sorry-ass mother. "Yeah, I was the only child and my parents gave me everything I wanted." I continued to lie, but felt as if I didn't have much of a choice. He owned a basketball team and I grew up in a trailer park. If he knew the truth, he'd probably send my ass packing before I could even blink. Fuck that...as close as I was to landing a rich man, that part of my life would just have to be taken to the grave.

"It seems like we grew up on the opposite side of the tracks," he said, as he let out a sigh.

"What do you mean?"

"I mean your life. You grew up privileged. I grew up on the south side of Houston, in one of the worst hoods. I'm from the streets. Never had anything because my mother smoked it all up. My father was a pimp and last I heard got killed by one of his hoe's husbands. When I was a little boy, the only dream I had was to own a basketball team. For some reason, I never wanted to play. I just wanted it to be mine so that I could watch it all day. When I got older, I worked hard until everything happened. All the odds were against me, but I still made it."

His life was my own.

It was for a slight second that I wished I hadn't lied about my past. I'd finally found someone who could understand what I'd been through. But we were still different. He wasn't ashamed of how he was brought up even talked about it with a hint of pride. But it was just something that I couldn't reveal. I was so disgusted about being trailer trash that I couldn't even find the good in it to use it as a *rags to riches* story.

He grew up poor.

Not me…I'd just stick to my story of growing up rich.

During our brief silence, he'd dozed off just that quick, even though it wasn't surprising to me. My pussy was known to put niggas in comatose states every now and then.

I guess Brice is just another candidate, I thought just before my phone started ringing. Jumping up like I was about to compete in the Olympic pole vault, I hurried over to my purse to pick it up so I wouldn't disturb Brice. The ID said 'Private.' A call that I didn't answer. I sent it to voicemail. Seconds later, it rang again with the same private caller. I had no idea who it could be. After sending the call to voicemail for the second time, I decided to put the phone on vibrate then placed it back in my purse.

Whoever it was would just have to wait. Besides, didn't they know I didn't like to be disturbed when I was with a new victim?

Chapter Thirteen

My phone vibrated.

And then stopped.

Did the same thing over ten times back to back. Whoever it was was relentless and refused to give up. Had been calling since the night before. I turned over and looked at the time which read 9:12 a.m. After looking at the time, I finally decided to get up and curse out whoever was fucking with my sleep. Anyone who knew me should've known I didn't even like to get up before noon most of the time. Besides, the new love of my life needed his rest too.

I crawled out of the bed and walked over to my purse ass naked. When I pulled out my phone, I couldn't believe that there were twenty-two missed calls. All private of course. *Who the fuck could it be*, I thought as I scrolled down the list. I had to find out who was damn near harassing me.

However, before I could do anything, the 'private number' called again.

This time I answered.

"Valtrex!" he said out loud. "You're taking Valtrex?" The question was rhetorical, one that really didn't warrant an answer, although I'm sure he wanted one. The man on the other end of my phone was Dr. Khan, and he'd obviously found the bottle of medicine that I intentionally left on his counter.

Herpes.

That was my big secret.

Had the STD for a while now.

I took Valtrex pills every day to reduce my outbreaks, but it wasn't long before another one would erupt. My shit was like clockwork. A week at the most and I would be blistered up. It wasn't a pretty sight. Vaginal discharge, headaches, sore muscles, fevers, the signs were all there. I had recurring outbreaks about eight times a year. Yeah…all because of one man's dirty dick, I had a disgusting STD that would be traveling with me for the long haul.

Damn.

"You have herpes?" he asked again.

I hope he didn't expect me to feel sorry for his ass. That's what the fuck he got for having unprotected sex with a patient. That's what he got for trying to just give me a measly thousand dollars. And that's what he got for telling me about what he'd planned to buy for his wife. He needed to be taught a lesson.

Permanently.

"Yes, as a matter of fact I do," I admitted, not able to elaborate any further. I was well aware that although Brice seemed to be knocked out, every shut eye wasn't asleep. I had to watch what I said. "Now, it looks like you might have it too."

"How could you do this to me?" Kahn screamed into the phone.

"Baby, is everything okay," Brice asked when he turned over and realized that I wasn't beside him.

I froze, then hung up the phone with Khan immediately. I didn't give a fuck that he might've been still talking, or that he was still trying to figure this whole thing out.

There was nothing else left to say.

He should've given me what I wanted.

"I'm fine," I answered, then walked back over to the bed. "Good morning." I kissed him on the lips and loved it. Even with the morning breath.

"Good morning, beautiful. Sorry I feel asleep on you last night."

I smiled. "Oh, it's okay Brice. That just let's me know how good my loving was. If we have sex, and then you decide to go run a marathon or some shit afterwards then we might have a problem."

He laughed out loud. "You know what I was thinking…that I can't wait to spoil you."

"Well, actions speak louder than words."

On the insides I was jumping up and down. *Jackpot! Baby, Jackpot*! I thought to myself.

"Then I'll say no more," he commented like he had a plan.

Brice picked up his cell phone that rested next to his head and dialed some numbers. After a few seconds of waiting, he told his driver that he would be ready to go shortly.

"Already?" I asked. "Why are you leaving so soon?"

"Don't worry, you're coming with me. I'm going to show you how a woman is supposed to be treated. "

Then out on nowhere it dawned on me.

Today was Monday.

"Wait, I can't do that."

He looked surprised that I'd turned him down. "Why?"

"My flight was scheduled to leave out this afternoon."

"So, I'll get you another flight out after we finish. Just relax. I'll take care of everything."

"Are you sure?"

"Did Michael Jackson used to be black? Of course I'm sure," he joked.

● ● ● ● ● ● ● ● ● ● ● ● ● ●

An hour later, both of us had showered, brushed our teeth with hotel supplied toothbrushes, and put back on the clothes from the night before. Something that I wasn't too cool with. I'd asked Brice at least three times to take me back to my hotel, so I could change but he wouldn't oblige. He told me that he would buy me whatever I needed. I decided to let it go after a while. Besides, I wasn't gonna be the same fool twice. This time, I wasn't passing up a free shopping trip.

"Are you ready to go?" he asked as he sat on the edge of the bed.

I straightened my hair with my fingers and put a few coats of lip gloss on.

"Yeah, I'm ready. Where are we going again?"

"It's a surprise, so just sit back and enjoy the ride."

We left his room and took the elevator down to the main floor. And just as I suspected, the Phantom was waiting right outside. All eyes were on us as the driver opened the coach style doors to let us in. Eyes that waited for their cabs to come and take them to the airport so they could go back home. Eyes that were envious that I'd obviously hit the jackpot and was riding away in style. We drove past the once busy Harrah's Casino, whose front doors had slimmed down considerably from the tourists who'd come just for the weekend, and headed straight to the Gucci store which was about five minutes away from the hotel.

I looked at Brice with a big cheesy grin. "Is this my surprise?'

"Why yes it is. You seem like a woman with style, so I figured this would be the perfect store for you."

Was he kidding me? Of course I had style. It was my middle name…right along with Gucci… Prada…Louie V. I had so many middle names. I reached over and planted a huge kiss on his lips. "Of course this is the perfect store. Let's go." I didn't even wait for the driver to open my door before I opened it myself, jumped out then walked toward the door.

A sales associate walked right over to us as soon as we stepped inside. She greeted me, but hugged Brice. She was very beautiful who seemed to be a little too familiar with him. I felt uneasy about that and wasn't sure why.

"Suze, this is, Mirror. Make her happy please. Get her whatever she wants," Brice stated.

"No problem, Mr. Towers." She smiled at me, grabbed my hand and promised to take good care of me as she led me to the shoe section first. I felt like Julia Roberts in the movie *Pretty Woman*, as he demanded three other associates to help me with my selections. They offered up compliments and did as much sucking up as possible without being obvious, but failed miserably. I was so happy when I saw Brice walking toward me.

"I still can't believe all of this is for me," I said, hoping he'd give me the indication that all of this would never stop.

"Believe me sweetheart." He came in closer, wrapped his hands around my waist and then whispered in my ear, "This is nothing."

I'd started to realize that was his favorite line because he said it quite frequently.

Suze walked up and interrupted our moment. "Do you know which shoes you'd like to try on?" she asked.

"I didn't even get a chance to look around yet," I replied.

"Well, I'm sure I can help you with that. What size shoe do you wear?"

"Seven."

"Just take off your shoes and I'll do the rest," she informed. Their customer service was something I wouldn't have gotten if I hadn't shown up with Brice. Guess it all depended on who you knew or in my case, who I was with. Moments later, all four of my little helpers each came out with a box of stilettos, sandals, boots, and even a pair of sneakers.

"She'll take them all," Brice informed, before I even had a chance to try them on.

"Brice!" I playfully shoved him on the shoulders. "Are you sure?"

"Yes, of course."

It felt so good not having to risk my freedom by boosting these type of items over the weekend. I was more relaxed than I'd been in a long time. While someone took the shoes to the register, Suze led me to the handbag department as Brice followed closely behind.

I was a certified handbag whore, and tried on every bag my poor shoulder could carry, until I ended up with three Hysterias in different colors, a black studded Babouska, and a suede Jockey bag just for fun. I couldn't wait to rock them when I got back home. Most of them had just hit the shelves.

Just as Brice made his way to the counter to ring up my merchandise, my phone started vibrating again. Looking down at the number, it didn't say private like all the other times, but I still didn't recognize it. I knew if I didn't answer, it would continue to ring while I was with Brice, and that couldn't happen. I had to excuse myself to take the phone call.

"Hello?" I asked professionally, just in case my voice could be heard in the store.

"You fucked wit' the wrong person. I'ma kill you bitch!" he

shouted. It wasn't hard to recognize his voice.

I wanted to make sure Brice was at a good distance before I responded. Should've just hung up, but I knew he would only keep calling.

"Why the fuck do you keep calling me?"

"Because I want my shit back!" KP yelled.

I continued to walk toward the other side of the store. "I already told you once before, I threw that fake-ass jewelry away. If you such a baller then just go out and buy some more. Just make sure it's real diamonds this time." I let out a small laugh.

"Bitch, you think dis shit is funny. You know what I tried to give yo' ass a pass, but I see you don't want it. You obviously don't know who me and my brother are. You better watch yo' back."

I looked behind me to make sure Brice wasn't paying attention, then laughed again. "Muthafucka please. Threats don't mean shit to me. Fuck you and your brother. You fake-ass wanna be rapper." I wanted to yell so bad, but couldn't.

"Let me...let me tell you somethin'." KP was so mad at my comment he could barely get it out. "I am a fuckin' rapper. *King Pen*, bitch! Just wait til' I drop dis' new shit. You gon' be back on my dick in no time."

"Keep dreaming asshole. Now, what you need to do is stop playing around and give your brother my number. Since he's the one with all the money, I need to holla at 'em," I said just before hanging up.

Chapter Fourteen

A week had passed since my trip to New Orleans and Brice and I had started spending some serious time together. The only time we seemed to be apart was when he had an important meeting to go to or when he got phone calls on a red Blackberry that he carried around. I wondered why the hell he would carry around a damn red phone...thought that was a little strange. But then again I guess he could carry around as many phones as he wanted. He was a busy man...the owner of a major franchise. But still it was the way he looked at me when he got the calls that made me a bit uneasy. Nevertheless, I threw all those feelings in the back of my mind because regardless of what strange calls he got, our connection was crazy. It was like we'd known each other forever. I even had to pry myself away from him to come to the boutique and get some paper work done. Not to mention, I hadn't boosted since New Orleans, so my store was running on empty. I knew I had to get some more inventory and fast. I just hoped I could stay away from Brice long enough to swipe some good shit.

While rearranging some of the fixtures in the store, a silver Bentley Coupe pulled up outside my store. I almost broke my neck trying to see who it was. Then seconds later, Brice emerged from the car.

"Oh shit. No he didn't!" I yelled, trying to fix myself up. "I know he didn't buy me my dream car!" I hurried to the door and walked outside even before he had a chance to come in. "Hey honey!" My smile was as big as the whole state of Texas.

"Hello sweetheart. You didn't even let me surprise you," Brice replied. He looked good in his Hugo Boss sweat suit.

"Not with that chromed out car." I hoped like hell that he would be handing me the keys any second.

"So, this is your spot, huh? Savvy Girl Boutique," Brice

looked around then smiled. "Nice name."

I could barely take my eyes off the car. "Thanks."

"So, who is your landlord? I know a lot of real estate developers in Houston. Maybe I could get you a deal on your next lease."

A deal? How about you pay the rent, I thought. "It's Smith Realty Consultants," I replied folding my arms. I wanted my body language to suggest that I didn't want to have this conversation. *So much for the car being mine.*

"Well, we have a game that starts in a about thirty minutes or so. Would you like to come with me?" I guess he got the hint.

"Umm...I haven't had anything to eat yet," I said trying to down play his invitation. *Of course* I wanted to go. I just couldn't let him know how pressed I was.

"Don't worry about it, we'll grab something to eat on the way there," he replied with an assuring smile.

I put my finger up, motioning him to wait a second, then ran back in the store to grab my keys and purse off the counter. I was back outside in no time. As I went to lock the door, my cell phone rang. I was tired of this shit ringing every time we were together. Normally, I would've ignored it, but I didn't want Brice to think I was up to some bullshit so I took a chance.

"Yes," I answered, knowing exactly who it was. The caller was private and only Khan kept calling this way.

"I hope my wife kills you!"

He was angry, as usual.

"Well Sir, thank you for the information. Maybe next time you'll be careful," I advised before hanging up and taking out the key.

I twisted the knob to make sure it was locked before following Brice to the car. I was so glad that we'd used a condom when we made love. I didn't want to risk getting him infected. I know a week was a short amount of time to say that I knew enough about him, but I felt as though I was falling for Brice and hard. I wanted to keep him safe. Something that nobody had ever thought about doing for me.

Just as Brice was opening the door for me, I heard a woman

calling my name from behind. When I turned around, I couldn't believe who was walking up the sidewalk. Why in the hell was she here? Why now? The bitch had awful timing.

"Do you know her?" Brice asked me with a slight look of disgust on his face. He stood frozen next to my door. Now, I was afraid to get inside. I didn't want to leave my man outside to hear her lies.

I quickly turned back around. Tried to ignore her. "Ah, no...I don't know who she is." I lied. I knew exactly who it was. It was my mother, and she was only a few feet away.

"Tyon...Mirror!" she called out again. She was getting closer.

"But I think she called your name," Brice announced with his eyebrow crinkled.

"Well...I mean there are a few homeless people down here who I help out from time to time so it could be one of them. Get in...let's go baby," I urged.

I knew it was damn near impossible to get Brice into the car and drive off before she walked up, but I was gonna try.

"Hey," my mother said, finally walking up to us. "I'm so glad I caught you. I know you're tired of me coming down here, but can you help your mother out a little bit today? My lights are about to get turned off. I'll pay you back when I get my check on the 1st."

I couldn't believe she was asking me this shit in front of Brice. I was so fucking embarrassed.

Brice seemed a little confused. "Is this your mother?"

I paused for a few seconds. "I don't know who this woman is. She's obviously deranged and has me confused with someone else." My face was cold as ice. "We need to go Brice." I didn't even wait for a response before scooting into my seat. There was no way in hell that I was going to tell him the truth.

Even though Brice still seemed a bit uneasy, he closed my door then gave my mother a quick glance before walking to the driver's side of the car.

"Why do you treat me like this?" my mother pleaded.

I never said a word. Never even looked her way. She didn't

deserve my attention.

"Umm…Miss she said you had the wrong person," Brice said coming to my defense. "Clear, mistaken identity," he added. After jumping in the driver's seat, he put the car in drive then pulled away nice and easy. This time, I managed to steal a quick look at my mother through the side view mirror. She just stood there looking pitiful. I could care less.

"Now that was interesting," Brice said turning the corner, "I wonder why she would think you were her daughter."

I had to say something so the situation could make some sense. "I mean, I've seen her walking around downtown before, but that doesn't make me her daughter. Maybe I just look like her or maybe she's just crazy. Trust me, I have no clue who that lady is."

"You know, I really don't feel sorry for people like that," Brice replied. "I mean, not to sound so harsh, but I think that I had it worse off than a lot of people, and if I could make it out, I think everyone else has a chance, too."

"Yeah, you're one hundred percent right."

"I know you can't relate because of how you were raised, but just trust me. You shouldn't feel sorry for those type of people."

Little did he know that I didn't feel sorry for *our* type of people. Never had. Never would. "Really, everyone else in the world goes and looks for a job. What makes them feel like they can just beg for our hard earned money all day? Don't get me wrong, I'm a very giving person, but God blesses the child that has his own, you know?"

I was so full of shit.

Had to be in this case.

He continued to talk while I stared out of the heavily tinted window hoping that he would never find out that was actually the life I'd lived not too long ago. That part of my life was dead, so why bring it up anyway.

● ● ● ● ● ● ● ● ● ● ● ● ● ● ● ● ● ●

Brice continued to talk about poverty, urban neighborhoods and getting an education until we reached the Toyota Center. A boring-ass conversation, but I tried my best to act like I was interested. I hated when he got all deep on me like that. Once I stepped outside the car, there was no red carpet waiting like I'd imagined in my mind, but the way we were greeted there might as well have been. Brice Towers was a king and this was his kingdom.

"Good evening Mirror, how are you?" I heard several people ask from a distance.

"Fine...thanks," I replied with a huge smile. I recognized a few people from New Orleans, and was surprised to see that they'd remembered me. That said a lot and made me feel like some type of celebrity. A feeling that seemed surreal. A feeling I could definitely get used to.

We were escorted straight up to the Brice's luxury suite by two huge bodyguards, and right before we walked in Brice decided to have a stern conversation with one of them. "Hey, Marcus do you see this face?" he asked the big man, while cupping my chin. The grizzly bear shook his head yes. "She is to be treated like a queen whenever she steps foot in this place, do you understand?"

"Got it Mr. Towers," Marcus responded giving me a once over and then a wink.

"Good because this one is special," Brice said, rubbing my shoulder.

I wasn't sure if I wanted to be referred to as 'this one' but it didn't matter. I beamed like a ray of sunshine...inside and out. Brice had a way of making me feel special.

Taking me by the hand, Brice led me inside his owner's suite, which was laid out; flat screen T.V.'s, red suede sofas, a huge glass top bar, beautifully framed Rockets paraphernalia, team pictures, everything was plush. Even the display of sesame-seared tuna, grilled steak, and shrimp cocktail was superb. I loved everything, except for the uncomfortable glances I kept getting from a clique of women dressed in their Sunday's best. I wasn't sure who they were, but if the bitches called themselves hating then it was a waste of time. They would be seeing a lot more of me, so they might as well brace themselves.

This is where I was supposed to be.

This is where I belonged.

While Brice shook a few hands and talked to some of his colleagues, I waved to the women and smiled. They rolled their eyes, turned the other way then whispered under their breath in return.

Petty-ass bitches, I thought then laughed out loud. I knew Brice would be introducing me to the women once he finished his conversation, so I had to make sure my voice was nice and proper. However, once his conversation ended, Brice grabbed my hand and led me straight to the view of the basketball court. This was the first time he hadn't gone out of his way to let everyone in the room know who I was. It was strange. Had me thinking that he didn't want the uppity-ass women to know who I was. A little offended, it was on the tip of my tongue to say something, but Brice spoke first.

"I'm so happy I met you Mirror," he said before kissing me gently on the lips.

The uneasy feeling I'd just had left faster than I could blink. "I doubt if you're happier than me." I leaned in to kiss him again, but stopped when I suddenly felt the phone on his hip vibrating.

Taking the phone out the holster, Brice looked at the number and then looked at me. It was the infamous red Blackberry. Again, the situation felt strange.

Brice tensed up and instantly pulled away from me. "I have to take this call."

Before I had a chance to say anything, he placed the phone to his ear and quickly walked out of the suite sending the women in the room into a cackling frenzy. A part of me wanted to run behind him to see what that phone call was all about. To see if there was something I needed to know, but I decided to stay in my lane.

Don't trip, Mirror, I told myself. This was the first time in my life that I'd met a man with some major paper, so I wasn't gonna fuck up my chances. If I had to get rid of a few bitches and fight for my man then so be it. This wasn't new to me. I'd done it countless times before. *Let the games begin.* Besides, Brice was more than worth it, and I didn't plan on losing.

Chapter Fifteen

She nodded her head.

Twice.

That was my signal that the coast was clear and that my time clock had just begun. I was in Neiman Marcus at the Galleria Mall and hungry to steal everything that wasn't bolted down. Normally I wasn't as anxious, but this time I had an inside connect so I figured I could get away with even more shit this time. Her name was Sabrina and she was the assistant manager. I'd grown up with her in Shady Grove and had bumped in to her a couple of weeks ago while strolling around in the store. Hell, she was the one who came to me with the idea in the first place. Even though she was a manager you know how the saying goes. You can take the chick out the hood, but you can't take the hood out the chick.

The operation was simple. I would grab everything that I wanted, including the items on Sabrina's wish list, and in return she would be the one to ring me up. The great thing about that was, instead of ringing up every item, she would only ring up one. Two at the most. Sabrina assured me that not only was she the only manager working, but that she was also giving the dude in loss prevention pussy on a regular basis so we didn't have to worry about the cameras. It was the perfect plan.

This is going to be too easy, I thought as I took my time going through each article of clothing. I checked the tags for the most expensive pieces that I could find and then held each one up to my body to see if it was something that I would wear. My boutique represented style and whatever I wouldn't be caught dead wearing, neither would any of my customers. Yeah, I was definitely a label hoe.

I picked up Zac Posen, Missoni, Peter Som, Jean Paul Gaultier and several other designer items that I knew were going to be big hits in the store. My hands were full of merchandise and it was then when I realized how lucky I was to have this hook up. Any other security would've been on me by now, but we had this dude, Sabrina was fucking, under wraps.

"Hello Ma'am, can I get a fitting room ready for you?" The associate held her hand out and without giving me the chance to answer the question, proceeded to grab the clothes. I jerked away and before I had a chance to say anything, I felt someone walk up behind me.

"Lindsay, I'll help her. Can you please go straighten out the Hudson jeans? I really need you in that section until you clock out, thanks." The chick looked at Sabrina kind of angrily as if she had taken her commission sale away. Little did she know my bill was free. "Do you have everything?" Sabrina asked me.

I looked down at the mound of clothes I had in my hand and shook my head no. "Why, what's up?" I asked, wondering why she seemed rushed.

"Nah, it's just that you don't want all of these sales associates to keep asking you if you need help. Makes a scene and then they're going to start wondering why I'm not saying anything."

"But you're going to ring me up like everything is all good, right? And the security dude, he's still down with everything, right?"

"Well, yeah…"

"So what the fuck is the big deal? Let me finish shopping."

"Just hurry your ass up," she replied impatiently. "There will be plenty other days like today. Don't fuck this one up because you're being greedy!"

She looked around.

I did the same.

She had gotten louder than we both expected and now we were trying to make sure that no one was eaves dropping on our conversation. From the looks of it, there was nobody around. I felt like she'd brought too much heat over to me, so I decided it was time to cash out. I'd gotten enough stuff anyway to hold me down for a minute. Figured that I would just come back next week to finish up what I'd started.

I followed her to her register and laid everything out on the counter. She rang up some of the clothes and typed a few things into the computer. She pretended to ring in other pieces and folded them all neatly to the side. I had no idea what she did and how she did it, but it was quick and my total for well over eight thousand dollars worth of shit was only five hundred and seventy dollars. Although, a good price I didn't even want to pay that much, but she'd rung me up for the cheapest item I had. I took out my wallet and handed her the cash for it.

She wrapped up most of the stuff in tissue paper, trying to keep the appearance that I was a real customer and carefully put each item in bags. I breathed heavily while watching my back. For me, my hook-up girl moved entirely too slow. I needed to talk to her about that.

Finally after waiting another five minutes, I headed to my car that I'd parked next to the dumpsters at the employee entrance. I popped the trunk and continued to walk a few more steps until someone from behind me spoke up.

"Excuse me Ma'am, can we talk to you for a moment?"

I froze for a few seconds then turned around slowly. "Yes, how can I help you?" I asked, with the smile that I was forced to muster up. I had to find a way to appear natural.

"My name is Officer Barrett, and this is Officer Grimes. Do you mind if we take a look at the merchandise that's inside your bags?"

I looked at both men who were in plain clothes and frowned. They must've been undercover officers working the store. "I absolutely do mind! No, you can't just take a look. What is this all about? I'm late to a very important meeting!" Beads of sweat began appearing on my upper lip. My underarms were drenched and my head immediately started pounding. Those were my warning signs. I was in trouble.

"Ma'am can you follow us into the office?" Officer Barnett continued.

"No! I said that I had a meeting to attend so if you don't want to tell me what this is all about, I'm leaving."

Barnett took a step closer, while Grimes put his hand on his gun.

"It wasn't a question. You were caught shoplifting and you need to follow us now. I'm just trying to avoid the scene, but if you want, we can take you back into the store in handcuffs."

"Shoplifting? I don't shoplift. I …"

"Save your story. Cameras don't lie. We have one of the managers, Sabrina, in the back right now talking to one of our other officers. She's telling a completely different story. Sabrina says that this was all your idea and that…"

"You're fucking lying! I don't even know a Sabrina!"

"You'd be surprised what people will fess up to when you tell them how long they'll be staying at our hotel called jail," the taller officer, Grimes spoke. "Sabrina's little boyfriend in loss pre-vention implicated her, she implicated you…etc, etc."

He and his partner laughed at the joke. I just stared. Didn't think that it was funny in the least.

"Especially when you have a record like she does. We've been monitoring her for a while. Yeah, it didn't take long for her to start talking at all, but with those types of people it never does," Barnett added.

Grimes reached out to grab me, but I elbowed him in the stomach. All of the bags dropped instantly. He didn't see that coming. I didn't see that coming either. Before I knew it, I was slammed down on the pavement and had the weight of one of the officers sitting on my back. The other one struggled to cuff me as I wiggled around trying to catch my breath.

"I can't breath," I screamed.

"Well, you should've thought of that before you assaulted an officer. Now you have a shoplifting and an assault on a police officer charge," Barnett stated.

I just felt like there was nothing else I could do and that the officer was right. That bitch Sabrina probably was in the security office crying like a bitch-ass snitch. I wanted to fuck her up. Didn't she know the number one rule in the hood was, *don't snitch.*

The officers handcuffed me, stuffed me into a police car, which was conveniently located only a few feet away, and drove me and all of my stolen merchandise to the station. This was the first time in my whole career that I'd ever been caught. There were always close calls, but never the real thing. I was finger printed, had my mug shot taken, and placed in a holding cell until I was able to make a phone call.

The cell smelled like wet mildew, and looked like it hadn't been cleaned in years. I wanted to take a seat somewhere, but after reviewing my options of sitting on the dirt covered bench, I decided to stand for as long as I could until my legs gave out on me. It was just me and a couple of other women in the cell, who were surprisingly minding their own business. Everyone looked deep in their own confusing thoughts.

"Mirror Carter, you can make your phone call now," a pudgy female officer said to me.

Who the fuck can I call, I asked myself when the holding cell opened. My bail had been set, but I had no way of getting out. I couldn't call my dumb-ass mother and the only other option I seemed to have was Brice. Incredibly, I'd remembered his phone number by heart, so when I walked out of the cell, and it was my turn to make a call, I dialed the familiar numbers as fast as I could.

He answered on the second ring. "Hello, Brice Towers speaking."

*"*Hello. You have a collect call from the Harris County Jail. Would you like to accept this call?" the automated operator asked.

He paused for a few seconds. "Uh…yes," I heard him say. The call couldn't connect fast enough.

"Oh my goodness, baby. Thank heavens you answered. Please you have to come get me out! They put me in jail and… it was all a mistake…please just come get me…I'm scared!" There was an uncomfortable amount of silence. I wondered if he was still on the line. "Hello?" I yelled. I'd hoped that the one phone call I received hadn't been disconnected. "Hello?"

"Yeah Mirror, I'm still here. What are you in there for?"

I suddenly hoped that the call had been disconnected so that I wouldn't have to answer that fateful question. I was so antsy to get out of jail that I'd forgotten about our initial contact. The moment we met.

"I was at Neiman Marcus shopping and they arrested me

for shoplifting and…"

"Are you serious?" His pitch was higher than normal.

"Look, can you please send someone to get me? I can explain everything then!"

"I'll be there myself."

Click was all I heard next. I suddenly felt like a child who'd been sent to the principal's office, and was waiting on their parents to pick them up. A guaranteed ass whipping. My stomach turned every which way trying to figure out which was worse. Being caught stealing at the store, or having Brice find out the truth. All of a sudden, staying in here didn't seem like a bad idea compared to the wrath of Brice. *Oh well*, I thought. There was nothing for me to do now, but just wait and hope that by the time he got here, he would have cooled down some.

● ● ● ● ● ● ● ● ● ● ● ● ● ● ●

Three hours later, I was free from the county jail. I didn't expect for it to take so long to get me bailed out, but couldn't complain at all. I was just happy that Brice had decided to come and get me. When we got into the car, I noticed that he wasn't being chauffeured as usual. Instead, Brice took his place in the driver's seat and pulled off.

He said nothing to me. Not one word. I was afraid to say anything as well. I put my fingers to my mouth and began ripping off each nail one by one. My nerves were getting the best of me and my French manicure was suffering for it. Felt like that ass whipping was coming any moment. Good thing I was old enough now and ready to defend myself, but there was something in me that would've preferred the screaming and shouting as opposed to the silent treatment. Fed up with him acting like nothing happened, I decided to break the silence.

"Where's your driver at?" I asked.

"Do you honestly think that I would want anyone to see me bailing you out of jail?" His voice had extra base. "Mirror, what the hell is going on? And don't feed me the bullshit!"

I'd never seen him act like this before, and by the tone in his voice, I had a lot of lies to make up.

"Well…see there was this woman in the store, who's the assistant manager. She and I dated the same guy a while back. They ended up moving in together, but he continued to call me, and she didn't like that. She started stalking me and I swear, if I'd known that she was working in the store, I would've never gone in there. I have a restraining order against her…"

"I'd like to see it."

"Like to see what?"

"I'd like to see the restraining order you have against her," he said calmly. He called my bluff and shut me down before I could go on.

"Wait, I'm not finished! I noticed her following me around the store and before I knew it, I was being hauled away by the police. I just know that bitch stuck something in my bags."

I looked at him and his face. It read he wasn't buying it. There was no ex boyfriend, no stalker, and no restraining order. Everything had been made up just as fast as I told it and he didn't believe one word.

"I remember when I first met you at Saks. The exact thing was happening. Mirror, I'm a very simple man and I believe that there are no such things as coincidences. You're a thief."

I was shocked. "How dare you!" I screamed, appalled. "You're just like everyone else! I worked hard for everything I have. I don't have to steal anything."

"Yeah well I find that hard to believe!" Brice shouted in my direction.

"Why…I got money!" I continued to make a fuss and while in the middle of making a point, his phone rang. The red Blackberry of course.

This time Brice didn't even hesitate to answer. "Hey," he said softly.

There was another woman on the other side of the phone. I could hear her soft tone clearly. Obviously, the volume was up too high. He fixed his mouth to tell me to be quiet, but instead pulled the car over to the side of the road and stepped out. He was tense. Just like every other time he answered that phone. I watched him as he paced back and forth and then finally smiled. Obviously smiling at something the woman on the other end said. Seemed to be having a good time. Seemed to be enjoying their little conversation more than he was enjoying my presence. After a couple of minutes he got back inside, and pulled off in silence.

"What was that about?" I asked, trying to get the heat off of me. Besides, it was about time I found what who the hell was calling on that fucking phone.

"Nothing!" He was short and seemingly overly frustrated.

"Oh it's like that? You got a bitch calling you and you let that ruin our time together?"

"What time? This isn't a fucking date. I just bailed your ass out of jail. If you had kept your sticky fingers in your pocket, I would still be in the office taking care of some business. Besides, maybe *that bitch* is more of a woman than you will ever be!"

I was shocked. "More of a woman? Wow…are you serious?" He didn't answer. Just kept his eyes on the road. I stared him down, trying to force him to look at me. Nothing ever happened. "Take me home!" I demanded, but it was too late. I initially had no idea where we were headed to, but when we pulled up at the Four Seasons Hotel it was all clear. To compensate for bailing me out, I had to repay him with some ass.

Chapter Sixteen

Parking his car next to the valet, Brice got out, but I stayed inside.

"Take me home!" I demanded again.

"Get the fuck out the car!" he shouted then banged his fist on the hood. I guess he'd already grown tired of my little tantrum. I'd never seen him so upset before. He was loud and had caused a slight scene, forcing people who didn't want to be nosey, look over to see if it was a domestic situation going down. I did as he said, but let myself out with a major attitude. Then followed behind him slowly as we went straight up to his penthouse suite.

Once inside, I wasted no time getting buck. "Why haven't I been to your house yet? You've been to mine," I stated like a little child. "Are you seeing someone? Is it the woman on the other end of that stupid-ass phone? Why is that shit red? Is she considered an emergency?" My questions could go on for days.

Brice walked over to the chair that was beside the bed and sat down before taking off his jacket and shoes. His body language said that he didn't want to have this conversation, but answered anyway. "You haven't been to my house yet because I'm afraid you might steal something!"

He succeeded with his goal…to shut me up. It wasn't an answer that I was expecting, but that's what I got.

"So that's what you think of me? You're gonna take those asshole's words over mine?"

And just like that, that stupid-ass phone rang again. It was the woman that he claimed was better than me. I could tell by the way he stared. His body shifted, like he wanted to talk to her, but was stuck here with me.

"Who is it? That bitch?" I asked as I walked over to him. "Go ahead, answer it!"

"Mirror, back up," he warned as I invaded his comfort zone.

"Or what?" I asked moving closer. "Answer your fucking phone! That's your bitch, right? Answer the shit then nigga!" The real me had been exposed. I had actually called Brice, the most professional and paid man I'd ever dated, a nigga.

Damn.

The phone rang several more times, then stopped. When it started again I bit my bottom lip. He refused to answer it in front of me, and I refused to allow him to play me. I snatched the phone out of his hand and ran to the bathroom at top speed. He chased after me, and damn near caught my ass just before I threw his phone in the toilet. Even though I knew the phone was too heavy to be flushed when I pushed the handle, at least it would have some serious water damage.

Brice pushed me out the way hoping he could save it, but it was too late. It sat at the bottom of the toilet like a sunken ship. He walked over to me, grabbed my shoulders and shoved me up against the wall. He put his face close to mine. I knew he was about to issue a threat.

"Let this be your first and only warning! If you touch my shit again, I'll break your fucking fingers!" With his hard grip on my shoulders, I smiled then leaned my head forward and placed my lips on his. Brice was angry, but didn't fight the wet kiss I'd planted on his juicy lips. He slowly moved his hands down to my waist and pulled me close to him.

I could feel the hardness of his dick as I rubbed against him, and continued to make love to his mouth. He stopped kissing me for a second before quickly removing all the clothes from my body. As I stood against the wall, he sucked my breasts, ran his tongue down to my navel and then continued the trail to my pussy. Before I knew it, he was naked as well, and within inches from my nest.

He moved closer until his lips covered every inch of vagina that would fit inside of his mouth. He licked. Then sucked. I'd stopped him the first time he'd tried to go down on me, but not this time. I knew it was possible to spread the virus to him even though

I didn't have an outbreak at the moment, but all of that went right out the window. The shit felt too good for him to stop. I was taking a hell of a chance, but it was worth it. He grabbed onto my ass and held me tightly as I began trembling. Brice worked harder knowing I was almost at my limit. He stopped, turned me around, bent me over, and stuck his dick deep in my zone. We both enjoyed the rhythm of my ass smacking up against his stomach every time he dove in and out.

Suddenly, he pulled his dick out and led me out of the bathroom to the bed. I laid down, threw my legs up in the air and spread them far apart, giving him as much pussy as I could at one time. He made his home between my legs and put his dick back in the hole where his tongue once mingled. Vigorously, he moved in and out, kissed me in my mouth again, and grinded harder.

In an instant, beads of sweat began to pour from of his skin and drip all over my body. He sucked on my breasts, while punishing my pussy with each stroke. He dug deeper and deeper until I was drowned in as much sweat as he was.

We both didn't say a word. Neither one of us wanted to give in. Didn't want the other one to know how good we made each other feel. I could feel my cum juices flow out of me and listened to the sound of the squishy noises my wetness made every time he moved.

After a few more aggressive pumps, he took his dick out of me and jerked it until all his unborn babies, laid on my stomach.

Damn, why didn't he leave it in, I thought. *A baby would be a guaranteed money maker*. At that moment, I wondered why we'd done it without a condom anyway.

He fell on top of me, squishing the cum in between us both and laid there until his breathing returned back to normal.

"I'm sorry," he said. "Please forgive my remarks from earlier. I've been a little stressed out lately." He took his hands and rubbed them over his face. He looked exhausted. "The only reason you haven't been to my house yet is because the whole thing is being remodeled. The construction is almost done though."

"Please just tell me the truth…are you married?"

He displayed a smirk that I was uncomfortable with. "No."

That was all he said with no added explanation. And then the famous *but* came. "But, I have a daughter who lives with her mother."

"Awww, you have a daughter? How old is she?"

I pretended to care.

"She's five."

"I bet she's a pretty little thing," I replied. "So, how's the relationship between you and her mother?"

"The relationship I have with my daughter's mother is great, but you would think with the money I'm paying her in child support, she wouldn't complain about anything."

"Well, when you're in love with someone, money is never an issue."

"Bullshit, money is *always* an issue. We were never in love, just fucked and she got pregnant. Now, she gets ten thousand a month in child support and she wants more.

Now I really wished he'd kept his dick inside of me.

But he already had a baby mother.

I would've much rather him said that he had a wife. A wife was constant. You knew what to expect out of the deal, but baby mama drama wasn't good. This bitch had it made and was still coming after him. And his daughter, a daddy's girl. She came first no matter what happened.

"So where do I stand in all of this?"

No answer. He just kissed me, passionately.

"Look, I know we've had a rough day, which ultimately caused our little argument. So, I think we need some time to ourselves, alone. Away from everyone else."

"Yeah. Things have been tense for me recently."

"I want you to take a trip with me out of the country. I need to get to know you even better. You know, spend some quality time together."

"I would love to," I said happy that we were able to clear up our little beef. Maybe this time I could really get to Dubai. "When should I be ready?"

There was no answer once again.

Instead, he began trailing gentle kisses along my neck.

Kisses that immediately ignited tingling sensations inside of me. At that moment, there was little need for anymore words. I was ready for round two.

Chapter Seventeen

I loved him.

And he was falling in love with me.

Even though it was going on a month since we first met, he was already doing things that proved that he didn't want to lose me. Like the week long trip to the Turks and Caicos Island he'd invited me to. It was initially a one day business trip that he'd extended several more days so that we could get away and have some fun. An amends for our first argument, and hopefully our last.

We arrived at the exclusive private resort, Parrot Cay, around three o'clock in the afternoon, less than two hours after leaving Houston in his private jet. Not my choice of transportation since most private aircrafts tend to crash, but who could complain when this was something that I was gonna have to obviously get used to. After all, I was becoming closer to being Mrs. Towers. Maybe we'd come back to the spectacular island for our honeymoon.

The beautiful one thousand acre island of Turks and Caicos was a celebrity attraction.

A place where all the A-Listers and billionaires vacationed.

A place where I was now a part of.

The Parrot Cay Resort was absolutely breath taking, and just like the baller Brice was, we checked into a three bedroom beach villa that rented for four thousand dollars a night. The villa was impeccably clean, and white fabric adorned every piece of furniture as if we were in heaven. The king sized canopy bed was draped with white fabric on all four posts along with a netting that was designed to keep the insects away. A sixty-inch projection T.V., tiki hut, personal butler service, spacious deck and a huge negative edge private pool were additional amenities.

Our villa sat only a hundred feet from the beautifully colored turquoise blue ocean and white sand that covered every inch of the paradise island. *Lisa Raye hit the fucking jackpot,* I thought as I unpacked my bags on top of the bed. Even though she and the Chief Minister of the Island were now going through a divorce, I was sure all the luxuries that came along with being his wife was worth it. I had dreams of doing the same thing one day. Hell, my dreams were coming true right before my eyes, even quicker than I could've ever imagined.

When we arrived at our villa a few hours before, Brice notified me of a meeting that he had to attend and suggested that I do some relaxing and settle in to our new abode. Since my unpacking had been completed, I decided to take a shower and get ready for the night. I took off my clothes and headed into the gigantic bathroom that awaited me.

Wrapping my hair up, I turned the shower on then waited for the steam to come seeping out of the glass doors before I climbed inside. I held my head back as the hot water poured down my body and into the drain. My headaches had started coming back, but this time I had a serious vaginal discharge and felt several blisters beginning to form around my pussy.

My outbreak.

It had finally arrived.

This was not the time to be alone with a man who had no idea that I had a serious STD, but I wouldn't have dreamed of passing all this up. I had it all planned. I would just tell him that I was on my period and he would understand.

They all did.

Nobody liked to fuck when Aunt Dot was in town.

We would just take this time to learn more about each other and what the future held for us. And if he got horny, I would suck him off until he was in a coma.

I grabbed a fresh wash cloth that was already laying on the shower wall and lathered it up with my mango body wash. The smell of fresh fruit filled the air as I coated my body with the juicy fragrance and made sure to avoid my sore, blistered vagina. I refused to make this an issue and would do anything it took for him not to find out.

We were going to be together.

Regardless.

If it was the last thing I did, I would make sure that he would be my husband.

I rinsed off all of the soap and suds that were left on my skin and turned off the water, which was so hot it left me red all over. Once I got out, I dried myself off with a plush white towel, which had a slight scent of lavender then walked over to the marble counter. Grabbing my mango lotion, I squeezed a handful into my palm, then rubbed the sweet smelling cream on my skin until my whole body was moist. Before I put on my underwear, I walked over to the toilet and sat down dreading what came next.

I'd held my urine for as long as I could. Using the bathroom during one of my outbreaks was one of the hardest things to do. I could never get used to it. I let the piss trickle down for a few seconds before I quickly tightened up. The shit stung like hell and I wasn't looking forward to letting the rest flow freely. I took a deep breath in and exhaled loudly as I let go again, this time all of it and shrieked in utter pain the whole time. I made a mental note to myself to watch my water intake for the rest of the trip.

My outbreak would last for a week.

It always did.

My daily little Valtrex pill, was no use to me now. I could take a vacation from the medication once my bumpy little friends appeared.

After getting off the toilet, I slipped on my sheer black La Perla bra and panties, then suddenly heard a noise coming from the front of the villa.

"Hello? Anybody there?" I asked the dead air. I shook my head as I reminded myself of the dumb white bitches in the movies who always said that shit. "Brice is that you?" Again there was no answer.

Stuck in the bathroom, the only thing I had to defend myself was a fucking brush, which would probably only make the intruder mad if I tried to use it. A few seconds later, I heard a noise again. This time it sounded like someone had bumped into a piece of furniture.

"I have a gun!" I screamed, hoping that whoever was trying to attack me would be afraid of the warning. For the third time, I didn't get a response and the shit was beginning to scare me. With my phone in the same room with the intruder, I had no way of calling Brice or anyone else for that matter. I was going to be left to defend myself.

Suddenly the bathroom door crept open at a slow pace, and I backed up feeling like this was the end. "If you take one more fucking step, I'm going to blow your brains out!" The door continued to open wider and then out of nowhere Brice stuck his head in along with a big grin on his face. "I'm going to fucking kill you!" I yelled while running over to him at the same time.

He removed his hands from around his back, revealing a dozen red long stem roses then placed soft wet kisses on my neck. I moaned.

"I was trying to surprise you, but I chose not to after you threatened to kill me with your imaginary gun." He laughed as I playfully hit him in the chest making the roses fall to the floor.

"Look what you made me do! They are so pretty." When I bent down to pick them up, he quickly positioned himself behind me and placed his hard dick on my ass. I stood up as fast as I could before he got any bright ideas.

I would've screamed in pain.

And he would've wanted to know why.

I turned around and kissed him in the mouth before he asked me any questions. Shit, I was glad that I didn't get blisters in my mouth like some people because things really would've been ugly. His hands caressed my body with gentle touches while I rubbed the back of his head, messing up the waves that were so neatly in place.

"You smell so good," he whispered in my ear. "Let me taste you."

"Ah…" I took a step back and stuttered a little bit. "I'm on my period. It just came on today…been irregular lately. Probably has something to do with the birth control pills that my doctor put me on. I'm going to get it checked out as soon as we get back." I knew that I was rambling on and on, but I was nervous. He looked at me with disappointment in his eyes, and didn't say a word.

"Are you mad?" I asked.

"Nah, not mad. Just a little messed up that we're all the way on this beautiful island and you can't fuck. It sort of defeats the purpose you know?"

I was surprised by his response, but didn't press the issue. "Well, I was thinking that we could take this time to get to know each other a little better." I looked in his eyes for some confirmation and got nothing. "Since we've met, all we've done is sleep together. I mean, we hardly know anything about each other. Let's just make the best of this and maybe later I'll suck on your candy for dessert." He seemed unimpressed with our new itinerary and walked out of the room.

"Get dressed," he demanded. "I'll meet you on the beach for dinner."

He left quickly without waiting for my response. I didn't know what to think of his demeanor, and I wasn't sure if the whole trip had been ruined, but I was determined to make things right. I grabbed my tight satin emerald green Derek Lam dress that I'd hung up in the closet and slid it on. It showed every curve that belonged on my body. I combed my hair down and decided not to wear any shoes since he had something set up on the beach. It wasn't everyday that my feet had the chance to meddle in white sand so I seized the opportunity. I put on a pair of authentic emerald tear drop earrings and headed out the door in less than ten minutes.

The skies were clear and the warm seventy-eight degree weather was like icing on a cake. As I walked toward the beach, the therapeutic sound of the ocean's waves filled the air, and it was then when I realized there was no one else around. No one else other than the candle lit table that Brice sat at along with a server that smiled when I arrived. Brice stood up to greet me and kissed my hand before I took my seat.

My smile was big and cheesy. "This is amazing!"

"Not more than you are," he responded before gently running his hand along the side of my face. His attitude had done a complete 360. I closed my eyes and took all of this in. I couldn't believe that I was actually in paradise with my prince charming

147

and that it wasn't a dream. "I have something for you," Brice admitted. He reached into his coat pocket and pulled out a black velvet jewelry case.

Handed it to me. And then waited for me to open it.

I held the soft fabric in my hand and rubbed it along my fingers before opening it. "What's in here?" I asked. Even held it up to my ear and shook it around.

"Just open it." He took a sip of the Louis the thirteenth in his glass, and clenched his teeth at the strength of the expensive cognac. The way the waiter kept his drink filled and made sure I stayed with a crisp bottle of water let me know that Brice had already ordered everything that we were having for the night. I took the case and pried it opened with my freshly manicured nails as Brice watched.

My jaw dropped in awe. "Oh my goodness, I can't believe you got this for me!"

I was excited and jumped up to give him a huge hug. The mixed-cut, three-row diamond bracelet that was designed by Donald Trump's daughter, Ivanka, was absolutely flawless. Just when I thought that our trip was going to be ruined, he redeemed it by giving me a girl's best friend.

I was in love with him.

And he was obviously falling in love with me.

"Do you like it?" Brice asked.

"Are you kidding me, of course." I took off the simple platinum bracelet that I had on and replaced my wrist with the emerald, marquise and princess cut masterpiece. "I've never been this happy in my life." I leaned over and gave Brice a passionate kiss before sitting back down. It didn't even matter that the waiter was still there. I wanted the whole world to know how much love I had for this man.

"Beautiful jewelry for a beautiful woman," he stated.

I wanted to say, 'Yeah, I'm a master of the four C's.' The bracelet had to be at least four carats, G in color and VS clarity. I took a guess and estimated the bling to be worth $18,000 or more. "Why do you treat me so good? I mean really…we haven't even known each other that long."

"Why not? You deserve it, right? It doesn't matter how long we've known each other. If the spark is there, it's there."

It wasn't long before the waiter brought us our entrees of garlic roasted chicken with red skin potatoes and spinach, then finally left us alone to enjoy it. When we were done, he came back over and cleared the table so that we could enjoy our dessert.

Crème Brulee.

My favorite.

"This is so nice. Us sitting under the stars, on the beach." I got up and went to sit on his lap. He welcomed me. "Look, I agree with what you said earlier. It doesn't matter how long we've been seeing each other, and that's why I think I'm falling in love with you."

He looked at me.

As if I had ruined his moment.

Didn't give me comment either. Just took another drink from his glass and for the millionth time, and grimaced at the strength of the alcohol.

"Did you hear me? I said that I'm falling in love with you."

"Yeah…I heard you."

"So, how do you feel about what I said? Are your feelings the same or…" I couldn't bring myself to finish the rest. I guess I wasn't really interested in knowing whether or not he loved me back. Men had egos and I knew that he probably didn't want to let me know something that important so soon. I knew the answer deep down inside. No one did things like this for someone that they didn't care about. He felt strongly about me, just couldn't admit it yet.

"Let's go back to the villa," he suggested, before lightly pushing me off of his lap.

"But we haven't even started on our dessert."

"Let's go," he demanded.

He wasn't the same. Maybe it was the liquor that was causing him to be so short, or maybe his meeting didn't go as expected, but there was something that was bothering him and I couldn't figure out what it was. Once we got back into our villa, he took a seat

149

at the edge of the bed. I climbed behind him and began massaging his shoulders.

"What's wrong baby? You seem tense."

"Nothing."

"You seem so distant like you're upset with me. Did I do something to you? Are you mad at me?"

He moved his shoulders from my grasp, got off the bed and started to undress himself. He never smiled, never laughed to let me know that he was just joking. There was something that was bothering him and getting the information out was like pulling teeth.

"Dance for me," he instructed as he laid back down on the bed, wearing only his Dolce & Gabbana briefs. It gave a hint of what I would be missing for the rest of the trip. His dick bulged out of his underwear, seemingly larger than it was before. Maybe because I knew I couldn't have it. I was feigning.

It took me a second to unzip my dress, but once I finished I slipped it over my head and stood before him in my sexy underwear. His eyes lit up as I began belly dancing to the sound of the ocean roaring. My big ass had taken over the show and my nipples stood hard underneath the bra. He sat up, pulled me over then placed his hands on my hips.

"Take it off," he whispered in my ear.

"I can't. Remember I told you that I was on my period. I don't want blood to get all over the white sheets."

"I don't care. I said take off your clothes." He didn't move and kept his eyes glued to my body.

Oh my God, I thought. *We can't do it. Not now.* "Baby, I'm cramping too. It's really not a good day for this." I crawled on the bed and straddled him. "Let me suck on your dick. I promise that it'll feel just as good." I put my hand on his manhood and felt it rise as I stroked it back and forth. To my surprise, even though his dick was now harder than a steel pole, he took my hand and threw it off of him.

"Are you hard of hearing? I said I want to fuck!"

"But I can't Brice. Why are you acting like this? We have sex all the time. Why can't we just chill and have a good time with each other?"

"Because I fucking said so. I brought your ass all the way to this island to fuck, and I want some pussy, blood or not!"

"But I…" Was all I pretty much got out before Brice hauled off and slapped the shit out of me.

I was shocked. The once calm and professional acting man had turned out to be fucking Dr. Jekyll and Mr. Hyde. I looked at him and placed my hand over my stinging face.

"I'm sick of you and your damn excuses. When I ask for something you need to get it or do it. No questions," he replied with a cold look. "I should just take your shit."

He tossed me off of him like a little doll and got off the bed. "I'll see your whining-ass in the morning," was all he said before he turned around and walked out, leaving me to sleep in the villa all alone.

● ● ● ● ● ● ● ● ● ● ● ● ● ● ● ● ●

The next morning I had to walk around the entire resort before I finally found Brice in one of the hotel's restaurants. He was eating breakfast, and obviously didn't have plans on me joining him. The situation was as awkward as the night before. Brice had never come back to the villa to take a shower or change, but had still found a way to be incredibly fresh and fly. Dressed in an all white linen suit and some white Gucci sandals, he sat across from me at the table reading the newest issue of Forbes magazine. I had on a crème colored linen dress along with the bracelet that he'd given me the night before. Walking up to the table, I couldn't wait to sit down. I had tons of questions.

"Brice, where did you go last night?" I asked, placing a piece of toast in my mouth.

"Don't question me," he answered, never looking up from his magazine.

"But I feel like we should talk about this. I'm sorry…" and just like that, the red Blackberry began to ring.

I could've sworn I destroyed that shit, I thought. He'd obviously gotten another one.

"Hello," he said as he got up from the table. "Yeah, the meeting this morning went great. We closed the deal and everything is a go!" He listened to the woman on the other end of the phone, mumbled a few more things, then hung up. Whoever she was seemed to make him happier than I could. He sat back down and continued reading.

"Why couldn't you talk to me about the deal? I asked you how everything went and…who was on the infamous red phone? I see you went and got another one or is that the same one?" I could tell he was getting angrier by the minute. "Is that bitch so important that you stuck your hand in the fucking toilet?"

I took my own cell phone out of my purse. "As a matter of fact, give me the number to that phone, so we don't have any more confusion." I had my fingers in perfect position ready to punch away.

He finally looked at me and laughed. "You've got a lot of nerve demanding something from me."

"Brice, why are you so cold all of a sudden?"

I didn't want to get on his nerves by whining as he said the night before, but I really was confused. I wanted to show him how much I cared.

"Look, there has been a change of plans. You're leaving to-morrow."

"But I thought that we were staying for the rest of the week. What happened…why are you switching everything up?"

"No, I'm staying. You're leaving."

His reply caught me completely off guard. I stood up. "Brice, what the fuck is going on?" I asked, leaning in a little closer to him. "Why the fuck are you treating me like this? Please, just talk to me. I'm sure whatever it is we can work past this. I don't want to lose you, just talk to me."

He looked around the restaurant like he was embarrassed. "Lower your fucking voice and sit back down!"

This time he stood up and walked away, I guess somewhere I wasn't allowed. Confused, I sat back down and followed his instructions like a little child.

Whoever was on the other end of his phone was responsible

for the stress in our relationship, and I was determined to not only find out who it was, but to also put an end to that shit once and for all. This is what I'd wanted my whole life…to be with a paid man, so giving up that dream wasn't an option.

Chapter Eighteen

"You have reached the Sprint PCS voice mailbox of..." was what I'd heard for the millionth time before hanging up my phone and tossing it across the bare floor. It didn't even matter to me whether the shit broke or not because I was already depressed. The leather couch in my living room is what I'd converted into my bed for the past week since coming home from Turks & Caicos. I felt awful about the way Brice and I ended things and I hadn't heard from him since he put me back on the plane.

Delta.

The muthafucka didn't even let me take the private jet back, but instead placed me on a commercial airline. I wasn't even in first class.

If only I knew where he lived, I could've gone over to plead my case. The only residence I knew of was at the Four Seasons, and I'd called there a few times as well, but they said he'd checked out. Thinking that them muthafuckas had told me a lie, I even drove down to the hotel to see for myself.

Big mistake.

Because of the huge scene I made at the front desk, I almost left out of there in handcuffs. No matter what avenue I tried, I couldn't seem to get a hold of Brice, and the shit was starting to take its toll on me.

Forcing myself to move, I got up off the couch and walked over toward my phone. When I picked it up off the floor, surprisingly it was still working. A few cuts and bruises is all it had. I dialed his number again.

And again.

And again.

I wasn't eating. Hadn't opened up the store, and hadn't gotten any rest. I'd stayed up night after night trying to figure out why he was ignoring me like this. The last time I'd checked my cell history, I'd called his phone close to eighty times over the last two days. Pressed wasn't even a good term to describe myself anymore. Hell, at this point, I was way beyond desperate and also determined to call as many times as I could until he answered. I wiped away the overflowing tears that started running down my face and called again.

"How could he do this to me?" I asked myself after taking a tissue to wipe the snot that had started to run out of my nose. "I thought he loved me." Plopping back down on the couch, I curled up into a ball and rocked myself, hoping to make some sense of it all. Just as quickly as everything had started between us, the emotions and the time spent together appeared to be at its end. My eyes, now puffy from the seven days of tears, were beginning to sting and my nose was now stuffy.

Maybe he's hurt, I thought to myself. It was the first time that conclusion had come up, but I was glad that I'd thought of it. I knew how upset he was at me during the trip, but then again that really wasn't a good enough reason not to answer his phone after all this time. Other scenarios began filling up my mind. Thoughts that he was possibly in a car accident, sick and in the hospital, or maybe something had happened with his daughter. My emotions went from sad and confused to sympathetic from what my mind was forcing me to believe. It helped keep me sane when insanity was creeping up. Fast.

Then out of nowhere it hit me. The only other place where Brice was guaranteed to be seen was a basketball game, and if he wasn't there, I could at least get some answers from his friends.

I gained some energy after coming up with a new plan of action and sat up once again. I reached over, and grabbed my laptop that was on the coffee table next to me and went to the Rockets website to see when the next game was going to be.

Tonight.

Against the Washington Wizards.

The game started at seven o'clock which meant I had a little less than an hour to get ready and over to the arena. It was also in a little less than an hour that I was going to finally get the answers I'd been looking for. Still a little weak from a lack of food, I managed to get off the couch and into my bathroom without passing out. Looking in the mirror, I realized how bad I really looked. Dark circles now rested under my eyes and everything seemed to be swollen from the constant crying.

I grabbed a wash cloth and soaked it in steaming hot water, before pressing it on my face to relieve some of the pressure. It helped a little bit, but I couldn't spend too much time with this issue. The clock was ticking and I had to get to the game on time. I brushed my teeth, took a five minute shower, and headed to the closet after all that was done. What I wore was important and frustrating because I was in a rush, but wanted to look my best at the same time. I ended up putting on a pair of vintage Marc Jacobs jeans that had crystals covering the pockets, a black ruffled shirt that exposed all of my cleavage and topped it off with the diamond bracelet Brice had gotten me.

My weave hadn't been wrapped up in a week and was now matted to my head. I turned on my flat iron and quickly sectioned off several pieces so that I could get it as straight as possible. When I was done, it didn't look like I'd just come from the salon, but it was presentable.

Moments later, I ran to the front door, put on my knee high black leather stiletto boots and grabbed my Louis Vuitton Mahina bag off the coat rack. Just before leaving, I took one more look at my rushed appearance. It wasn't the way I wanted Brice to see me after our week long hiatus, but it would just have to do. Winning him back, meant more to me than winning a beauty pageant right now.

• • • • • • • • • • • • • • • • • •

I arrived at the Toyota Center exactly seven minutes later, which was good time even with all the bumper to bumper traffic. I could normally make the short trip in four from my downtown apartment. After parking my car in the congested garage, I walked as fast as I could in-between the eager fans to the ticket booth.

"Hey you can't cut me…hey!" someone yelled when I

stepped in front of them and up to the counter.

"I'm not cutting anyone," I replied in an attempt to calm the crowd. "My man owns the team. You know him right…Brice Towers? I don't have to wait in line sweetie. So if you'll just excuse me."

That didn't satisfy them.

And I didn't give a fuck.

I turned back around then smiled at the woman who sat behind the little glass. She was badly in need of a dental plan. "Hello. I'm Mirror Carter."

She looked at me as if she didn't even want to be there. "Well, *Mirror Carter*, you have to wait in the line just like everybody else," she replied, exposing her missing front tooth.

"No, you don't understand. I'm Brice Tower's girlfriend and…"

She started to laugh.

Right in my face.

As if what I'd just said was a joke.

"Sweetheart, whoever you are, like I said the back of the line is over there," she stated sarcastically.

She pointed.

I looked behind me to see where she was pointing to. There had to be at least fifty people in the line and I refused to be one of them.

"Can't you just call someone to give them my name? Everyone knows who I am and…"

"Look," she said cutting me off again. "I don't have time for this. It took me three buses to get to this no-good ass job, so I don't care who the hell you are! Besides, if Mr. Tower's is your man, you call him yourself. As a matter of fact, if Mr. Towers is your man, you shouldn't have to swindle your way in through the front. You know… the way us regular folk have to do it." I couldn't believe all the shit that she was talking.

"Fuck you!" I told the toothless bitch.

"Yeah well, I'll see you at the end of the line," she replied laughing like a damn hyena. "Next!"

The guy behind me bumped into my shoulder making me

stumble back slightly.

I looked at him with an evil expression before turning my attention back to the rude-ass woman. "When Brice hears about this, I'll make sure that this is your last day at work."

"Like I said, the back of the line is that a way!"

She pointed as and I walked to the back, defeated. There were a couple of snickers from the people I'd passed just moments before, but little did they know when I got in, they would all see that I really was the shit.

Fifteen minutes later, I made it back up to the ticket counter and paid for the cheapest ticket they had. I had no intentions on ever sitting in the seat, but I had to buy it just to get in. Once I got past security, I headed straight up to the luxury suites where Brice and I had watched the game before. When I was a few feet away from the door, I was so excited to see the bodyguard that Brice had introduced me to my first time at the game, I didn't know what to do with myself. Thinking that this whole night was going to be a struggle, I felt a little bit at ease with everything now. Brice had instructed him to treat me like a queen so I knew that I was in good hands.

There was a gang of people, mostly women, trying to get into the room, so I pushed my way to the front and held my hand up so that the bodyguard could recognize me. When I walked up to him, I smiled and placed my hand on his arm.

"Marcus, I'm so glad I saw you. You wouldn't believe the hell they put me through trying to get in here, but I made it. Is my baby inside?"

"Ma'am, please step to the side," Marcus rudely stated, never acknowledging that he even knew me. "I need everyone to move away from the door. If your name is not on this list, you will not get in!"

What the fuck does he think this is, a club? "Hey, remember me? Brice's girlfriend, Mirror Carter?" I asked.

"Sweetheart, if your name is not on this list, you're not getting in this room."

He looked on the list.

My name was not there.

He then took his big arms and pushed me to the side like I was one of the other groupie bitches. He wasn't respecting the fact that Brice was my man and that his ass had specific instructions to treat me like royalty. I would have his job as well. Wasn't he the least bit surprised that I even knew his name in the first place. I wasn't going to let these muthafuckas treat me like this and get away with it. I managed to make my way back over to where Marcus was and decided to try my luck once again.

"Do you think that you can go get Brice for me, and tell him that I'm out here? This is all a big misunderstanding and I'm sure he'll clear it all up."

"I don't bother Mr. Towers. If he wanted you in there, your name would've been on the list and since it's not, my job is to make sure that you don't bother him. So, if you don't leave now, I'll make sure that you are personally escorted out of the arena. And I'm not going to repeat myself," he said, this time giving me eye contact.

Just when I thought I didn't have any tears left, my eyes managed to well up. I turned and walked away defeated before he had a chance to embarrass me any further. At first I told myself to leave, to walk out while I still had a little bit of dignity, but then I decided against it. Even though it was a risky move, I'd already decided to try my luck when the game was over. Maybe after all the groupies left I would have a chance.

I had the worst seats in the entire building.

Nose bleeds.

That's where I was headed.

It wasn't long before I got to my section and made myself as comfortable as I could in the hard plastic seat. No hors d'oeuvres, no plasmas and no classy conversations going on like in the suites…just hard plastic seats. The roars of the fans and the excitement of the game was just the opposite of how I was feeling. I felt like a stranger in my own home. Once accustomed to having floor seats, anything else seemed so foreign. I sat in a daze for the entire first half of the game and tried conjuring up ways to get in Brice's suite. In my mind, I knew this was my only chance to get to him because bumping into his ass on the street was something that would probably never happen. Besides, it's not like we ran in the same circle. He was already at the status that I was trying to get to.

And then the arena lights dimmed.

Half time.

I stood up, prepared to try and get into his suite one more time. Prepared to be turned away. Prepared to be thrown out into the streets. I was prepared to do all I could not to lose him, even risking humiliation.

"Attention all you crazy Rockets fans. Before you all go grab your popcorn and hot dogs, the owner of the team has an important message just for you…" the animated announcer said, over the speakers just before Brice's face appeared on the huge jumbotron. The crowd erupted into cheers once again as a mixture of emotions went through my body. I wasn't sure whether to be happy about finally seeing his face or mad that he could talk to all these people, but wouldn't answer my calls. At least I knew that he was okay.

"Hello. I just want to take this time to thank all the Rocket fans for supporting us through the seasons and never giving up. This is going to be our best season yet and we promise to give you everything we have. Can anybody say NBA finals?"

Again there were thousands of cheers.

I smiled.

Was happy to see him happy again.

He continued, "And now I want to make that same promise to a very special person in my life." The monitor now showed the face of a woman with a familiar face. She had diamonds dripping from her ears, neck and wrist and the biggest smile in the whole fucking place. She was more than a familiar face, it was Alexa. The stuck up bitch, who always came into my store. The bitch who now sat in front of the man I loved.

"What the fuck is going on?" I asked out loud.

"I know," an older woman next to me said with a huge smile on her face. "Isn't this beautiful?" I looked at her and rolled my eyes.

And then it happened. Brice got down on one knee while Alexa covered her mouth with her hand, just as shocked as I was.

"I've loved you since the moment we laid eyes on each other. You're the mother of my child," then he paused to rub her stomach. "And we have another beautiful one on the way. I can't imagine my life without you and I wanted to know if you would do me the honor of being my wife?" he asked, holding up a ring.

The diamond was so fucking big people in Austin could probably see it.

Tears streamed down her face.

Tears streamed down my face.

I could've sworn I saw tears stream down his face.

I could tell he loved her.

"Yes...yes," she answered, then swung her arms around him and hugged him tightly.

Hold up...she is married, I thought then looked up at the monitor. "Wait, she already has a husband!" I yelled to the top of my lungs. The older women along with a few other people sitting in my section all turned around and looked at me like I was special.

But then at that very moment, it made sense. This was the reason why Alexa never had on a ring when she came into the boutique. This is why she'd never confirmed who her husband was every time I asked. Now, she was gonna be married. To my man. This bitch was about to fuck up all my hopes and dreams.

When the arena lights came back on, I became nauseous at the sight of everyone going wild. The fans were happy for them, not realizing that my heart was being broken in the process. The last image I saw was of Brice kissing his daughter right before the monitor switched to basketball highlights.

I didn't even get a chance to react to what I'd just seen before the announcer quickly came back on. "Mr. Towers on behalf of the Houston Rockets and all the dedicated fans, we want to say congratulations!"

Several people in my section began to clap.

I didn't.

"Now, ladies and gentleman, I want you all to put your hands together for the newest sensation on Bankroll Records, Houston's own recording artist, K-I-N-G P-E-N!"

The way the announcer said that shit irritated me, but I had

to admit I thought someone was playing a joke until I saw King
Pen running out onto the middle of the court.

My mouth dropped. *I can't believe this nigga is performing
at half-time*, I thought as his ass started waving his hands from side
to side. *Whoever authorized this shit needs to be fired.*

"What up, Houston. How y'all feelin'," KP asked the
crowd. "Yo' I wanna give a shout out to my big brother. Thank you
fo' finally hookin' me up!"

I sat there and watched his dumb ass for all of five seconds
before my mind went back to more important things, Brice. Besides, I'm sure the crowd would be setting off an alarming amount
of boos any second.

I immediately grabbed my purse and bumped into anyone
in my way as I headed back to the suite. I wanted answers, and
wasn't going to leave until I got them. When I arrived, the asshole
bodyguard, Marcus was still standing at the door, this time along
with Patrick, Brice's good friend. *Finally, someone who really
knows who I am. I'm sure he'll tell me what's going on,* I thought
as I walked up and interrupted their conversation.

"Hey Patrick, I'm so glad that you're here. Can you please
tell me what the fuck is going on? Where's Brice? I need to speak
to him!" Marcus' mood changed instantly when he saw that I was
back and still trying to get in the room.

"I told your ass that if you came up here one more time, I
was gonna have you put out," Marcus informed.

I paid him no attention. "Patrick, please just clear this up
for me. Tell him who I am, and that this is just a big misunderstanding. I need to speak with Brice, its important!"

"Brice is done with you," Patrick announced just before the
suite door opened up. I never got a chance to defend myself. His
daughter ran out first and then I saw Alexa.

She was on cloud nine.

With that big ass diamond ring covering her finger.

I couldn't hate. She looked good…not pale like she normally looked. Her skin looked extremely tanned like it had been
kissed by the sun. Oddly, Brice was darker than normal himself.

He held Alexa's hand closely as all of her girlfriends trampled behind them. Even Carmen was in the bunch.

"How could you do this to me?" I screamed, making every-one stop what they were doing to see who was making all of the noise. "How could you do this to me?" I started walking closer to them, but was swept off my feet by Marcus.

"Mirror? Is that you?" Alexa asked, probably wondering who I was talking to. She let Brice's hand go and started walking over to me when Brice quickly pulled her away. Alexa shook her head. "But Brice I know her."

"But I don't," he replied. "She's obviously unstable and wants attention. Let them handle it. I can assure you that she'll be in good hands."

"Let me go!" I screamed, making an even bigger scene. I tried to wiggle my way out of Marcus' big ass arms. "Let me go!"

He put me in a slight choke hold and carried me away like a new born baby. Alexa just stared at me, while their daughter pointed probably wanting to know why the crazy lady was scream-ing like that.

It was because I was fucking her daddy.

And he was getting married to someone else.

"Brice!" He ignored me. Never even looked in my direc-tion. I felt helpless and suffocated. As if someone had just buried me alive. I screamed his name again and again until I was immedi-ately thrown out of the building and into the street. His silence spoke volumes.

"Don't you get it? He doesn't want you anymore. You were just another fling, so move on," Marcus advised.

I got up off the ground and dusted myself off. That was just it. I couldn't.

Chapter *Nineteen*

I made it home in one piece.

Had driven on the road like I was intoxicated, the entire way. Tears blurred my vision and the compulsive thoughts that filled my mind were the reason that I couldn't seem to drive in a straight line. But I still managed to make it home in one piece. Because I'd been thrown out during half time, there was probably another hour or so before the game was over, but that didn't stop me from trying to get in contact with Brice again.

And so I dialed his number.

Over and over again.

I would serial call his ass until he answered, turned it off for good, or either changed his number. I was still stunned that he'd proposed to Alexa in front of thousands of people. I didn't even know that he was her man. Her baby father. He was who kept her fly at all times. She was obviously the one who always called on that red phone.

I kept dialing his number, knowing that at this point, he wasn't going to answer, but I had to let him know that he couldn't get rid of me that easy. That I wasn't a bitch that got thrown out on the ground like trash. I kept dialing his number, to remind him that he still loved me. So that every time he saw my name on his caller ID his heart would hurt as much as mine did. He could act like he didn't care, but I knew that he had feelings for me.

Then out of the blue, I realized the phone had stopped ringing.

There was an awkward silence.

"Hello…Brice?" I said hoping to make some kind of connection before the phone hung up. "Please, say something. Anything."

"If you don't stop calling my fucking phone, you're gonna

be sorry."

"Baby please. Why are you doing this?"

"It's over between us."

His voice was firm, his breathing slightly heavy.

I had to think of something else quick. Something that would turn the tables. Even if it was to surrender just for the moment. "Okay, I understand. I obviously wasn't the one for you, and I can respect your decision."

He didn't say a word.

"Can you at least come over my house one last time? So we can talk face to face for some closure? I at least deserve that much, right?"

While Brice sat silent on the phone, I prayed that he would agree to come over. I was sure that when he was in front of me, I would have a chance to change his mind about all of this.

"And what if I don't?" he finally asked.

"Well, if you don't, I'm sure Alexa really wants to know how you and I are acquainted. You know she shops in my boutique *all* the time." I hated that a threat had to be my next move, but I was running out of opinions.

"You bitch."

"I wasn't a bitch when you were fucking me."

"I'm on my way, but trust me this is the last time." And with that he hung up.

I ran around my apartment like a chicken with its head cut off, trying to straighten up a bit before he arrived. Soiled tissues covered the place where the floor used to be and junk had been thrown everywhere during my week long temper tantrum. I had to make sure my baby was comfortable, so that he didn't want to leave.

About fifteen minutes passed and just as I was picking up the last empty tissue box, there was a knock on my door. Quickly sliding the box behind the couch, I ran up to the door. I was trying to mentally prepare myself not to break down, but it wasn't working. I could feel myself melting as I grabbed the door knob and slowly opened it. When he took a step inside, I didn't waste anytime flinging my arms around him, just as Alexa had done. The only difference, Brice pushed me off of him and continued to walk past me and into the apartment. Slightly lowering my head, I closed the door and followed him.

"Baby, what's going on? What happened to us?" I asked. I attempted to hold his hand, but he immediately let go and backed up again, putting more space in between us. He didn't want to be touched by me and that hurt.

"Mirror, there was never an us. I just met you a couple of weeks ago. Don't get me wrong we had a good time together for the most part, but that's as far as I ever intended to take it."

I was crushed. Had never had a man say that to me before. "A good time together?"

"Look, I don't really understand what the big deal is. We were never serious and…"

"Never serious?" I raised my voice because I wanted him to hear me clearly.

"Yes…never serious…"

"What do you mean we were never serious? What about the shopping sprees and the trip. The time that we spent with each other, and you telling everyone to treat me like a queen! Doesn't that sound like something serious to you?"

He smiled.

And then started to laugh.

Not a laugh as if to say that he was just joking about everything, but a laugh letting me know that I was playing myself.

"Sweetheart, don't you remember me always telling you that *it was nothing*. I treat all the women I fuck to a little something. How else would I get any pussy?"

"But…"

"But what?" he asked. His face was so serious. "If it wasn't you in New Orleans then it would've been someone else. Consider yourself lucky. You just happened to be stealing at the right place at the right time." He laughed again.

"But I thought you loved me!" I shouted before pushing him with all my strength. He stumbled back and then regained his balance. I walked up on him again and pushed him harder. "I thought you loved me!"

"I never loved you. You're not that type. You're not Alexa."

When I went to push him again, he grabbed a hold of my shirt and jacked me up before backing me against the exposed brick wall. Forcefully, I swung at his face, catching him a few times in the eye and then scratched his neck.

"Bitch are you fucking crazy!" he yelled before letting me go and tending to his wounds.

And then just that fast, I stopped all my commotion and looked at him with tears in my eyes. I couldn't believe he'd told me that I wasn't the type of woman he would ever fall in love with. That I wasn't Alexa. I couldn't believe after all we had, he would say something like that.

"I'm sorry," I said, wiping my tears away. "You're right. I misread what we had going on and should've discussed it with you first before assuming."

I walked over to him, placing my hands around his waist for a hug. This time, he didn't resist. He surprisingly just relaxed and let me hold on. I kissed him on the neck, where the scratch was.

And then on his cheek bone.

His chin.

His lower lip.

Kissed him until my lips touched his.

I closed my eyes and imagined us together one last time as I rested my right hand behind his head.

"One last time. Please, just give me one more time with you," I pleaded.

I kissed him some more.

He opened his mouth slightly.

"Oh, so now you want to give me some pussy?" he asked in between my short kisses of affection. "If you had given me some in Turks, I might've kept you around a little longer."

I was crushed. "Then why did you take me?"

"For ass," he admitted with a smirk.

I couldn't believe he'd just said that, but I had to keep my cool. He'd lied about everything just to get in my panties. I'd definitely gotten played.

"I'm not bleeding anymore. I just want to feel you in me one last time."

It was the perfect time to make love again since my outbreak had gone away, and my pussy was back to normal. I tugged at his pants until I got them unbuckled and they fell to the floor. I fell to my knees shortly after. Pulled his dick out his briefs and stuck it into my mouth.

I licked.

Sucked.

Tugged at his dick while he stood there. Trying to stroke him into changing his mind about his future. Trying to suck him into wanting me into his life. This was my most important performance of a lifetime and I wanted to win the award that he had so recklessly given to someone else. My head bobbed back and forth as I slobbed him down, deep throating every inch of his dick that my tonsils could take. His dick started to throb and I wanted to feel him inside of me before he came all over the place.

I stood up. "Take off your clothes," I instructed him. I did the same.

Still not putting up a fight, Brice quickly got undressed then walked over to the couch to sit down. I straddled him while he grabbed my ass and held onto it, like he knew this was going to be our last time. My pussy dripped with anticipation as I rubbed it against his dick, hoping to be able to slide it in without any resistance. But just before I put it in he stopped me. Moved me off of him.

"What's wrong?" I asked as he got up and went for his pants.

"Condom."

Oh now this muthafucka wants to wear a condom again. I bet it's because of Alexa.

Brice went in his pocket and took one out, before breaking the package open with this teeth. He then took the greasy condom out, sliding it on his dick with ease. He walked back over to me and laid me down on the couch. I don't even think Brice waited five seconds before sliding it and thrusting his dick inside my pussy as far as it could go. Using a force that he'd never used before. Like he was proving to himself that he didn't love me.

That I was just a fuck.

He fucked me harder, jabbing me with his shaft that didn't seem so magical anymore. I dried up slightly, making his plunges a little more painful.

"Owww…" were the words that replaced the constant moaning I was supposed to be screaming.

"Ahhhh…wait….go…slower…"

"Shut up bitch!"

With each wince I made, he pushed harder and all I felt was painful burning. In an attempt to get him off of me, he pushed his body weight on top of me even more and wrapped his hand around my neck. Closed his hands around it tighter while I scratched his chest, hoping that he'd let me go.

The S&M shit turned him on.

Could've turned me on if he wasn't so forceful.

I gasped for air and continued digging my nails into his body while he fucked me even harder. He clenched my neck tighter as I tried prying his hands off of me, one finger at a time. And then he stopped. Took his hands from around my neck and threw me on the floor, making me bump my thigh on the coffee table. Flipped me around to my stomach and shoved his dick in my ass.

I screamed.

So loud that he pushed my head into the floor to make me stop.

Brice grabbed my hair and pulled it, causing the thread from my weave to loosen instantly. He fucked me in the ass for less than a minute before finally reaching his peak.

"Ahhh…shit!" he yelled while his body jerked violently. His arms stiff as ironing boards.

It would've been nice if we were able to cum at the same time, but I guess he had other plans. Plans that he didn't bother to include me on. After getting out a few more jerks, Brice finally pulled out then got up and walked away like I was some type of prostitute. All I could do was lay there and watch him walk into my bathroom and come back out several minutes later. He didn't waste any time putting his clothes back. Just stood over me after he was done.

"That's what you wanted to do to me in Turks?" I asked.

"I did. I truly did," he replied with no emotion. "But luckily Alexa was at the hotel in another villa all along, so she took care of me that night."

My mouth dropped open.

Wide open.

I knew that pale bitch looked tanned earlier, I thought. "So, Alexa was really there? At the same time?" I asked in a daze.

He laughed. "I was at breakfast in a fresh outfit the next morning. How else would I have done that?" He continued to laugh. "There was never any meeting. I just told you that whenever I was with Alexa. Told her the same thing when I was with you."

All types of thoughts began to run through my mind. "What about the All Star Game? We sat courtside. There were cameras."

He shook his head. "What about it? Alexa wanted to go with me, but I didn't want her there, so I sent her to Paris for a week. As far as the cameras...my money is long Mirror. I pay people when I don't want my picture taken," he proudly stated. "Besides, everybody knows me by now. When they see me with a new piece of ass, they know to keep a tight lip."

I thought about the massive steak knife waiting silently in the kitchen drawer, then smiled. I'd taken a life before. No one knew but me, and it's something I wasn't ashamed of. However, the more I thought about it; that would've been too good for him. Too fast. He needed to suffer nice and slow.

"Why are you marrying her if you can't keep your dick in your pants?" I asked.

His face seemed to light up about the subject. "Because I love her, and I know she's not out to get my money like the rest of these money hungry bitches...like you."

I was floored. If he thought Alexa wasn't out to get his money then he was a fucking fool.

"Now, that was your closure," he announced, before walking to my front door.

"No, wait. Let's talk about this!"

He ignored me. "Don't fucking call me again." And with

171

that, he walked out and closed the door behind him.

I couldn't move. Couldn't believe that I'd let everything go wrong. Couldn't believe I'd let him get away with it. And then...it hit me.

I never heard the toilet flush.

I got up, walking as slow as possible to the bathroom. Managed to get a glimpse of the black and blue bruise on my thigh. I went over to the trash can and saw no trace of the soiled condom and then I peeked over into the toilet and saw that it was still floating in the lemon colored water.

I picked it up with my two fingers and saw that it still carried his sperm inside of it. This was gonna be worth all the drama that I'd been through today. Even though I would've rather given Brice my life long disease to get him back for fucking me over, this was going to be the next best thing.

"Too bad I don't have a fucking turkey baster," I said out loud. It was the perfect opportunity to be knocked up right along with his perfect little Alexa.

I laid on the bathroom floor and poured his cum all on my pussy, rubbing it in as good as I could. When it was completely empty, I flushed the condom down the toilet and walked back into my living room. I picked up the phone and dialed three numbers.

"911 what's your emergency?"

"Hello," I screamed into the phone. "I've just been raped!"

Chapter *Twenty*

Distraught.

Violated.

I couldn't believe he'd raped me.

Well, that's what I wanted everyone to think.

I sat at the detective's desk trying to seem distant from it all, like I thought a real rape victim would feel. Tried hiding how excited I was that Brice would finally get what he deserved for fucking with me.

"Mirror, my name is Detective Jodi Moore and I'm going to be working with you concerning your case. I know this must be hard for you, so I appreciate you coming down to the station. We have to get you over to the hospital to administer a rape kit before any evidence gets lost. But before that, I have a couple of questions for you just so the hospital staff will know what to look for. After your exam, we'll continue on with the rest of our interview."

I never looked her in the face, but saw that she was beautiful from the moment she walked through the door. Tall, dark, and skinny, she looked like a run way model. Her hair was a chestnut brown tint and cut short like Rihanna's. She was fly…for a cop. I kept my eyes darted toward the floor the entire time she spoke and then made myself cry. Had been doing that off and on since I'd arrived at the police station.

Detective Moore bent down next to me and asked, "Who did this to you?"

"It was my ex-boyfriend, Brice Towers. You might've heard of him. He's the owner of the Rockets. I don't know what happened, he was just so angry…and I said stop…screamed no…cried out in pain, but he just wouldn't stop!"

"I know the questions I'm going to ask you might be a little uncomfortable, but I need to ask them unfortunately. It's crucial to the case." She paused and pulled out her pad and paper from her back pocket, positioning it to write. "What did he do with his penis? Where on your body did it touch you and where did he ejaculate at?"

I wiped a few tears from my left eye then answered the question as if I were holding a conversation with the floor. "He made me suck his penis first then he raped me. My vagina...my rectum. The ejaculation is all over my vagina."

"Did he perform any sexual acts with his mouth?"

I shook my head. "No, but he forced me to kiss him and when I turned my face, he hit me." I started rocking myself to seem like I felt uncomfortable about talking about my assault.

"I need to know what your prior sexual activity was before tonight. Who have you been with? Did they use protection?"

"He's the only one I've been with. There was no one else. I was faithful to him."

"Okay, I think that's enough for right now. I have an unmarked squad car that's going to take you to the emergency room so we can get more physical evidence. We also need to move fast. In these situations, time is of the essence."

I stood up and wrapped my arms around my stomach then walked slowly out of the station. Once outside, I was quickly escorted to the car that was waiting for me.

"I'll meet you at the hospital," was the last thing I heard Detective Moore say before she drove away.

Ten minutes later we pulled up to University General Hospital. I was put into a wheel chair and whisked away into the emergency room. Detective Moore arrived shortly after, and began talking to the heavy-set nurse who was scheduled to do my exam. When the detective caught me staring at them, she snuck me a reassuring smile that everything was going to be okay.

As soon as they were finished comparing notes, I was led into an examining room by the nurse and asked to undress while standing on a large sheet of butcher type paper. She explained to me that the paper had been placed there in the event anything fell like, hairs, fibers, etc., then it would be carefully collected and placed into the kit. I guess that was why the 911 operator instructed me not to bathe, douche, brush my teeth or even wash my clothes before I spoke to the police. If I didn't have proof, then Brice couldn't get charged, and that was an absolute no-no.

After taking a urine sample, the nurse instructed me to get up on the examining table and place my feet on the stir-ups. Following her instructions, I crawled onto the table, but kept my legs closed refusing to let her in. Of course I was still acting the part of a rape victim.

"Sweetheart, I know this is difficult for you, but we need to get this done. This is how we'll be able to put whoever did this to you in jail." Yes, jail. That muthafucka needed jail time. Kahn KP did too, along with his brother and that bitch, Nurse Kahn. I'd set them all up if I had to.

I shook my head, letting her know that I understood and went along, placing my feet where she wanted. She took an ultraviolet light and scanned my entire body with it, helping to locate undetectable semen or saliva.

When she was finished with that, she checked me for bruises then began swabbing damn near every part of my body. She combed my pubic area for hair samples, and scraped my fingernails to collect any tissue that might've been left behind. After that was done, she labeled each swab and sealed them in containers with evidence tape. At that point, they were placed in separate envelopes before being put into one large white envelope.

When that portion of the exam was done, she took out a digital camera and began taking pictures of the physical injuries I had. The bruising of my neck and my thighs were taken first along with some other black and blue marks I didn't know I had.

"I know this is rough, but the worst is over now," the nurse said softly. "The only thing that we have left to do is the blood test and…"

"Why do I have to have my blood drawn?"

"It's routine. We check you for any infections or sexually transmitted diseases you may have contracted. We also give you preventive medicines like a tetanus shot and emergency contraceptives. It will only take a few minutes, trust me. This will be all over soon," she assured me.

"Oh, that's great because I think he definitely might've given me something. There were sores or some type of blisters on his penis, like he might've had herpes or something." I couldn't help but smile when I came up with that lie.

Ten minutes later, we were done with everything...finally. I was given an unflattering purple sweat suit to put on since my outfit had been seized for evidence, then waited until Detective Moore made her way back into the room.

"Hey, how are you feeling?" she asked me.

I didn't answer.

I'd cried rape. The answer should've been obvious.

"They've offered us a counseling room here at the hospital so I can talk to you a bit more. Follow me," the detective said.

"Whatever." I was tired of this shit already, and was ready to go.

"The sooner we get this over with, the sooner we can get you home." I followed her into the hospital's counseling room, which was surprisingly nicer than I'd expected. I took a seat on the couch. She did the same.

"Okay, Ms. Carter. I need you to recount the events that led up to the attack."

I cleared my throat and began with my long and detailed story. Something that I was tired of talking about already. Once I was done, I looked at the Detective with a serious expression. "So, when is the arrest going to be made?"

She looked around the room like we were being watched, then leaned in my direction. "I shouldn't be telling you this but...," she looked around the room again. "Once the Chief found out about your case, and who's involved, he wanted me to wait until the DNA results came back before we even attempted to make an arrest."

I was furious. "What? But that could take weeks!"

"Yeah, I know." Detective Moore let out a huge sigh. "Let's just say the Chief and Mr. Towers are very close associates."

I was speechless. Didn't know what else to do. I wondered if the Chief was on Brice's payroll as well.

"I might lose my job for this, but I plan to arrest him anyway," Detective Moore stated.

My eyes lit up. "Really?"

She shook her head. "My sister was raped and killed a few months ago, so let's just say I'm not too fond of men who think they can do whatever the fuck they want, especially rich assholes like Brice Towers."

I was ecstatic. "Thank you."

"Just make sure you keep this between us," she replied. "Now, we're all done here. Do you have a relative or anyone that you can stay with tonight?"

"No, I just want to go home."

"Okay, well let's make sure you get there safely."

The entire ride back to my apartment I was quiet. Mute. Didn't have much to say when Detective Moore tried to make small talk, and said a few dry cop jokes. Didn't she know that I was tired of talking for one night? I was appreciative of what she'd planned to do, but I still didn't have shit to say until somebody arrested Brice's ass.

Once we pulled up, Detective Moore walked me upstairs, and made sure my apartment was secure before finally leaving, which I was more than happy about. It had been a long night, and I was completely exhausted. All I wanted to do now was climb in my bed, go to sleep and dream about Brice and Alexa dying. It didn't matter how, just as long as it was a slow, horrific death.

● ● ● ● ● ● ● ● ● ● ● ● ● ● ● ● ●

The next morning I woke earlier than usual. It was just before eight o'clock. I wanted to get my place cleaned up before I got started with my day. After I showered and put on a comfortable Juicy sweat suit, I heard my house phone ringing. I hardly gave that number to anyone, not even to my men, so I knew it must've been important. I answered it right away.

"Hello?"

"Ms. Carter, this is Detective Moore. I just wanted to let you know that we made the arrest and…"

"Oh my God, that's great! When did this happen?" I asked, overwhelmingly excited to hear the news. The detective had kept her word.

"Late last night. Turn on your television. It's breaking news and on almost every news channel."

I ran over to my flat screen and turned it on to the first news channel I could find. She was right. It was a media frenzy.

"The owner of the Houston Rockets, Brice Towers, was arrested late last night while attending an engagement party at Rockefeller Hall and charged with sexual assault," the reporter informed. "Mr. Towers was released from jail on bond just over an hour ago, and has yet to release a statement. We've tried to obtain the name of the young woman, who implicated Mr. Towers, but that information has not been released as well. We did however speak to Police Chief, Harold Hunt who says as of now no sufficient evidence has been found against Mr. Towers, but that department plans to conduct a thorough investigation…"

I'd heard enough. "How come he's out of jail?" I asked Moore who was still on the other end.

"Because he has money, but believe me, one way or another he's going to pay for what he did to you."

"No, he won't pay! He'll pay his way out of this like everyone else does. Shit, look at Kobe and R. Kelly. Money talks!"

I hung up.

Pissed that his ass was already a free man.

I put off cleaning for a while so that I could bask in the glory of watching the recap of Brice being hauled off in handcuffs the night before. I watched in satisfaction as microphones were shoved in his face for answers that he didn't have.

His team of lawyers all cried how innocent he was and that he didn't have sex with me. Little did they or the Police Chief know that fucking excuse would all come crumbling down once they saw the evidence. Alexa would hurt as much as I did when she found out that he'd fucked me right after asking her to be his wife. She would now find out the truth about her man.

Once I had enough of the news, I turned off the T.V. , ready to continue my cleaning spree, and that's when the banging on my door began.

"Open this fucking door bitch. I'm going to kill you!" he yelled from the other side of the door. "I'm going to fucking rip your head off! You think you can fuck with me...I will ruin you!"

I might've let Brice in had he not said all that shit, so I decided that the smartest thing for me to do was to talk to him through the door.

Weren't his lawyers smart enough to tell him that he shouldn't be seen at my house? "This is just the beginning muthafucka! I'm the queen of this shit. Threats don't scare me. You think that you can just leave me like that? Marry some other bitch and I'm supposed to be okay with that? Fuck you!"

I walked away from the door while he kept yelling and turned my surround system up as loud as I could until I couldn't even hear myself think. I was the one with the upper hand now and wasn't about to give away my power again.

He continued to bang.

"Get the fuck away from my door!" I yelled over the loud music. When he didn't oblige, I thought to myself, *fuck this*.

I picked up my cell phone and proceeded to dial Detective Moore's number when a call came through on the other end. I hoped like hell it was one of my neighbors who'd heard the commotion, and had already called the cops for me.

When I hit the talk button, I immediately heard a lot of noise and sirens in the background. "Hello...may I help you?"

"Yes, this is Fire Chief Evans. I'm looking for a Mirror Carter."

"This is she," I said, wondering why the fire department was calling me.

"We were told that you were the owner of Savvy Girl Boutique. Is that correct?"

"Yes, it is. Why what's wrong?" I could sense the urgency in his voice.

"Ma'am, we need you to come down here right away. I'm afraid your boutique has been set on fire!"

Chapter Twenty-One

Out of breath.

Couldn't believe my eyes.

It had taken me an hour to finally make it to the boutique, all because I had to wait until Brice stopped banging on my fucking door, and finally left. Ten o'clock in the morning and my store no longer existed. The hundreds of gallons of water that it took to put the massive flames out now flooded the downtown streets. Fire trucks, police cars and yellow tape now replaced where my customers used to stand. The situation was beyond fucked up.

"This was no accident," the fire chief told me. "This place was set on fire with gasoline. There's no question that it was intentional."

My face tightened up and my body became tense. One because the chief was in desperate need of a breath mint, and two because Brice was the first name that popped up in my head. I knew for a fact he was responsible for all of this. *Yeah, he definitely paid someone a shit load of money to handle this.*

The chief looked at me as if he knew what I was thinking and asked, "Ma'am, do you know of anyone who could've been responsible for this? Anyone that wanted revenge against you for any reason?"

I thought about it for a moment, then took two steps back and covered my nose. I thought about ratting Brice out, but decided against it. I had my own revenge that I wanted to implement, so calling out his name wouldn't be enough to satisfy me.

However, before I could even open my mouth, I noticed Kippy's BMW slowly driving by. As we made eye contact, I could see the big-ass smile plastered across her face, just before she picked up speed. Shaking my head, I made a mental note to pay

Bubba for all Kippy's information, so I could track her down, immediately.

"No. I have no idea who would want to burn my place down," I cried. At that point, I really didn't.

I looked at the burnt Savvy Girl sign and took a deep breath of the thick black soot that stained the air. Everything that was once inside: my merchandise, the furniture, the memories...everything, was gone. Destroyed by the flames. What had been my livelihood for over a year had now been demolished in seconds. I had no idea what I was going to do next.

Over the next few hours, I stayed at the scene while trying to sort this whole mess out. The realty company that I'd been leasing from had to be contacted and I let the fire department know I would do that part as soon as I went back home. One o'clock came faster than I expected, and I wanted to get back home to figure all this shit out.

I hadn't eaten all day.

Hadn't eaten all day yesterday.

Come to think of it I didn't have much to eat throughout the week either.

Stress caused it, and no matter how hard I tried to force myself, I knew I wasn't going to be able to hold anything down. Sad, anger, and hurt had replaced my hunger. Now, I just wanted to sleep my emotions away for as long as I could. I wanted to come as close to dying as my sleep would let me. Wanted to run as far away from my problems as I could.

I drove past several different restaurants, but didn't stop. Instead, I drove straight home. The bed was all I had in mind as I parked, walked into the building and headed up to my floor. Once there, I noticed that there was a note taped to my door. I peeled it off and unfolded it to see what it said. Within seconds, my eyes were two times their normal size. It surprised me to see the big bold letters that graced the top of the paper.

EVICTION NOTICE.

Thought that there had to be some kind of mistake, that is until I saw my name printed on the document as well. *This shit is crazy*, I thought to myself as I struggled to get my keys out of my bag.

"First my fucking store, and now this." The idea of going to sleep was now out of the question until I could get this mess straightened out. Finally able to find my keys, I put them in the door and turned the knob.

When I walked through the door, I almost passed out at what I saw. I stood frozen in one spot, unable to move. The entire place had been trashed. My leather couch along with pictures that once hung on the wall had been slashed. My flat screen T.V., which was now on the floor had been smashed, my laptop, destroyed and the hundreds of books that used to sit on my custom made bookshelf were torn to shreds. I ran to my bedroom and found it the same condition. Completely destroyed. My bed, all of the clothes in my closet, purses, and my shoes were no longer useable.

"What the fuck is going on!" I screamed to the top of my lungs. I couldn't for the life of me figure out who could've done this. It would've been obvious to blame Brice for this too, but it seemed like too much damage for one person to handle, especially all in the same day. My mind recounted all the people that I'd done wrong, and who could've been responsible for this. Going by my track record, it could've been anyone.

Over ninety-five percent of my apartment had been destroyed in some way or another, and the cost to get all the shit replaced, was quickly estimated to be well over a hundred thousand dollars. A hundred thousand that I didn't have.

And then I realized something.

This hadn't been a break in.

There hadn't been any sign of forced entry when I walked through the door. Now the real confusion started to seep in. While my mind raced to figure out who was responsible for this, I grabbed my cell phone out of my pocket and called the management office.

"Towers and Associates. Mike speaking."

Towers and Associates? What the fuck happened to The Lieberman Group? "Hi Mike. This is Mirror Carter and I live in apartment 1720." My voice was shaky.

"Yes Ma'am. How can I help you?"

"Someone has broken into my apartment and did a lot of damage to my property. I need to come and take a look at the cameras that are in our hallway. I need to see who may be responsible for this."

"Oh, I'm very sorry to hear that. Did you say apartment 1720?" he asked. I could hear the sounds of papers being shuffled around in the background.

"Yes. What time can I come?"

"When did this break in occur?"

"Today, within the last four hours or so I guess."

He paused, sighed and then confessed, "I'm sorry, but the cameras were being serviced all day today…since this morning. We don't have a recording of anything after six a.m."

"Are you fucking serious? My place is supposed to be under surveillance at all times! You mean to tell me there's nothing you can do about it!"

"Ma'am, we're not the police. I suggest you call them if you need to file a report." I was getting ready to curse his ass out for the inconsiderate comment, but he beat me to the punch. "However, before you go, I just wanted to know if you received your eviction notice today?"

I'd almost forgotten about that shit. "Oh yeah, what the fuck is that about?" I asked, thankful that he'd remembered to even bring it up.

"Our records show that you're six months behind on your rent and…"

"What the hell are you talking about? Your records are wrong! I'm current on everything. You need to look back over all your *records* and get this shit straight!" The truth was I'd fucked the shit out of the owner of the building, Carl Lieberman over six months ago so I wouldn't have to pay the two thousand dollars it cost to live in this bitch every month. Carl was in his late sixties. Had owned the building for years. Told me everything would be taken care of. Maybe it hadn't.

"Sir, you obviously don't know what you're doing. Get Carl on the phone so he can straighten this shit out!"

"Well Ms. Carter, I'm sorry to inform you that Mr. Lieberman passed away last week. The building along with the management company has been taken over by Towers and Associates. I'm the new apartment manger," he informed.

"Towers…as in Brice Towers?" I asked.

"Yes." He paused for a brief moment. "Listen, Ms. Carter I'm sure Mr. Lieberman kept great records, but right now it's showing that you haven't made any payments over the last six months. If you happen to have any of your receipts showing proof of payment, I'll be happy to take a look at them. Otherwise, I have no choice, but to give you two days to catch up on your delinquent payments."

"Look, check this out you fucking faggot…"was all I was able to utter before he hung up on me. *I can't believe that muthafucka gave me two fucking days to leave?* I thought as I tossed the phone on the couch then paced around the floor. I had no receipts to show him, and the only proof of payment was in the form of pussy popping. That kind of currency was only good in Carl's world.

But then it dawned on me. Even if my rent had been paid, it probably wouldn't have mattered. Brice had found a way to buy my fucking apartment building, so there was no doubt in my mind that I would be evicted…regardless. How he'd managed to pull that shit off in a short period of time was beyond me. I had to give him his props. He was good.

Suddenly, I stopped pacing. I grabbed my chest like Fred always did on *Sanford and Son*. "Oh, shit. My money!" I yelled running toward my bedroom. There was fifty thousand dollars in my crib that I'd stashed away for a rainy day, and because that was all the money left to my name, it was raining like a muthafucka.

Rushing into the bedroom, I got down on my hands and knees then looked under the bed where I kept my safe, but nothing was there. Thinking I might've overlooked it, I looked again, this time placing my hand under the bed for some assistance. I wanted to feel something. Wanted the safe to mysteriously appear, but it didn't. It was gone. Small enough to pick up, it would be useless to anyone who didn't know the combination, but obviously they didn't care. I quickly got up and grabbed my chest again. My money, along with all my jewelry had disappeared without a fucking trace.

Damn.

Everything had been taken away from me. Nothing made sense. A single tear ran down my cheek as thoughts of someone invading my personal space ran through my mind.

They say that stress is the number one cause of death.

I felt like I was almost there.

I was beginning to feel lightheaded with every moment I stayed inside the apartment that was obviously no longer mine. Hell, I didn't need two days to leave. What was the use of stopping the inevitable anyway? With no money, there was no way I could come up with six months worth of rent. Why get embarrassed and let my neighbors see me getting evicted? It was time to go.

Without a dime to my name, I went to my closet and searched through the piles of shredded clothing, before spotting a few t-shirts and a pair of Citizens jeans that were still intact. I threw the clothes over my shoulder then walked over to my armoire to see if the psycho intruder had cut up my panties too. However, before I had a chance to open one drawer, I noticed several little cards lying all over the floor. Cards that I hadn't noticed before. Cards that oddly stuck out like a sore thumb.

When I walked over and picked one up, rage consumed my body instantly. It was a business card that read: *Towers and Associates.*

I started to sweat. My heart pounded a mile a minute from how angry I was. Now everything was coming together, even down to the cameras. Obviously, Brice had requested that the cameras be turned off so someone could come into my apartment without being seen. I looked down at the card again, wondering why he'd decided to leave so many. I got the fucking point with one.

"I'm going to fucking kill you Brice!" I yelled like he was listening. "You can't fucking win playing with me…this shit is war!"

Chapter *Twenty-Two*

Over the next few hours, I drove around town with absolutely no direction. Had no one to turn to, no one to ask for help. The only thing that kept me going was the fact that I still had my car. If all else failed, I would just have to sell it in order to get some money, or even buy a cheaper car. Although riding around in anything less than fifty thousand wasn't something I looked forward to, now wasn't the time to be choosy. I was gonna have to stick this shit out until something else came through. Just when thoughts of me hitting rock bottom began to surface, the name of someone who might be able to help me appeared in my mind.

Bubba.

I grabbed my phone off the passenger's seat and tried calling the pawn shop. There was no answer. Bubba didn't have a cell phone, so before I had a chance to think, I turned the car in the direction of the hood and drove straight toward it. A fifteen minute drive wasn't normally something that would've bothered me, but with no money, gas was going to be a problem. Had to watch where I went and make sure that it was only necessary that I go.

I considered this to be necessary.

Bubba was my only hope.

As I crossed the threshold of the pricey area of downtown to the poverty ridden south side, I saw the reflection of what I was becoming, walking along the streets. Homeless women, wishing that they had a roof over their head, begging for money. I was still in utter shock that within a day, the sky had fallen down on me. Now, I was one of those homeless women, wishing that I had a roof over my head, and on my way to beg for money.

But it wouldn't be this way for long. Had promised myself that the day would never come when life would kick me back to this place again. I was here, but I refused to stay. After pulling up to the pawn shop, I got out of the car and walked to the front door. It was locked, but the lights were still on.

I pushed the buzzer.

And then pushed it again.

It wasn't long before Bubba's voice finally came over the intercom. "What you want girl, I'm closing up!"

"Bubba, please let me in."

"I don't need anything you selling right now," he replied.

"Oh, no. I'm not selling anything. I need to talk to you. Please let me in," I pleaded.

There was a long pause before he replied. "Alright girl. But make it quick."

Seconds, later he buzzed me inside. I knew that my time was limited and I had to say what I wanted before he detected some bullshit. Bubba was a hard man, but always had a soft spot for me. I needed his help and even if he didn't want to give it, I knew eventually he would.

"Thanks for letting me in," I said walking up to the counter.

He looked at me with a frustrated expression. "What do you want?"

"Bubba, somebody burnt down my store, trashed my apartment, and stole all of my jewelry, money…"

"Who you did wrong?" he asked, while straightening out his inventory.

"No one," I lied. He looked at me and grunted. I guess he could tell.

"I doubt if all that shit happened to you and you ain't do nothin' to *no one*. You reap what you sow."

"Okay, I don't need your lessons right now. I need your help!"

"You better watch your tone when you talking to me girl," he demanded before stopping everything that he was doing. I'd obviously stepped out of line when I raised my voice, and he put me back in my place...quick.

He was my elder.

And I was supposed to respect him.

But I'd learned not to respect anyone. I'd learned that people weren't meant to be trusted. Also, that the people who were the closest to you were always the ones who hurt you. That lesson was something that had proven to be true in my life.

"I'm sorry. I just need your help."

He went back to organizing his merchandise. "What kind of help."

"I need information on Brice Towers and his fiancé, Alexa. I need to know where they live and the phone number if possible." I was scared to mention the next statement, but had to do it. "I know this type of information normally costs, but I don't have any money." I spoke up before he could contest. "But...but I'll pay you back. I promise."

I looked desperate.

I was desperate.

"What they do to you?" he inquired. I was surprised he never mentioned anything about his fee.

That was a first for Bubba. I wasn't used to his concern. Normally, when I wanted background information, he just provided it. No questions asked.

"He's the one who did this. He's the one who took my money, set my boutique on fire and..." I stopped and looked away as tears welled up in my eyes. Hopefully Bubba could see how emotional I was because it wasn't an act. Every time I even thought about what Brice had done, I became more and more furious. "I'm going to make him pay for trying to fuck up my life!"

Staring at me for a few seconds, Bubba walked over to the cordless phone that he kept on top of the jewelry case then picked it up. After dialing a few numbers, he looked at me one last time before walking into the back of the store. I had no idea what was going on.

"Who the hell is he calling?" I asked myself. I tried my best to be as quiet as possible so I could somehow make out what he was saying, but couldn't hear a thing.

He walked back in the room about three minutes later, and handed me a piece of paper. "Consider this a favor. It normally takes my people a little longer to get information for me."

"Thank you so much," I said, grabbing the paper. I was an

immediate hater when I looked down. "So, that muthafucka lives in Rivercrest." One of Houston's most exclusive subdivisions. Homes that started in the two million dollar range. My stomach dropped at the fact that he was living the fairy tale life I wanted.

"I'm getting ready to close," Bubba warned. I could tell by his mood that the next time he opened his mouth, he was just blatantly going to tell me to get the fuck out.

"Okay, okay, okay I'm leaving, but before I go, I need one more thing."

He was completely annoyed. "What?"

"Money," I replied in a low voice. He looked at me with eyes that screamed no. "Please, Bubba. I swear to you, I got about thirty dollars left to my name, but that's not even gonna last me through the night." As a last resort, I knew I could always offer Bubba's kinky ass some pussy in exchange for money. But I really didn't want to do that. Him and I had a different kind of bond. One that was special.One that I didn't want to ruin.

Again, without putting up much of a fuss, Bubba went in his pocket, took out five twenty dollar bills then handed it to me.

"Um, do you think that I can have a little more?" I knew I sounded ungrateful.

"No, and if you keep fucking with me, I'll take that back!"

"Bubba, but you don't understand…"

He let out a heavy sigh. "Look, come back tomorrow, and I might be able to give you a little more. Now get out of here before I change my mind."

Satisfied with that answer at least, I walked out of the door and got back into my car. Laughed because I was still driving a Benz in these conditions. Cried because it was where I would sleep for the night. I knew Bubba was good for his word. He'd give me some more cash, but I didn't know how much it was going to be. Had to save what I could until I figured out what my next plan would be.

My imagination got the best of me and I knew I wasn't going to be able to sleep soundly until I got my revenge. So I put Brice's address in my GPS system and followed the directions for the sixteen mile drive. Cried my eyes out to Mary J. Blige's song, *I*

Never Wanna Live Without You, off her My Life Album the entire drive.

> *I never wanna live without you baby*
> *I wanna be your lady*
> *Your love is so amazing*
> *What is this feeling*
> *I can't sleep at night*
> *Just thinking about being without you*
> *Work 'til I'm tired and I can't eat a bite*
> *Cause I know someday you're going away*

Mary's lyrics were perfect after finding out you'd been played. Perfect for when you were seconds away from slicing your wrists. Those tears lasted until I arrived.

Rivercrest Estates.

Home of the rich and famous.

I drove nice and slow to Crestbend Way then made a quick left. Creeping up the street, I made my way to the third house before my navigation informed me that I'd reached my destination. I stopped the car immediately, looking at the two story six car garage home with an overwhelming amount of jealously. Here I was, in front of a luxury mansion and I wasn't a part of it.

I should be the one living here not her, I thought to myself as I placed the car in park and turned my headlights off. *This shit was supposed to belong to me!* I had no idea what I was going to do, but would sit here until I figured it out.

A white Maserati Gran Turismo sat in the huge driveway.

Another car of my dreams.

A car I'd never seen Brice drive. My mind instantly started to wander. I was daydreaming of what Brice and I would've been doing right now in the house that he built for me. Tucking in the children…maybe read a few bed time stories, and then cuddling up with each other before retiring for the night.

Right before more thoughts came to mind, I saw the front door open. I sat up to get a good look at who it was. *This is too fucking good to be true*, I thought while I watched Alexa carry her sleeping daughter to the Maserati that was supposed to be mine. It killed me to watch her, especially once she put the little girl in the backseat, and revealed her pregnant stomach. It wasn't poking out too far, but I was pissed off just because I knew it was there.

I ducked down, trying not to cause any suspicion as she got in her car, backed out of the driveway, and drove off. I placed my car in drive, but kept the lights out and proceeded to follow her. The thing about living in these rich neighborhoods was that they barely had any street lights, which was a good thing when you were on a mission like me.

As I continued to follow her, I remembered passing over a bridge on my way to Rivercrest, that wasn't too far from where we were. As crazy as it sounds, I said a silent prayer to God hoping that she wouldn't turn off, and continue in that direction. If so, that was when I would make my move.

You really should've found your own man Alexa, I thought, keeping a good distance behind her. The last thing I wanted was for her to detect anything.

Five minutes later, we approached the bridge, and I quickly got into position. It was now or never, so I floored my foot on the gas pedal and turned my headlights on bright, ramming my front end into the back of her car. It didn't even matter that I was about to fuck up my Benz again. Seeing her ass die was worth it.

The Maserati immediately started to spin, and I watched as she struggled to gain control. I wanted to hear her cries for help. Wanted to hear the daughter's cries of confusion, so I quickly rolled down my windows. When her car finally came to a stop, I backed my car up several feet. Once I thought I was far enough to cause some major damage, I slammed my foot on the gas pedal again.

This was for everything that I'd lost. I guess to Brice, this would be his equivalent. Losing his future wife and children would be like me losing a place to live and ways to survive. He would finally feel the sense of loss I felt when he left me for her. I now possessed the power to make him feel exactly what I felt when this shit all started.

My car slammed into hers again, banging it up against the weak metal rail that was obviously saving her from a deep drop into the water. I wanted her dead and it just wasn't happening. I needed to do it again. Wasn't going to stop until I got the perfect results.

"Oh my God. Somebody help us!" was all I heard coming from her car.

Suddenly, I could see a pair of headlights in the far distance, and knew it was headed toward us. I needed this shit to work this time so I could make a clear get-away.

Backing up my car for the third time, I could hear Alexa screaming for help and calling Brice's name at the same time. I had no idea why she'd decided to call out that muthafucka's name. She must've thought he was about to save the day, like some fucking superhero. Shit, little did she know that nigga was only a womanizing asshole, who'd fucked over the wrong one this time.

After making sure I was even further away, I locked my eyes directly on my target before pressing the gas pedal all the way to the floor. This time the sound of a huge splash in the water was like music to my ears, the moment I drove away.

Chapter Twenty-Three

I flew down the dark road going seventy miles per hour with one of my headlights hanging on by a thread. Part of me wanted to slow down so I wouldn't get pulled over by the police, but I knew I had to get out of the area before they came looking for me. I jumped on the expressway and headed back toward the southwest part of town. Even though Bubba had given me a hundred dollars until the next day, I didn't want to spend it getting a hotel room, and would've rather died first before going to my mother's house. I needed to save the money because it was all I had to my name. I knew that I could put it to better use so I decided to sleep in my car. Needed to be on the low anyway and what better place to hide out in other than the hood.

I pulled up to a Citgo gas station that was several blocks away from Bubba's and parked in the back. Still shocked at what I had stooped to doing, I reclined my seat and turned off the car. It was close to eleven o'clock by the time my mind stopped replaying. Replaying the fact that I was now homeless. It was the position I'd been telling myself I would never be in again since I was a teen. Guess I was finding out the hard way that those were promises you simply couldn't make to yourself.

Never knew what tomorrow would bring anyway.

Would've never guessed in a million years that my tomorrow would have looked like this.

I adjusted my body several times until I was able to find a decent sleeping position. No organic chenille blankets, no eight-hundred thread count sheets, no flat screen to watch. My leather seats would just have to do. I felt defeated by my life, my love, and this seat. The leather that once seemed so soft was now unbearably hard against my skin and there just wasn't enough room for me to stretch out. Thoughts of being laid out in the back seat sounded appealing, but I had to be on point. Needed to be ready to pull off or run away if danger came; and in these parts, danger was always lurking around.

I watched as fiends walked around the back of the store, trying to find loose change on the ground or anything they could pick up to sell. Prostitutes brought their johns near my sleeping quarters to suck dicks or get fucked. It was apparent that I'd found a fucked up place to lay my head. With the intentions of staying up all night to watch my back, my eyes became heavier and heavier and I was out before I knew it.

● ● ● ● ● ● ● ● ● ● ● ● ● ● ● ● ● ● ●

I woke up to grey skies and drizzle, disappointed that I was still in the same spot. I hoped this shit was just one big dream. But the reality was…it wasn't just a dream. It was my reality that had gone terribly wrong.

Stretching my arms, I yawned a few times before looking in the rearview mirror, which was enough to make me burst out in tears. I looked like shit. Hadn't seen myself look this way in a long time. Didn't want to see myself looking this way. My eyes were puffy and red, my face, blotchy. I was allowing all of this to beat me down and my physical appearance showed it.

Breath stank.

Had to pee.

Wanted to freshen up.

There was no way I was going back to the pawn shop or anywhere else with those issues.

Raising my seat, I turned the car back on then drove around to the front of the Citgo. Normally, I liked to park my car directly in front of the store, but the space was taken, so I had to park closer to the gas pumps. Knowing I wouldn't be in the store too long, I only took twenty dollars from the money Bubba gave me, along with my cell phone then hopped out of the car. Even though I wasn't in the best neighborhood, I'd hidden my purse pretty good, so I didn't feel a need to take it along with me.

After walking into the store, I made my way over to the small toiletry section and picked up some tooth paste, a tooth brush, Dove soap and some deodorant. However, when I went to pay, the cashier was busy ringing up a customer and had five other people waiting in line.

"Fuck this. I'm not waiting." I simply walked to the ladies' restroom, locked the door and laid out all my products on the sink.

It was disgusting.

Felt like this was where all the fiends came to wash their asses.

I wanted to walk out and try this again once I found a cleaner place, but my time was drifting away. Didn't know what today held for me and besides, I was funky. Was able to smell myself outside of my clothes and that was something I definitely couldn't deal with. Still in the same velour Juicy sweat suit from the day before, I slipped the jacket off and turned the water on in the sink. The pressure was extremely low, which told me that this was going to take longer than I'd anticipated.

Avoiding the mirror at all cost, I opened up the package of Dove, then lifted up my arms. Placing the bar of soap under the water I made sure it had a nice lather before rubbing it under my right armpit. It wasn't long before I did the same to the left. After rinsing them both off, I went to grab a paper towel.

There were none.

No toilet paper either.

"Shit!" I yelled out in frustration.

Using my jacket to dab my arms dry, I realized that I wasn't going to be able to wash anything else under these conditions, so I made the decision to go somewhere else once I finished up with Bubba.

"Hey, unlock the door!" a woman ordered from outside. I was holding up three stalls and she obviously needed to use one of them. "What the hell are you doing in there?"

"Wait a fucking second," I yelled back while I rushed to put my jacket back on. I grabbed all of my products and unlocked the door as an angry crack head ran past me and straight into a stall.

"Go use the bathroom somewhere else next time!" I had the

audacity to say before I walked out.

When I got to the front of the store, there was still a long-ass line of people with coffee, donuts and cigarettes in their hands. Everybody looked frustrated. The line never seemed to move. Again, not wanting to stand in line, I walked back over to the toiletry section. Pulling a ghetto move, I placed the used items back on the shelf and walked away like I'd never even touch anything.

Happy that I'd saved a little bit of money, I walked toward the front of the store and stared out one of the huge glass windows. I'd only been in the store for a few minutes and the skies seemed to be much darker than they were when I first came in. The drizzle had turned into a steady rain and I could've sworn I heard thunder rolling around in the air. Interrupted from my daze by a customer who accidentally bumped into me, I decided to leave out and get to my car before it started to rain any harder. Quickly, I stepped outside the door, and tried to cover my head.

Damn, this weave is really gonna look like shit now, I thought trying my best to get to my car. However, once I walked in the direction my car was parked, I instantly stopped in my tracks.

Looked around.

And saw nothing.

The Mercedes Benz that once sat a few feet away from the pumps all banged up, was now gone. I had no fucking clue as to what could've happened to it. More importantly, how someone managed to take my shit so quickly. Even the repo man didn't come that fucking soon. I couldn't believe it. My money, purse, and my driver's license were all inside. All I was left with now was twenty dollars and my cell phone.

I was fucked.

In the ass.

Without lubrication.

All over again.

"This shit can't be happening to me!" I hollered.

But it was.

For the life of me I couldn't figure out who was doing this shit. Running down the list of people once again, it could've been anybody. But how they'd managed to keep finding me was another puzzling question.

I couldn't even call the police. I was scared that if they found the car, they would connect it to the accident. And at this point, that was the very last thing I needed to happen. I now stood where my car once was and allowed myself to get soaked in the rain, which now seemed to be coming down even harder. I had no choice. I walked back to the store slowly. Looking around, hoping that by some mistake I'd parked the car somewhere else.

I hadn't.

When I reached the dry, warm store, I instantly went off. "Somebody just stole my car. Did anybody see anything?"

Nothing.

Not one word came from anyone's mouth. Not even the slow-ass cashier.

"Are you all fucking listening to me? Did any of you see somebody get into my car? It was a Benz...parked right out there by the gas pumps." I pointed outside.

This time, I managed to get a few head nods, but still nobody spoke up. Even though, I wanted answers it didn't surprise me that everyone in the store was following the no snitch rule.

I wanted to burst out in tears, but kept my composure as I grabbed the phone out of my pocket and called Bubba. There was no answer. I knew there was no telling when he was coming in to open up. I tried several more times to reach him, but each time got no answer.

I knew that I couldn't stay in Citgo until Bubba finally arrived, so I had no other choice, but to go to my mother's house who only lived a few blocks away. Contemplating on whether I should walk, my inner diva told me no, so I walked back outside and hailed a cab that was waiting for business.

"Where are you headed?" the African man asked me as he put his newspaper down and clicked himself into the seatbelt.

"Shady Grove Trailer Park," I replied while looking out the window. I had now hit rock bottom and swore revenge on all who'd put me here.

"You realize that's only a few blocks, right? It's not even a mile."

I snapped. "Of course I know it's only a few blocks, *Uhm Foo-Foo*. Just drive the fucking car!"

"You don't have to be insulting," he responded before driving up the street and around the corner.

On my short ride over, I looked out of the window and shook my head at the filthy area. Reminded me of a cemetery and the people who lived here looked like the living dead. "I gotta get my shit together because there's no way in hell I'm coming back here," I told myself right when the driver pulled up to the trailer.

After giving him five dollars for the $4.17 fare, I hopped out of the car and heard him say something in his native tongue as he drove away. I was more than sure he was cursing me out, for the eighty-three cent tip, but that beady headed muthafucka could kiss my ass. Shit, I only had fifteen dollars left, and planned to spend it wisely.

I stood in front of my mother's trailer, not wanting to go inside. Would've rather thugged it out in the rain, but I knew that wasn't possible. I didn't have anybody else to call for help. One thing I knew for sure though was that whoever was after me, would never think to find me here. I walked up to the door and turned the knob.

Locked.

This bitch's door was never locked.

Ever since I was a little girl, my crazy mother always kept the door unlocked every time my sorry-ass father did one of his famous disappearing acts. She would always say that he didn't need to struggle when he decided to come back home. Every time I thought about how pressed she used to be for that man, even after all the shit he did, it always pissed me off. She was such a fool.

"Cookie!" I screamed as I banged on the door trying to get her attention. I was now so wet that it looked like I'd jumped into a swimming pool. I needed to get inside. Lightening now accompanied the thunder and the conditions were getting dangerous.

"Cookie, open the fucking door!" I yelled again.

Climbing through a window was out the question as they were all covered in bars to keep the local intruders out. I continued to bang against the fragile door as hard as I could until my fist became sore.

Maybe I should try and knock this muthafucka down, I thought looking around the junky-ass yard. I knew there had to be something I could use.

I guess after all the commotion, one of her neighbors lifted up her window to see what was going on.

"You looking for Cookie," the woman asked. She appeared to be in her thirties, and struggling with a substance abuse problem. Most of the people that lived here were, but at least they had somewhere to stay for the night.

"Yeah, I'm her daughter. Where is she?"

"She moved out. Been a couple of days now. Came over to say goodbye, but never said where she was going." She stopped to scratch her head. "You should get back in your car and get out of this rain fo you get sick."

After her unwanted advice, she closed her window back down and left me to my own thoughts. However, before my mind got a chance to wonder, my cell started to ring.

"Hello?" I asked. It was a private number, but I didn't care. I was desperate and hoped that whoever it was would be able to help me.

"So, you're a trailer trash bitch, huh?" a woman said on the other end of the phone.

"Who is this?" I asked wanting to know who had found out about my life.

"You fucked with the wrong person! I'll make sure that you end up where you started off…with nothing!"

And then the phone went dead.

I still had no answers.

Sounded like it could've been Doctor Khan's wife, but the voice was clearly being disguised so I wasn't sure. After all the happy homes I'd destroyed, it honestly could've been anyone. Besides, after all the shit I was going through, I was tired of trying to figure out all the threatening phone calls anyway. I looked around, wiping the rain from my eyes, to see if someone was watching me. I was almost positive that whoever made this call was responsible for taking my car. My cover had been blown and I was no longer safe. Needing to find a way inside, I walked around the back of the trailer and hoped that the back door would be unlocked. It was. Obviously her dumb-ass had failed to use her brain again.

I walked into a hell that was still fully furnished. "How the fuck did she move and with what money?" I asked myself as I noticed that everything was exactly the same. It was almost as if I were reliving my childhood. The stale smell of old rags and the dingy furniture that I'd grown up with still lingered along with the mounds of old shit she hoarded.

I was soaking wet from head to toe and I would've rather died than to bathe in this piece of shit. Didn't really want to sit down either. I tried calling Bubba a few more times but still got no response. There weren't many options left. I had to stay here until I could get in touch with him.

Taking off my clothes, I hung them on her kitchen chair to dry then continued to look around. With just my underwear on I stood in one place. The memories that this trailer brought back were too excruciating to bear. Every time I stepped foot in here, it felt like it had all happened just yesterday. And just when I thought I'd gained a little strength, I started to lose it. I was having a panic attack. It felt like the walls were closing in on me, all from my memories of what he'd done to me.

Took my innocence away. My virginity.

All before I was twelve years old.

I might've ended up normal had my child molesting father not touched me. Fucked me like a nigga fucks his bitch. Told me to do the things that my mother couldn't satisfy him with. Forced me to grow up before my time.

Herpes.

My father was the one who'd actually given it to me.

I just blamed it on Rich and every other man who I fucked without a condom, just to try and block the truth out of my mind.

Bending over, it felt like I couldn't catch my breath. I was losing it and didn't know how to bring myself back to a normal sense. Wasn't even sure if that was possible for me anymore, or if I was doomed to the curse of insanity for the rest of my life.

Like my mother.

Like my father.

I cried so hard that I began to gag on the spit that got caught in my throat. It felt like I was suffocating. Had to get out of this haunted house before it killed me, or worse…before I killed myself. I threw the wet clothes back on my body and ran back out of the house. I needed to find my mother. I wanted to pay her back like all the others. Just another name added to my list. My death list. Revenge would be mine.

As I continued to walk, a local dope boy who was getting dropped off by a cab quickly ran over to me before the cab even had a chance to drive away.

"I got the best shit around here," he said, getting ready to show me whatever he had.

"Do I look like a fucking fiend to you?" I yelled, with tears still streaming down my face.

"You're not?" he asked confused.

He was serious. I looked at myself through the window of the cab and could've very well mistaken myself for one too. I decided against arguing with him and hopped into the cab.

"I need to go to Bubba's Pawn Shop," I demanded. "And yeah, I know it's not that far, so don't tell me that shit." There were questions I had that only Bubba could answer

Surprisingly, the driver cleared the meter just before pulling off, never saying a word.

My phone rang again.

Private.

"What!"

"Awww…why did you run away? You don't like living in trailers anymore?"

It was the same woman from before.

"Who the fuck is this?" I asked, looking out every window.

Whoever kept calling was definitely following me. Watching my every move. Taunting the fact that I was clueless as to what was going on. And then out of nowhere, the phone died. I looked down at my cell, and shook my head. Now, my battery was dead. This was definitely the start of another fucked up day. I turned around and looked out of the back window of the cab to see if anyone was following us, but didn't see anyone. I was nervous, but tried my best to act as if I wasn't.

When we pulled up at Bubba's shop, I noticed that the lights were on which was a huge relief. He was finally open. Running out of money and places to go, the last thing I wanted to do was walk around with a stalker on my trail. After paying the cab driver, I got out of the car and ran toward the shop. The rain continued to pour down, but I no longer cared. Nothing mattered anymore...except revenge. Everyone would pay for the shit I was going through.

I pushed the buzzer several times back to back, hopefully indicating that this was an emergency. And surprisingly it must've worked because this time Bubba's voice never came over the speaker. He just buzzed me in.

Once inside, however he didn't say anything. Just looked down and pretended to be straightening up shit that didn't need to be straightened. Didn't mention how wet I was or how crazy I looked. Didn't seem to notice me at all.

"Bubba, somebody stole my car. I need some more money."

He ignored me. Like I hadn't said a word.

"Bubba, do you know where Cookie is?" I walked up closer to him, to a distance where I couldn't be ignored. "Bubba?" He finally looked at me and shook his head again. Like he was disgusted.

"Dis the last time you welcome in here. After dis, I cant give you nothin' else, hear?" He was stern. Used a tone that he'd never used with me before. I was confused.

"Bubba what's going on? Why are you acting like this? I really need your help right now. I promise to pay you back when I get back on my feet."

He shook his head. No, negative is what he wanted to say. He lit a cigarette, poked it in his mouth and pulled before saying, "I can't do it."

Before I had a chance to plead my case again, he pulled out fifty dollars and handed it to me.

"Bubba, I don't think you understand what's going on. The hundred dollars that you gave me was in the car when it was stolen. Please, I really need more money. I need to know where Cookie is."

"Dis the last time you hear," he replied before picking up the cordless phone and walking to the back of the store.

This time, I knew exactly what he was doing. I guessed my sob story had worked. But I was still confused as to why Bubba didn't want me back in the store. I knew I had a tendency to piss people off, but I'd never done anything to hurt him. Now that I think about it, I guess he really was the only friend I had.

He returned back to the counter a few minutes later with another piece of paper.

My mother's new address.

"Thanks," I said, sadly. He didn't answer me back. Pretended as if I were invisible. "Bubba, don't you hear me? What's wrong?"

"Don't come back here!" was what he yelled before leaving the counter, headed to the back of the store again. He never looked back.

I shook my head in disbelief wondering why he was acting like this all of a sudden. The only person in the world that ever gave a damn about me was now acting like I was some begging-ass family member. I thought he really cared for me. My emotions were welling up once again. Anger and sadness were the shadows that followed me as I walked out of the store.

I stood on the sidewalk as the rain poured down and raised my hand to get the attention of another cab that drove by. I was surprised to see this many cabs in the hood, even though it worked in my favor. When the driver pulled over to the curb and stopped, I immediately hopped in.

"Where you headed?"

"I want to go here," I replied, after handing him the paper with my mother's address.

The driver turned around and stared at me. "You want to go to Sugar Land?" he asked suspiciously.

"Yes."

"You do know it's about twenty minutes from here. I'll need a deposit up front."

"Do you do this shit to everyone? Just drive this fucking car and I'll pay your dumb-ass when we get…"

"Listen," he demanded. "This is my cab and my rules. I'm not driving all the way out there for you to tell me you don't have any money, so either you can give me that shit now, or you can get the fuck out!"

I caught a reflection of myself in the window I stared out of, and saw what he saw; a broke bum bitch that was tired and worn from the cards life had dealt her. Couldn't say I blamed him either because I wouldn't have trusted myself if I were in his shoes. Hating the fact that I had to give in, I handed him the fifty dollars Bubba had just given me and continued to look out of the window as he drove away. It didn't even matter if that was enough. It was all I had.

I knew in my heart that today would be the last I ever saw Bubba again and surprisingly, it bothered me. I'd taught myself not to have feelings for anyone. It had been my survival guide. Broke my own rule by letting Brice in. Thought he loved and cared for me too. Thought we had a future together. "After I deal with my mother, he's next on my list," I told myself.

Chapter *Twenty-Four*

"Hey…lady! Lady…wake up, we're here!"

I opened my eyes and realized I'd fallen asleep during the long ride. I barely remembered pulling off from the store, but we were here nonetheless.

"This bitch can't be living here," I shouted out loud as I gazed out of the window at the brick house. Figured Bubba had fucked me with some bullshit information, and sent me on a wild goose chase. He knew I didn't have money. Besides, my mother could never afford to live in a place like this.

"What's the fare?" I asked, never taking my eyes off the house.

The driver glanced at the meter. "$43.67." When I finally looked at him and held my hand out for the change, he laughed. "I hope you don't think I would drive all the way out here and not get a decent tip."

"I don't give a shit what you thought. I gave you fifty dollars to bring me out here, and the fare was only forty-three. Give me my change!" I would've never imagined in a million years that I would be arguing over six dollars.

He laughed again, ignoring my demands. "I don't have all day. Are you getting out or what?"

At that point, I didn't have the strength to debate with him anymore. I also didn't have anywhere else to go. I didn't even have enough money to get back to Shady Grove. With my back against the wall, I let myself out of the car and closed the door. He drove away within seconds, leaving me in front of a house that, my mother couldn't have possibly be living in.

Sugar Land, Texas.

CNN profiled it as one of America's best places to live. With my phone dead, I knew I needed to get in contact with Bubba somehow to curse his ass out for giving me the wrong information. I began walking to the house to see if anyone was home. Was going to ask to use the phone and hoped that they wouldn't see me as everyone else did; a begging bitch.

I rang the doorbell and waited for an answer while checking out the surroundings. I noticed the perfectly trimmed yard, which was the total opposite of how my mother kept her shit. Muddy, sloppy, filthy was what she was used to. Would've felt uncomfortable with anything else. This was definitely not her house.

While my back was turned, still admiring the yard, someone opened up the door. I turned around and dropped my jaw when I found out who it was.

"Cookie?" I asked, still not believing what was right in my face.

She looked me up and down with a reflection of satisfaction in her face. I could tell that she was glad to see me doing as bad as I looked. "What are you doing here?" I asked with a blank expression.

"Maybe I should be asking you that, *Tyonka*. You're the one who came uninvited." When I didn't respond she looked at me again. "Well, since you're here come in." She opened the door and stood to the side. Just before I walked inside, she gave up a little smirk then closed the door behind me.

Who's fucking house is this? I thought admiring the chandelier which graced the front entrance. I followed her past the living room, that was filled with a full entertainment system, a leather sectional, and expensive artwork that sat on the walls. She led me to the kitchen. Stainless steel appliances were all that surrounded me and the smell of homemade lasagna filled the room.

"So, what are you doing here, again?" Cookie asked me.

She crossed her arms over her chest and waited for an answer. She looked good, like she was finally sober. Like she was a pivotal player in the community. She looked like the mother that went to PTA meetings and took their child to church on Sundays. However, I wasn't buying the façade. She'd obviously put on a Halloween costume and hid the woman who she really was.

"What am I doing here? What in the hell are you doing

here? Whose house are you in, Cookie?" I questioned as I continued to look around.

"Even though it is none of your damn business, this is my house!"

She walked over to *her* oven and opened it to check on *her* food. I still couldn't believe how spotless *her* place was. Nothing was out of order.

"Did you go to rehab?" I asked. It was the only possible excuse for the drastic changes she'd made in her life.

"Yes I did. Been trying to tell you that for a while. Every time I came to your store, I wanted to tell you, but you just wouldn't listen. Oh, and as a matter of fact, I'll give you their card so that you can take a visit. Looks like you started fucking with that shit! That's what people do when they love someone. They make sure that they get help."

She laughed at her own sarcasm and then took a seat at the glass dining room table.

"I don't fucking need your help bitch, and you want to talk about love? True love would've killed the man you called your husband the first time you saw him sleeping with your fucking daughter. He took my fucking virginity!"

The sarcastic grin she had on her face, had now disappeared. I'd hit a soft spot that she didn't expect me to talk about.

"You bitch!" she yelled as she rose from her seat. "He never wanted to do that to you. He told me you seduced him!" I watched as her hand started to shake, probably wishing at this point that she had a drink to calm her nerves.

"And you believed that shit. Why did you always take his word over mine!"

"I watched you. Even when you were little, you were always a fucking whore. Always prancing around him trying to get his attention. What man wouldn't give in to that kind of temptation?"

"But I was only twelve years old and he was my father!" The tears started to rain down my face harder than it had rained all day. I'd become weak and felt my knees beginning to buckle.

"Fuck him being your daddy! He was my husband and you

took that away from me!"

"But I was only twelve years old," I repeated, trying to remind her again as if she didn't remember. "He raped me every
week for two years straight and you knew about it! It's because of
him that I have fucking herpes!" Cookie's face showed no emotion
while I was barely able to control mine. "Tell me…tell me he
didn't get that shit from another woman on one of the little vaca-
tions he always took from us!"

"Stop lying. Your little whoring-ass was fucking everybody
in the trailer park. You gave that shit to your father!" Her face
seethed with jealousy and her shaking had increased.

I couldn't believe that after all these years my mother was
still in denial about what my father did to me. "He raped me! You
were my mother. I would never let that happen to my daughter. The
man that hurt her would be dead and…"

"But you took care of that for us all…didn't you?"

I paused.

It was the first time in more than a decade that she'd ever
mentioned anything about his death and implicating me in the
process. I guess she knew all along that I was the one responsible
for killing him. It was my twelfth birthday, and instead of taking
pictures of me in front of my birthday cake, I'd taken a life. The
day he took his last breath was the day I'd had enough of him
touching me like a man touched his wife.

Cookie was depressed for years after Doc died and I could
never understand why. It was her shadow I saw at my bedroom
door on the days that he wanted me. She knew. The whole time she
knew what he was doing to his own daughter, and never did anything to stop it. Almost seemed to encourage it just to keep him
happy. I remembered him always threatening to leave her, and
whatever the argument between them was about, led him to me at
night. I was the negotiation.

"You no good bitch!" I growled through my teeth remem-
bering the nights I wished I was dead every time he was on top of
me. Even having days where I woke up, disappointed. Disappointed at the fact that I was still living.

He'd died from the Ajax cleaner that I'd slipped into his

daily cocaine fix. After the autopsy came back, the cops thought my mother was responsible at first, but eventually ruled it as a bad drug deal. I was relieved when they changed their focus to the local dealers in the neighborhood. They never suspected me though. At twelve years old, I was a murderer. And as sick as it sounds, it's an accomplishment I'm most proud of.

"I knew you would do anything to break us apart. You were always an ungrateful bitch, never wanting to see us happy!"

After she uttered those words, it was as if I had been snapped back into reality. For some reason, I thought that I was going to get some type of closure in regards to my past, but I'd forgot who I was dealing with. The house, the furniture, the cleanliness all fooled me into thinking that she was someone else.

I'd been sadly mistaken.

This bitch was still fucked up.

I closed my fist, ready to knock her fucking head off, until suddenly there was a knock at the door.

"Who is that?" I asked.

She ignored my question and quickly walked toward the front of the house. Suddenly, I heard the open door. "Yeah, she's here," Cookie advised someone. "What took you so long?"

I searched around the kitchen for something to protect myself with. Quickly and quietly, I took a few steps over to the counter and grabbed a kitchen knife, placing it carefully inside the back of my pants. There was no one in the world that could've known I was here other than Bubba and the cab driver, so I didn't know what the fuck this was about. Definitely smelt like a set up. Moments later, she walked back into the kitchen and my heart stopped beating when I saw that it was Brice. He followed her closely.

"There she is, baby," my mother said, pointing in my direction. She then placed her hand on his lower back and rubbed it gently.

My eyes immediately widened. *Wait a minute, I knew this bitch…* I couldn't even get the rest of my thoughts out before Brice kissed my mother on the mouth.

"The lasagna smells good. I can't wait to dig in," he said,

giving her another small peck.

"It's almost done." She looked at him and smiled, like she was infatuated. I hadn't seen her this way since Doc was alive.

It felt like my heart had dropped into my stomach. I couldn't believe that this shit was happening. My mother and Brice? Hell no.

Brice turned to me, and frowned. "So, you tried to hurt Alexa and my daughter?"

"No," I answered then shook my head. "I actually tried to kill them! As a matter of fact they should be dead."

He stepped a little closer toward me, but still not within arms reach. I could tell it took everything in his power not to attack me. "The only one dead is my unborn child."

"Well, I guess one out of three ain't bad," I replied with a smirk. I knew my devious comments were risky, but didn't care. I wanted him in pain...just like me.

Brice banged his fist on the counter. "Bitch my fiancé and baby girl are both in fucking comas because of you! On life support damit!"

Good, that means both of them are on their way out, I thought.

My mother sat off to the side enjoying every moment of the drama. I looked at him and then her, still trying to figure out how they'd connected with each other. How they might've been fucking each other.

Brice let out a wicked laugh. "Did you like what I did to your apartment?"

"You fucking bastard! I knew that was you!" I yelled. "Thanks for all the business cards."

"Yeah, I thought that was a nice little touch," he continued, "I got you evicted too. Since I bought out the whole building, it wasn't hard to do. I told you I wasn't the one to fuck with. Oh, and what about your car?" He looked over at Cookie. "That was fun watching her come outside to an empty parking space, don't you think?"

The more he taunted me, the angrier I became. I glanced over at my mother who was smiling from ear to ear like this was

212

some sort of fucking game. "How do you know her," I asked, pointing to Cookie. I was tired of trying to make some sense out this shit.

"Bubba always comes through when you need him, huh?" Brice responded.

I was shocked. Couldn't say a word.

"I paid Bubba to get me all your information. That's when I found Cookie. She told me everything I needed to know about your wanna-be ass. Now, I know how you really grew up. How you killed your father. Shit, how you slept with your father," Brice continued. "Who would've thought the sweet homeless woman in front of your store that day would turn out to be your mother?"

I wanted to walk over and punch her ass in the face. "So, what does fucking her have to do with anything?" I asked.

He smiled. "Mirror, you know how I am when it comes to women. Your mother provided me with some good information, and some good head. In return, I provided her with a nice place to stay, some money, bought her a new wardrobe. You know how it works. I don't mind throwing my money around, as long as I can get what I want. "

I looked at the woman who gave me birth, and just shook my head. "You've always put a man before me."

"Don't get mad Mirror," Brice teased. "You of all people should know how shady people are when it comes to money…and very large sums can be even more persuasive." He was right. I couldn't argue about that. "But I can tell you one thing though. Bubba has a soft spot in his heart for you. He wasn't trying to tell me anything about your life. He also didn't want to call me when you went to the pawn shop earlier."

I looked at him with wide eyes. "That's right. I was the one Bubba called today. I was the one who gave him this address. I wanted you to come here, and for the right price, I got Bubba to set you up."

Even though I wondered what conniving plans Brice had up his sleeve, and why he wanted to lure me here, he was right once again. When it comes to money, nobody could be trusted.

Suddenly, Brice's phone began to ring. The red phone.

Shaking my head, I knew damn well Alexa's ass couldn't be calling from a fucking coma. I stared at him with anticipation, hoping that he would answer. He did.

"Yeah," Brice said. "Everything is going according to plan. Trust me you'll be happy with the results." After laughing out loud for a brief moment, he hung up then looked back at me. "That was my brother, Wolf. Or you might know him as King Pen."

I was completely floored. Couldn't say a word.

"You know, I had no idea you were the bitch my little brother wanted me to handle a while back. I can't believe it took us this long to put the shit together, but I'm glad we finally did. Now, getting rid of you is going to be even more fun."

I swallowed...hard. Thought about the knife again when Brice directed his attention toward Cookie.

"I guess your daughter really is a slut. First she fucked my brother, then yours truly," he said, pointing to himself. "She probably thought he had some money. Not realizing that I make him earn everything he gets from me, even his spot on my label."

Looking at Brice, now it all made sense. That's why he looked so familiar to me in New Orleans. He was the one on all the pictures inside KP's house or whoever paid the fucking mortgage there.

"See, it's bitches like you who give women like, Cookie a bad name." Brice continued to talk shit.

I'd heard enough. It was time to retaliate.

"Well, since you know so much, did you know that I paid Bubba the *right price* to find out where *you* and *your* precious family lived?" I asked. "If I found them before, I can find them again."

I could tell I'd hit a nerve by the way he shook his leg. "Is that a fucking threat? Do you think I'm going to let you get away with trying to ruin my life?" he asked. "Bitch, don't let the fancy suits fool you. I know how to put in work."

"Yes, please consider that a threat. Besides, I'm not finished ruining your life. You might want to go get a check up to see how many times your herpes might flair up each year. " This time Brice looked at me in shock. "That's right, nigga. That's what you get for fucking me without a condom." I shot my eyes toward

Cookie. "And if you're fucking him, I hope you catch it this time."

"You're such a devious little bitch!" she yelled, finally breaking her silence. "Why try to end his happy home because he didn't want anything to do with you anymore? You're nothing but a fucking whore. Always have been...always will..."

Without any warning, I ran over and punched her right in the face.

Shocked everyone that I had made that move.

Shocked myself that I didn't cut her instead.

I was able to get a couple of more blows in before Brice pulled me off of her and quickly carried me to the other side of the room. My arms flew all over the place as I tried maneuvering from his grip.

"Get the fuck off of me!" I yelled.

He brought his hand up to my neck and wrapped them around the bruises that he'd just given me a couple of days prior. I gasped, choked, and coughed for help as I felt the blood being rushed up to my head.

"I wanted you here so I could kill you!" Brice yelled with a deranged expression. "You deserve to die!" He twisted my neck even tighter. It wasn't long before I wasn't able to make any sounds. I became dizzy, but managed to get a quick glance at his face. Saw the determination to end my life in his eyes.

Before he squeezed out every ounce of life I had left, I reached behind me and pulled out the knife that was still lodged in the back of my pants. He never saw it coming as I crammed it into his stomach. He let me go…immediately.

"You bitch!" he cried out while I backed up. I watched as he slid to the floor helplessly not knowing what to do next. Blood was everywhere.

"I need an ambulance here now!" I heard my mother shouting into the phone. "My daughter, Mirror Carter, has just stabbed a man in my house and I think she's going to kill me too!"

I couldn't believe that this bitch had snuck away and called the police on me. I knew I had to escape. I ran over to her, snatched the phone out her hand and hung it up.

"I hope you rot in hell for the rest of your life!" she cried out just before I landed my fist right on her chin, causing her to go down as well.

While Brice laid on the floor, struggling to survive, I dug around in his pockets, looking for his car keys. Once they were jiggling in my hand, I spit in his face and ran out of the house as fast as my legs would take me.

I hopped in his Bentley and backed out of the driveway like a professional driver, then pulled off. Moments later, I made my way out of the development just before a team of authorities rushed past me to solve a crime that I'd just committed.

Chapter Twenty-Five

I was sweating bullets trying to get away from the scene as fast as I could without looking suspicious. I knew that I had to figure something out, but with no money or cell phone it looked impossible. Suddenly, I looked in the passenger's seat and saw that Brice's phone was still in the car. I picked it up and just held it in my hand as I mentally went down the list of anyone I thought would give me some money. Then again…out of all the men I'd ever fucked with, there weren't many who would've accepted my phone call, so the list seemed to be getting shorter. However, there was one name that stood out. I dialed the number, hoping he would still help me.

"Khan's Plastic Surgery Center. How can I help you?" the receptionist answered.

I paused, contemplating to myself if I really wanted to go through with this, but quickly remembered that I had no other choice.

"Hello?" the receptionist answered again.

"Um yes, I was wondering if Doctor Khan was busy right now."

I needed to talk to him, apologize for what happened between us, and then ask him for some money. I knew that I had a lot of nerve trying to contact him after the whole herpes thing, but I was positive I'd make him get over that. In the past he'd never been able to resist me, so this time wasn't any difference.

"I believe he's with a patient right now. Is there a message I can leave for him?"

"Well, is Nurse Khan in today?"

"As a matter of fact she's out for the rest of the evening."

That was my go ahead to book an appointment. It wasn't

him I'd have to worry about, it was that angry bitch. "This is an emergency. I think the saline in one of my breast has ruptured. Please, I need to see him right away!"

"Absolutely, what's your name?"

"Um…I'd rather just come in if that's okay with you."

"Yeah, but we need to pull your file for him so that you're not waiting around all day."

"When is the appointment?" I asked her, ignoring her question.

"Well, we just had two cancellations. So, feel free to come in right away."

"Okay, I'll be there!" I hung up the phone and hopped on the expressway and straight to his office. I was determined to get out of town before my face was plastered all over the news. I needed to get myself together to be able to be at my full strength when I attacked again. There was a part of me that hoped Brice had died while another part hoped he'd made it through. That's not how I wanted him to go. He just needed to suffer.

After the twenty-five minute drive, I pulled up to Doctor Khan's office. Looking around, I realized that the receptionist was right. Nurse Khan's car was nowhere to be found. I was free and clear to walk in without a scene being made. Jumping out of the car, I made sure no one was following me before making my way inside. Heads turned as soon as I walked into the office, and I couldn't say I blamed them. I still had on the same dirty sweat suit, and I'm sure I smelled even worse. Making my way to the reception area, I waited for about two seconds for the young lady to get off of the phone before speaking up.

"Hello, I'm Mirror Carter. I just made an appointment about twenty minutes ago."

She looked at me and blatantly rolled her eyes before finishing up the call. Once she was done, she never gave me eye contact. Just continued to type something on her keyboard, with a slight smirk. "Mirror Carter? No, I don't see an appointment for you and the doctor is booked up today."

"But, I did make an appointment. You just told me he had two cancellations and that I could come right in. Remember the girl with the ruptured breasts?"

She seemed to care less. "No, I don't. I actually just got back from lunch, so that was obviously someone else you spoke with. But, regardless we don't have any openings. I can schedule something for you in the morning though."

"Why the hell are you playing games? I need to see him now!"

The patients sitting in the waiting area were now engrossed in our conversation, trying to figure out what was going on.

"Please lower your voice when you're speaking to me," the receptionist asked in almost a whisper. She seemed to want to confront me, but not at the cost of causing a scene. I used that to my advantage.

"I want to see him now and I'm not leaving until I do! It's a fucking emergency!" I yelled.

She looked into my eyes, not wanting to give in, but really had no other choice. It was a smart decision on her part because the next time I had to speak, it was going to be replaced with my fist. I didn't have time for any bullshit.

"Sure...follow me," she finally instructed as she got out of her seat and led me through the door that separated the waiting area from the examination rooms. I walked closely behind her, trying my best to see if I could find Kahn before she stuck me in the room. Thought if he'd known I was in the office, he would've rushed to see me, wondered where I'd been, and given me anything I asked for. But that wasn't the case. The bitch stuffed me in a room a few seconds later.

"He'll be with you when he can. Like I said earlier, he's booked."

She closed the door behind her, leaving me to look at the plain white walls. Magazines were my only other entertainment, but the thoughts I had running through my mind were enough to keep anybody busy. I sat down in a chair beside the examining table, and buried my head inside my hands. The situation with Brice was all I could think about. Now, there was no doubt in my mind that he was responsible for burning down my shop. However, the whole thing with Bubba and my mom really fucked me up.

219

Even though my mom had always been a bitch, I had no idea she would stoop that low, and the fact that Bubba had turned on me broke my heart in two. I'd done so many people wrong and played so many dangerous games, that I guess this shit really was my payback. I just wished it didn't hurt so bad.

Before I knew it, twenty minutes had gone by and there was still no sign of Kahn. I hopped up out of the chair and began pacing around, trying to figure out whether to stay and continue to wait for him, or if I was going to walk out and cause another scene.

"Fuck it. I'll find Kahn myself," I said out loud. However, just as I was about to walk out the door, the knock that I'd been waiting on finally came.

I sat back down, trying not to look as confrontational and said, "Come in." It was as if the door opened in slow motion and instead of the doctor, in walked Nurse Khan.

Damn.

"Mirror, I'm so glad you came to me instead of me having to find you," she announced before closing the door. She walked closer to me. "I knew that was your voice when you called. It took all that I had to conceal my excitement."

Shit that was her crazy-ass on the phone instead of the receptionist? I'd been set up once again.

I quickly jumped out of the chair and stood up. Didn't know what she had up her sleeve, but from our other run ins, I knew that this bitch had heart. I didn't put anything past her.

"Back up! This shit didn't have anything to do with you!" I wanted to let her know that this beef was between me and her husband. It was personal, and all business.

"Oh, but that's where you're wrong. This has everything to do with me. I take it personal when you screw my husband, and then I have to be tested for herpes. It's personal. Very personal. Did you like what I did to your store?"

I looked at her with a confused expression. "What are you talking about?"

"The fire I started." Nurse Kahn let out a devious laugh. "I know, I know...shocked me too that I was capable of such a thing, but it turned out to be so much easier than I thought. Gasoline seemed so old fashioned when I first thought of the plan, but it ended up doing the job perfectly."

"But you couldn't have been the one who burned down my store," I said still shocked at her confession. *It had to be Brice.*

"Why can't you believe it? Oh, what a stupid question. I'm obviously not your only enemy." She looked at me and smiled. "I used my husband's money and had you followed. Then I started following you myself. But the crazy part is there was someone else following you too."

I listened to her story like a well behaved student.

"But, let's not get it confused. It was me, who destroyed your store. I refuse to let anyone else take the credit for that."

She walked closer, trying to block me in. I got my hands ready to punch the shit out of her if she took one more step. And then that's when I saw it. It was a needle that she had tucked in her hand. Didn't see it when she initially walked in.

"I tried warning you before that I would do anything to keep my family together, but you wouldn't believe me." She began positioning the needle like it was a knife and stabbed me in the upper arm, injecting the liquid into my blood stream. I never got a chance to defend myself.

Epilogue

Cold.

Hungry.

Fighting for survival.

"Get the fuck out of my spot and don't let me have to tell you that shit no more," the homeless woman threatened as she pushed me out of her way.

I stumbled back trying my best to regain my balance after I dropped what scraps of food I found back into the garbage can. This had been her home for years and now here I was intruding on her territory just trying to survive.

To this day I had no idea what doctor Khan's wife had injected me with, but when I woke up, I was in a mental institution being evaluated. From what I was told by the doctors at the hospital, I'd apparently been picked up off the streets by the police, butt naked and talking to myself. I couldn't remember my name, where I had come from, or the lifestyle that I was used to. Had no idea who I was and where my clothes had gone.

It had been weeks since they let me out of the hospital, but my mind hadn't been functioning right ever since. The same streets that I said I would never come back to again, were now where I lived, and the same homeless people I told to fuck off were now my neighbors. I knew in my heart that I didn't belong here, but I couldn't prove it. I knew in my heart that I really wasn't crazy, but I couldn't prove that either.

As I walked around trying to find another trash can that didn't belong to anyone else, I looked up and shook my head.

There it was.

Another muthafucking billboard of King Pen.

I'd seen one on every other street corner.

I guess he was blowing up.

I guess I'd fucked up.

Even though I'd gone from riches to rags, I vowed to myself that I wouldn't be in this position for too long. I was determined to get back on top. Determined to have the finer things in life. Determined to be paid. This wasn't the end for me. I would definitely be back.

IN STORES DEC '08

The saying, I Love New York, brings chills to Cinnamon LaBelle's heart. For her, New York is a place of hatred, brutality, and self-destruction.

With her life on the line, she takes her new gritty environment in Brooklyn by storm. New tensions surface when she enters a new brothel where every conniving tenant is for herself. Conflict heats up when Cinnamon figures out she has to become just as ruthless and treacherous as her co-workers.

Determined to end up on top, she uses her luscious body, and undeniable street skills to rake in the cash, and turn her life around. One problem lurks in the darkness; pimps don't lay down easily. Cinnamon ends up running for her life with the possibility of being put six feet under.

IN STORES NOW!!

Meet **Jewel**l, a five foot nine diva, who was born with a silver spoon in her mouth and an American Express card in her hand. Sadly, when her bank account turns cold, she resorts to a dangerous, ridiculous scam only to maintain her rich girl status.

Meet **Nadia**, the youngest and least paid of her crew. She spends money like crazy to distract herself from the painful reality of being broke. By hook or crook, she sells her soul to the highest bidder only to keep what little paper she has.

Meet **Tori**, the hustling diva of the west. Vegas hadn't seen a devilish, by any means necessary chick until she showed up in town ready to show off her manipulative skills.

Together, they take the streets of Vegas by storm. Between chasing money, scamming men, and hustling the system, they vow to stay on top. The girls get desperate when chaos strikes and come up with a corrupt scheme to certify them as rich girls for life.

COMING FEB '09

Danette Majette

Essence Magazine Bestselling Author
of **DEEP**
brings you...

Never before has there been a
novel that keeps you on edge,
drooling at the mouth, and totally
satisfied. Good Girl Gone Bad is
sure to be a classic.
- *Azarel*

GOOD
Girl
Gone BAD
DANETTE MAJETTE

IN STORES FEB '09

MAIL TO:
PO Box 423
Brandywine, MD 20613
301-362-6508
FAX TO:
301-579-9913

ORDER FORM

Date:	
Phone:	
E-mail:	

Ship to:	
Address:	
City & State:	Zip:
Attention:	

Make all money orders and cashiers checks payable to: **Life Changing Books**

Qty.	ISBN	Title	Release Date	Price
	0-9741394-0-8	A Life To Remember by Azarel	Aug-03	$ 15.00
	0-9741394-1-6	Double Life by Tyrone Wallace	Nov-04	$ 15.00
	0-9741394-5-9	Nothin Personal by Tyrone Wallace	Jul-06	$ 15.00
	0-9741394-2-4	Bruised by Azarel	Jul-05	$ 15.00
	0-9741394-7-5	Bruised 2: The Ultimate Revenge by Azarel	Oct-06	$ 15.00
	0-9741394-3-2	Secrets of a Housewife by J. Tremble	Feb-06	$ 15.00
	0-9724003-5-4	I Shoulda Seen It Comin by Danette Majette	Jan-06	$ 15.00
	0-9741394-4-0	The Take Over by Tonya Ridley	Apr-06	$ 15.00
	0-9741394-6-7	The Millionaire Mistress by Tiphani	Nov-06	$ 15.00
	1-934230-99-5	More Secrets More Lies by J. Tremble	Feb-07	$ 15.00
	1-934230-98-7	Young Assassin by Mike G.	Mar-07	$ 15.00
	1-934230-95-2	A Private Affair by Mike Warren	May-07	$ 15.00
	1-934230-94-4	All That Glitters by Ericka M. Williams	Jul-07	$ 15.00
	1-934230-93-6	Deep by Danette Majette	Jul-07	$ 15.00
	1-934230-96-0	Flexin & Sexin by K'wan, Anna J. & Others	Jun-07	$ 15.00
	1-934230-92-8	Talk of the Town by Tonya Ridley	Jul-07	$ 15.00
	1-934230-89-8	Still a Mistress by Tiphani	Nov-07	$ 15.00
	1-934230-91-X	Daddy's House by Azarel	Nov-07	$ 15.00
	1-934230-87-1-	Reign of a Hustler by Nissa A. Showell	Jan-08	$ 15.00
	1-934230-86-3	Something He Can Feel by Marissa Montelih	Feb-08	$ 15.00
	1-934230-88-X	Naughty Little Angel by J. Tremble	Feb-08	$ 15.00
	1-934230847	In Those Jeans by Chantel Jolie	Jun-08	$ 15.00
	1-934230855	Marked by Capone	Jul-08	$ 15.00
	1-934230820	Rich Girls by Kendall Banks	Oct-08	$ 15.00
	1-934230839	Expensive Taste by Tiphani	Nov-08	$ 15.00
	1-934230782	Brooklyn Brothel by C. Stecko	Dec-08	$ 15.00
			Total for Books	$

Shipping Charges (add $4.25 for 1-4 books*) $ _____

Total Enclosed (add lines) $ _____

* Prison Orders- Please allow up to three (3) weeks for delivery.

For credit card orders and orders over 30 books, please contact us at orders@lifechaningbooks.net (Cheaper rates for COD orders)

*Shipping and Handling of 5-10 books is $6.25, please contact us if your order is more than 10 books. (301)362-6508